BOOKS

Bears, Bicycles and Broomsticks [a book for children of all ages]

The Legend of Joe, Willy and Red

SCREENPLAYS
The Legend of Joe, Willy and Red
Hacker's Raid
Talltree

TELEVISION [pilot]
ACT [Acute Care Transport]

SHORT STORIES
Molly
A Call To Arms
A Mouse In The House
Henry Gets Hungry
Henry Meets Monty Mountain Lion
Henry's Wild Adventure
Shoes For Pinky, Bubba and Roscoe
The Kindergarten Incident
Randal Learns To Swim
Desperate
Tarzan Trouble
Wally Weasel
Buford Decides To Retire
Melinda [award winner]
Stranger On A Black Stallion
Oasis
Visions
Badge Of Honor

WORKS IN PROGRESS
Hacker's Raid [western novel]
Bears, Bicycles and Broomsticks [vol-2]
The Kudzu Chronicles [screenplay]
Silent Runner [sifi novel]

The Legend of Joe, Willy and Red

Table of Contents

Chapter 1	*August 1933 - The Adventure Begins*
Chapter 2	*Unwanted Baggage*
Chapter 3	*And A Texan Makes Three*
Chapter 4	*Tracking Joe*
Chapter 5	*The Chicken Pen Incident*
Chapter 6	*The Birth Of Willy The Con*
Chapter 7	*Gone Again*
Chapter 8	*Josiah Nathaniel Wilson*
Chapter 9	*Following The Same Trail*
Chapter 10	*Bad Press*
Chapter 11	*The Truth Shall Set You Free*
Chapter 12	*The Look Alike*
Chapter 13	*A Ghost Town Full Of Booty*
Chapter 14	*Over Here Boys, I Think I've Found Him!*
Chapter 15	*Rejected, Again*
Chapter 16	*Mister William Conrad Bains - Dupe*
Chapter 17	*From Banker To Con Man*
Chapter 18	*The Great Escape*
Chapter 19	*The Fight*
Chapter 20	*The Farmer's Wife*
Chapter 21	*Joe And The Restaurant Owner*
Chapter 22	*Capaloni's Real Killer*
Chapter 23	*Welcome To San Francisco*
Chapter 24	*The Next Morning*
Chapter 25	*The Address*
Chapter 26	*The Proposition*
Chapter 27	*The Shortcut*
Chapter 28	*The Man In The Car*
Chapter 29	*Mistaken Identity*
Chapter 30	*The Last Hoorah*

Epilogue

From The Author

This is a book I've wanted to write for some time.

During my travels as a yonker I was privileged to have the experience of illegally riding the rails, being chased by railroad bulls who taught me words I'd never used before and staying in some of the hobo camps along the way. While in each of these camps I partook of some of the finest cuisine I've ever eaten, along with the hospitality of some of the greatest liars to ever spin a yarn. Gentlemen one and all.

It was this education that allowed me to wander back in time to tell you about the Legend of Joe, Willy and Red.

I want to thank, Matt Brown, Dawn Brown and Ed Liebmann for helping me with the cover pictures. Thanks guys....

I want to thank my editors, Linda White and Howard Bellew for their invaluable help. I'm not much on punctuation.

I also want to thank my good friend, Rob Krabbe, who not only put the words into book form but also designed the cover.

And last but by no means least, I want to thank my wife, Christine for her encouragement and belief in me.

Happy reading,

Jared McVay

Definitions

Hobo: After the civil war, many of the survivors walked around the country with a hoe over his shoulder, looking for work. They became known as, 'Hoe Boys.' But during the depression, the name was changed to, 'Hobo.'

Cinder Bull: Railroad Detectives, or Guards hired by the railroad to keep people from riding their trains for free. Many were hired because of their brutality.

Helper: An extra engine attached to long or heavily laden trains to help pull or push freight cars.

Hooverville: A name attached to hobo camps because then President Hoover was blamed by most of the country as the person responsible for the depression.

Grapevine: A way of communication between the people along the hobo trail - either by word of mouth or signs and posters placed at strategic spots for others to see.

Handed a match: A method of telling someone they weren't wanted in a particular camp and to light their fire elsewhere.

Homebrew: Homemade beer.

Bathtub gin: Illegal homemade alcohol.

Bootlegger: A person who sells illegal alcohol.

Speakeasy: An illegal drinking establishment.

Jake leg: Affecting the legs from drinking bad alcohol, making a person walk with jerking motions.

Bar of soap in a sock: Used as a weapon, like a sap or black jack. Left no exterior marks.

Tender: Person who shoveled coal into the belly of the locomotive engine.

Prologue

During the fall and rise of the great depression when the United States was at war with itself - a country seemingly gone crazy, there was a saying among the working class people.

"You can't get into the poorhouse because it's already full of millionaires."

In the year 1932, one out of four people were out of work. There were no jobs to be had and very few people had any money. Men from every part of the country and every walk of life swarmed the land, hitching rides on the freight trains, living in hobo camps, or Hoovervilles as they were called; named after then, President Hoover, the person blamed for our country's problems.

It is estimated that by 1933 there were over one million five hundred thousand destitute men and a few women riding the freight trains, seeking work of any kind, many needing money to send home to wives and hungry children that had to be left behind.

Mixed into the hordes were the criminals who were runaways from chain gangs, prison escapees, along with other law breakers seeking to outdistance themselves from the long arm of the law.

There were also a few who fled to the rails to escape the injustice of being wrongly accused of crimes they didn't commit, such as the men in this story.

Three men from three different parts of the country and three different lifestyles are forced to flee their homes and follow the hobo trail where they are thrown together in Colorado; forming an unlikely trio which turns into a bond of friendship stronger than many who are blood brothers. Although their romp across the country from Colorado to San Francisco is fictitious, along with the love triangle that takes place when they find a woman, unconscious in a boxcar, most of the happenings could be true.

And like many of us, just when we think things are finally going our way - the fickle finger of fate steps in with other plans which turn out to not be in our favor.

The Legend of Joe, Willy & Red

Chapter 1

August 1933
The Venture begins

After a week of riding the rails Joe Wilson found himself in an empty boxcar on a freight train that would carry him into the Rocky Mountains of Colorado, safely away from the mob and the New York City Police Department.

Standing in the doorway, Joe nodded at the ten hobos hiding in the timber who were waving encouragement at him, then turned his attention to the passing landscape. Instead of the tall skyscrapers, there stood white skinned aspen with their gold leaves shining brightly, surrounded by tall green pine trees standing majestically as far as the eye could see.

Replacing the smells of the city, like automobile exhaust, people stench, and the rancid smell of garbage, was the pleasant scent of pine.

Inhaling deeply of the fresh, cool mountain air caused Joe think of the thick cigar smoke in the poolrooms and the stink of diesel oil down on the docks - neither of which he would miss. It also brought to mind memories of things he'd rather leave buried in the past.

Joe stepped inside the empty boxcar and lit a cigarette, then blew the smoke into a rag to keep it from being seen as it went out the open doorway. Glancing down, Joe noticed a large bug crawling across the floor of the boxcar. It was a big, ugly looking beetle of some kind about the size of his thumb and since he had no one to talk to he decided to talk to the beetle.

"Say there, Mister Beetle, you got ah minute? I sure could use somebody to talk to and you seem to be the only one here."

The beetle stopped his journey across the floor then slowly turned his head in Joe's direction, his beady little eyes looked up at Joe as though he was interested in what Joe had to say.

Joe took a puff of his cigarette and blew the smoke into the rag, then said, "I'd bet that when the news hit the streets about Tony Capaloni getting his-self whacked, there must'a been ah whole bunch of people who hot footed it down to the morgue to check for themselves to make sure it was him. And I'll bet a dollar to a donut every one of 'em went home feelin' relieved when they found out it was true and thankin' their almighty or whoever it is they pray to, for answerin' their prayers. And I'll betcha come Sunday, every one of'em puts ah little somethin' extra in the church box."

The beetle stood dead still, eyeing Joe as though he was transfixed by every word Joe had to say.

Joe took another puff from his cigarette and then continued. "I personally know of at least twenty people who would have thrown a party and more than likely did once they knew for sure Tony was ah goner. I'll tell ya for a fact mister beetle, if most folks had to choose between associating with Tony or an ill tempered snake - the snake would win hands down."

The beetle crossed his pinchers back and forth as if he was agreeing with Joe and then moved on toward the back of the boxcar where he might find something to eat.

Joe grinned as the beetle walked away. "Nice talkin' to ya friend, and thanks for listenin'."

There was no remorse in Joe for Tony Capaloni. The man had deserved to die. He knew of more than a dozen people who had been visited by Tony and ended up disfigured, crippled or dumped in the east river after Tony had gotten through with them; and not one conviction. Payoffs to certain policemen and judges had kept him on the street as the mob's main collector.

The Legend of Joe, Willy & Red

It didn't matter whether it was protection money or a high interest loan. If you didn't pay, Tony enforced the penalty clause.

The first time he only broke something, like fingers or your nose, or if he was in a bad mood that day, he might slice off your ear but always with the promise of something crueler next time. And Tony was always nice enough to describe what next time meant; poke your eyes out, cut off your tongue or maybe even breaking your back, after which you still were obligated to make your payments at an even higher rate of interest.

And if none of these things worked, Tony would take things to the next level by dumping one of your family members in the east river, alive, with weights on their legs.

But now that Tony could no longer make their lives a living hell, a whole lot of decent people - and some not so decent would sleep much easier for a while; at least until the mob got themselves another collector.

The rub was, Tony's demise had been pinned on him and both the mob and the New York City Police were looking for him. But the truth was, he, Josiah Nathaniel Wilson was innocent, but had absolutely no way to prove it.

The undeniable fact was, there had been at least twenty men in the pool hall who could and would, if pressured, testify that he had given Tony and his two thugs a sound whipping, inside the pool hall less than three minutes before Tony was found stabbed to death in the alley.

And if he didn't know better, he just might believe he was guilty, too. But he did know better and that was his dilemma.

Knowin' was one thing, but provin' it was a different story altogether. During the past week he'd thought about it constantly. No one could have known they'd bump into each other in the pool hall. And even if they had, there should have been nothing more than the usual insults thrown back and forth. And for sure, he never contemplated killing the guy - even if he was the scumbag of the earth and deserved to be buried alive.

Joe finally convinced himself that on the spur of the moment, someone with a grudge had seized the opportunity and killed Tony Capaloni out of hatred or revenge or whatever - but who?

It would take an adding machine to add up all the people who hated Tony bad enough to kill him, makin' it hard to pin the actual killer down. But with him and Tony havin' their disagreement just minutes before sure made it easy to blame the murder on him. Coincidence – maybe; maybe not. He just didn't know.

Suddenly the train lurched and began to slow down causing Joe to consider the possibility that he might have been seen when he boarded the train back just this side of Denver. It was also possible the bulls were planning on beating him half to death and dumping his body out here in the middle of nowhere. He'd heard stories.

To his relief, that wasn't the reason the train was slowing down.

Ole #106, an ancient coal and wood burner out of Denver, headed for Salt Lake City was being challenged by the first of many long mountain grades.

"More coal!" the engineer, a large man with bloodshot eyes and soot stained handlebar moustache yelled at the tender. His head hurt something fierce from drinking too much who-shot-john last night and he was not in the best of moods.

With the back of his dirty shirt sleeve, the coal tender, a short, fat, stub of a man, wiped the burning sweat from his eyes as he shoveled more coal into the belly of the engine while trying hard to keep his breakfast in his stomach where it belonged. Why in God's name he had allowed the engineer to talk him into a drinking match last night, he would never understand as sweat rolled down his face and dripped from the end of his nose.

The Legend of Joe, Willy & Red

Ole #106 seemed tired, straining against hauling one hundred and three freight cars up the long, steep grade without a helper. The engine grumbled loudly, bemoaning the job ahead as it laboriously climbed the mountain, leaving a long, thick column of coal smoke marking its route; the only blemish in the otherwise gloriously clear sky.

Sixty-five cars behind the engine, Joe stuck his head out of the boxcar doorway just far enough to see forward.

Still some distance away at the top of the mountain Joe saw what appeared to be a red water tower. He tried to judge the distance and time it would take the slow moving train to reach the town. Timing could be critical to his remaining healthy.

All the hobos back in the Denver camp had warned him against riding ole #106 and if he did in spite of their warnings, he was to make sure he got off before the train reached any town limits. They had been very emphatic about the viciousness of the cinder bulls on this particular train.

Many of the trains could be ridden without much fear of anything worse than being run off or a few days in jail. In some places there was the chance you could be put on a work gang fixing roads or picking fruit, but that was mainly in the southern states. Back east they might put you in the penitentiary for thirty to ninety days - but a few trains like ole #106 had reputations that made it a very dangerous train to ride.

"The bulls on 106 search every car and they is meaner'n ah pit full of angry rattle snakes," Blinky, a frail little man who was constantly blinking his eyes, had said. "And if they catch ya, they're gonna maim ya fer life if they don't kill ya first. And they'll laugh all the time they do it, too. I'll tell ya, you won't catch me ridin' that train for any amount of money, no sir, not me. I want'a go on livin' and walkin' on both legs."

But he hadn't taken Blinky's advice. His main concern was to get as far away from New York City, as fast as he

Jared McVay

could and this train was headed west, now. Just as he'd started for the train one of the other men had grabbed his arm.

"Be careful, Joe. The next time I see ya, if I ever see ya again, I don't want you to be like me."

Joe stopped and peered down at the man for a long time, debating in his mind what to do. The bulls on ole #106 had caught him in a boxcar and when they finished with him he had to be taken to the Denver County Hospital. Some men from a nearby hobo camp had found him when they'd heard his cries for help on their way to board the train, which in turn may have saved their lives.

The bruises that covered his body were nothing compared to his back being broken - which left him in constant pain and a bent over cripple for the rest of his life.

Joe felt sorry for the man but he had his own agenda to deal with, and right now his only concern was getting off this train without being seen, before it made the town limits.

Grabbing his knapsack, Joe leaped far away from the slow moving train, landing on the run, moving with the speed of a much younger man and in three long strides Joe stood inside the dark shadows of the nearby pine trees, peering over his shoulder. To his relief, no one was in pursuit.

Chapter 2
Unwanted baggage

Suddenly from a little closer to town, but still near the tracks, the sound of a high-pitched voice shattered the quiet. It was a man's voice, desperately pleading for his life. Joe's body went rigid, a quiver tingling his spine - the image of the man with the broken back racing to the front part of his brain.

"Please stop! Don't kill me! I promise I'll never ride this train again! Oh God, please stop! Help! Please! Somebody help me!"

It became instantly clear to Joe why no one had chased him. They had seen the other guy first and from the sound of it the man was getting a whole lot more than he deserved just for ridin' in an empty boxcar on ah lousy freight train that was noisy, dirty and had no comforts of any kind other than keepin' ah body out of the weather. Taking a beatin' for somethin' like that just didn't seem right.

From what the men back in Denver had said, bein' beat ta death by the bulls in this area was not an uncommon thing and here seemed to be evidence of what they'd said.

So far, during the short time he'd been on the hobo trail, barely a week now, he'd been chased a few times, but never caught. Seein' for his-self men who were crippled for life or not right in the head any more, caused Joe to use caution and a lot of plain ole common sense whenever he rode the trains.

After eluding capture by the police and the mob, winding up dead or crippled at the hands of some two-bit thugs who called themselves railroad detectives was not in his plans. Besides, when it came to brawlin', he was not unfamiliar with the art of knock-down-drag-outs. They would be in for a big surprise if they ever cornered him. Absently Joe touched the bulge in his jacket pocket where a

Jared McVay

sock with a bar of soap in the toe, waited to be called on for duty. Effective as a blackjack or a sap, but not illegal to carry. A little something he'd learned in the bars down on the docks.

Indecision over just minding his own business or try to help this guy clouded his mind.

"This guy ain't my problem, nor is he my responsibility. Why should I risk my neck? It ain't my fault the guy is in trouble - except maybe technically. I guess we may have gotten off the train about the same time and maybe they saw him first. Or maybe the other guy was closer, or slower, or looked like easier pickings. Maybe they didn't even see me get off the train," Joe said to the trees.

"Who was it that said, 'don't stick your nose into something that ain't none of your business? Somebody musta' said that."

So why was he still standing here, he wondered. He already had more troubles than he wanted. Could be it wasn't near as bad as this guy made it sound. Maybe the bulls would just rough him up a little, maybe a couple of lumps and then go on their way if the guy would just stop that infernal yellin'. But the man didn't stop.

A different set of pictures flashed into Joe's head, pictures of his drunken father beating on him and his mother and before Joe realized what he was doing, he found himself standing not fifteen feet from the scene, watching from behind a tree.

"Please stop! Oh God, please stop! Help, please somebody help me!"

Two large men around Joe's size - six feet tall and close to two hundred pounds, were alternating between kicking the man and beating him with clubs. And both men appeared to be enjoying their work way more than they should be. As he felt his jaw tighten, Joe's hand touched the bar of soap in the sock that rested in his pocket.

Both men were grinning and laughing. The bull facing Joe's direction had mean eyes, reminding him of Tony Capaloni.

Why was it, Joe wondered, that bullies, men who purported themselves to be tough guys, only seemed to pick on non violent people, folks they knew wouldn't give them any trouble. And just to make sure, these bullies traveled in packs of two or more, always outnumbering their victims; like Tony Capaloni and his two henchmen; two men to hold the victim while Tony worked them over.

It was obvious they had taken the easy prey this time. Being as fat as the man was, he had to be slow getting off the train and for sure not a fast runner. He'd barely gotten into the trees before the bulls were on him and it was apparent the man had given them little or no resistance. The man was lying on the ground, curled into a ball with his arms up around his head allowing them to kick or hit him at their leisure.

To the bulls, this guy was not a flesh and blood, air-breathing man. To them he was nothing more than an object that could be used as an example to anyone else who thought they could ride their train.

"Damn," Joe muttered to himself. "Why do guys like this even attempt to ride the trains?"

The answer was simple, the depression. This man was not unlike thousands of other guys who were looking for something or running from something, with little or no knowledge of what he was getting into.

Without thinking more on the subject, Joe ran from his hiding place behind the tree, covering the short distance in a few long strides; the loose end of the sock with the bar of soap in it swinging in an arc in his right hand. When Joe got close he smashed the bar of soap against the side of the nearest bull's head.

The man had looked up, but too late to duck as the homemade blackjack did its job. The bull grunted as his knees buckled and he sprawled face first into the dirt, unconscious before he hit the ground.

As Joe spun to face the second bull, pain radiated from the left side of his neck. The glancing blow from the second bull's nightstick rocked him off balance; causing him to fall to one knee, pain rushing down to his shoulder.

Joe made a feeble attempt to swing the sock at the man's leg and missed. Being off balance, Joe began to fall and put out his left arm to brace himself, but the arm had gone numb and was useless and he fell face down into the dirt then rolled over onto his knees in an effort to stand up.

The second bull jumped back to avoid being hit, but when he saw Joe fall, the man charged Joe with the intention of kicking him in the ribs.

What happened next shocked both Joe and the railroad bull.

The fat man sat up and grabbed the bull's leg that was extended backward. And instead of throwing the bull off balance, the fat man bit the bull on the calf of his leg with all the force his jaws could muster. The second bull let out a long and painful scream.

Joe clambered to his feet and added to the man's pain by kicking him squarely between the legs, smashing the family jewels. The man's eyes went wide as a strained, almost inhuman cry erupted from his mouth. The sound lasted just long enough for the man to go to that place of darkness where extreme pain takes you. Before the bull sank to the ground, unconscious, Joe was dragging the fat man to his feet.

"Run, get outta here, now! Head into the forest."

The fat man hesitated for only a moment, then finished getting to his feet and without a word, ran into the forest. Joe took one last look to make sure no one else was nearby, and then he too ran into the shelter of the trees.

Moving his left arm back and forth as he ran, Joe ascertained the damage to be minimal. His left neck and shoulder muscles had been bruised, but they would heal in a few days at most.

Ten minutes later Joe stopped momentarily to check their back trail. If the trail was clear he figured he could take a short breather and let the fat man catch up.

Nothing stirred beyond the laboring fat man who stumbled along fifty feet or so behind. Joe motioned for the fat man to hurry - and when the man finally came running up, Joe said in a low voice.

"It's a good thing nobody is chasing us or the buzzards would be fightin' over your dead carcass about now."

The man leaned against a tree, huffing and panting, unable to speak as loud noises came from somewhere deep inside his chest. His face was drenched in sweat and for just a brief moment Joe was almost able to feel sympathy for him, almost, but not quite. People like him shouldn't be out here if they can't take care of themselves; Joe thought to himself and then realized the foolishness of such thoughts.

The trains and camps were full of guys just like this guy, forced from their home because of this damn depression, traveling down not only unfamiliar roads, but living lives totally foreign to them. They were like lost sheep wandering around in a world full of hungry wolves. For most of them this was the first time they had ever had to endure anything beyond a structured lifestyle.

As far as Joe was concerned, it was Hoover and all the men like him that was the cause of the depression and the state this country was in, and he wasn't alone in his thinking.

Unlike the little fat man and so many others just like him, Joe felt he was better off than most of them. Being a man who walked alone had its good points. It meant he had no one depending on him to worry about, no ball and chain dragging him down, forcing him to feel obligations he didn't want to feel. Being a loner meant the only person he had to worry about was Josiah Nathaniel Wilson and that was a full time job.

After a couple of minutes the fat man was able to breathe somewhere close to normal again and was finally able to speak.

"I can't. . . thank you... enough for what. . . you did... You saved my... life. Those men would have... killed me."

Without a word Joe turned and headed deeper into the woods; walking this time instead of running to allow the fat man to keep up, hoping there were no railroad men searching the woods. An angry mob might do things they would regret later.

The rest of the day was spent wandering through the forest from east to west without finding any evidence of a hobo camp. Nor did they run into any railroad men searching for them, which meant the injured men were too embarrassed to tell anyone what had happened, or they made up some big story to cover the truth. Either way, Joe didn't care so long as they left him alone. Calling attention to himself was the last thing he needed or wanted right now.

The moon was just visible low in the eastern sky and the sun had not yet departed behind the tops of the trees to the west as Joe and the fat man emerged from the forest and stood on the east bank of the narrow river. To the east, the first glimpse of night was approaching and in the west, day was just beginning to depart; not yet dark, but not full daylight either. It was early evening, when those few men who were fortunate enough to still have a job, hurried home to their families and an evening meal.

For some, being able to relax on the front porch swing to enjoy a bottle or two of homemade beer, or a glass of homemade wine was the best part of the day.

It didn't matter that prohibition of alcoholic beverages was the law of the land and had been since January of nineteen twenty - after the ratification of the eighteenth amendment a year earlier, which wouldn't be repealed until later this year in December.

The Legend of Joe, Willy & Red

Though many people respected the law, there were many, many more who sought the comforts of the thousands of speakeasies found across the nation. From the largest cities to the smallest towns, they came to forget their troubles, guzzling bathtub gin, while making rich men out of the bootleggers and makers of illegal alcohol. Tell a man he couldn't have something and he would do everything in his power to prove you wrong.

As a matter of fact, earlier that very afternoon behind a house near the outskirts of town, Joe had crept into a root cellar where he found not only Mason jars of canned meat, green beans, and potatoes; Joe also found several shelves filled with bottles of homemade beer - of which he requisitioned four bottles after sampling one bottle there in the cellar, just to make sure it was fit to drink.

Beer making was an art, especially homemade beer. Homebrew was the popular name for it and whoever made this batch had done himself right proud. It was some of the best beer Joe had ever tasted. Joe figured whoever made this should go into the beer making business if prohibition ever ended.

Joe did not however mention anything about his discovery to his short, fat, tag along traveling companion. Not that it was a secret, but the fact was, conversation between him and the fat man had been a bit one sided. Joe would instruct him to stay put while he scouted around. The man would nod; sit on a log or stand quietly leaning against a tree, then follow him again when he returned. Which made perfect sense to Joe. The less noise they made the better he liked it.

No more than two hundred feet from where they stood on the rocky riverbank, a railroad bridge made of steel with columns of rock cemented together spanned the narrow river west of the town. By it's look and design it had been there for a long time and would stand there for years to come. The river was narrow, no more than thirty feet at the widest place with a rocky bottom and shoreline.

~ 13 ~

From somewhere far away amid the higher elevations melted snow ran between the banks as it traveled down the mountain. Trout, exhilarated by the cold, fresh, fast running water, leaped high into the air from time to time. Crows and hawks swooped down trying to grab the leaping fish. Sometimes they won, but mostly they failed, cawing or screeching at the missed prey as they flew away looking for another fish jumping into the air.

Looking around, Joe saw an outcrop rock on the far side of the river just at the edge of the tree line. It was a huge boulder that would not only shelter them from the wind, but hide their fire as well. It was nearly ten feet high, twenty feet long and close to twelve feet thick and protected by pine trees on three sides. Plus, it was only a hop, skip and a jump up the river from the rail road bridge, which made it easy to scramble up the bank to board the train before it had a chance to pick up much speed - if that's what he decided to do, which was still undecided because of his extra baggage.

Besides, it would be a chancy roll of the dice to try and ride the train this soon. If those two bulls had alerted any of the others, the head bull may have put on extra men in the hopes of catching them and settling the score. Joe decided it might not hurt to wait a bit and see how things went.

Before actually making a final decision on whether to use this spot as their camp for the night, Joe scrutinized the forest and railroad track area in the direction of town, listening for people sounds. He saw no human movement and heard only the gurgle of the river, the splash of the fish and the sound of birds. This will do, Joe thought. Yes, this will do nicely, safe from prying eyes and protected from bad weather.

"We'll be spending the night here, so do you think you can find us some dry wood so I can start a fire?" Joe asked in a bit of a harsh tone. "I don't know about you but I'm hungry."

Looking directly into Joe's eyes, the fat man said, "My name is William Conrad Bains."

Grinning broadly William stuck out his hand and waited for Joe to shake hands and introduce himself.

Time seemed to stand still as they stood there staring at each other. Joe Wilson definitely had not been prepared for introductions or conversations or any kind of talk for that matter. This, William Conrad Bains caused Joe's temper to rise. Not once, not even once had he inquired about the man's name, nor did he care, and for sure wasn't gonna offer up his own name.

First it would be a name. Next came a handshake and then a bunch of idle talk and bingo, before you knew what happened you were brothers with a common cause and a lot of other crap that came along with it, like feeling responsible for each other's welfare.

Well not him. He wanted no part of it. He would remain what he'd always been, a loner with no one to care for but himself. He was not now, nor had he ever been, nor had he ever wanted to be, his brother's keeper. And he wasn't about to start with this little fat man in a dirty three piece suit standing there grinnin' like ah Cheshire cat with his paw stuck out.

Ignoring the stretched out hand; with a great deal of testiness in his voice, Joe finally said, "Yea, right, whatever."

William slowly lowered his hand and unsure what to do next, just stood there waiting for the man to make the next move.

Finally, Joe said, " So, now, Mister William Conrad Bains, sir, do you think you can find enough courage to wander around out there all alone in that big ole forest and find a small arm load of firewood while I start putting a camp together so we can have a little heat and a bite of supper? What'ya think; can you do that one little thing?"

Joe could see by the look on the man's face that his feelings had been hurt, but he would get over it. The last thing he wanted was some hero worshiper following him around, always bringing up the fact that he'd saved his life. No, it was better to stop it now before anything got started. Tomorrow morning they would go their separate ways and that would be the end of it.

Turning abruptly, Joe walked over and dropped his bag on the sheltered side of the boulder and then began looking around for some stones to make a fire pit with as he watched out of the corner of his eye as the little fat man walked slowly into the forest.

William Conrad Bains felt insulted but held his tongue. Not only had the man not taken his hand, as was the friendly thing to do, he had not offered up his name. Plus, the man had talked down at him and he didn't like being talked down to. It reminded him of his former boss, high and mighty Bill Davis. In fact, that was the same way Bill talked to all of the people that he considered to be the little people of his tightly run ship - the Minneapolis State Bank where until a few days ago, he had been the head teller.

Vivid pictures of his fellow employees working in constant fear as they sneaked peaks over their shoulders, hoping and praying the bank manager was focusing his attention elsewhere flashed through his brain. Of course there were two exceptions, the handsome, slick talking John Axel who was made loan officer even though he didn't have the seniority. And then there was Miss Fiona Bedletter, who everyone but Bill's wife knew she was Bill Davis's mistress in the disguise of his secretary.

As William walked through the forest picking up firewood, he talked to a nearby squirrel.

"Bill Davis is such a bigot, always strutting around like he was so much better than the rest of us, standing there in his windowed office like he was god-almighty, with his chin stuck out, rocking back and forth on his heels, hands behind his back like that English guy, Captain Bly standing on the poop deck of his ship, just waiting to hang somebody from the yardarm.

And if you were summoned, Mister Bill Davis made a big deal about marching you into his office and closing the door so no one could hear, but leaving the blinds open so you would be in plain view for everyone to see while he chewed you out for some minor infraction or a new rule you'd broken because he'd just made it up. And always with the threat of being fired, and how tough the job market was right now, and how lucky you were that he was in a good mood or you'd be down the road."

The squirrel barked at him, then scurried up a tree.

With the exception of maybe John and Fiona, William couldn't think of anyone at the bank who had a kind word to say about Bill Davis. William chuckled as he spoke to a bird sitting on a nearby limb.

"Maybe I should write Bill's wife an anonymous letter and tell her all about the lunch time activities between her husband and a certain Miss Fiona Bedletter. That would put a crimp in his style and put him in the hot seat for a change. And I'm sure everyone at the bank would love to see his wife reading the riot act to him."

The bird ruffled its feathers and shook it's head as though the thought gave it a chill, then chirped and flew away. William smiled and waved as he turned back to the work at hand.

As he searched for suitable firewood, William thought about the dutiful employee he'd been and how in the course of a few minutes he had not only lost his job but had been threatened with spending time in prison for a crime he hadn't committed. Then less than two hours later his wife, to whom he'd also been faithful, walked out on him. In what seemed like no more than the blink of an eye his entire life had disappeared. How could that have happened without him seeing it coming?

William took a deep breath of air and tried to pull himself back together while he collected an armload of dry firewood. It wouldn't do to dwell on the past just now.

Jared McVay

Maybe sometime in the near future he could find the time to figure out what had happened.

As Joe had watched William disappear into the woods he wondered what tragedy had befallen this gentle little man in a three piece suit that could be so terrible that he would rather face the dangers of riding the rails and this type of life rather than what he faced back home, then reminded himself it was just a passing curiosity and none of his concern. As he headed for the river to collect some rocks for his fire pit he told himself,

"From now on me bucko, no more pickin' up lost strays."

After placing some medium sized rocks from the riverbank in a circle under a small overhang that jutted out from the boulder so the fire would be protected from the weather and also hide the glow of the fire, Joe also placed a couple of flat rocks inside the circle at strategic spots that would allow him to set the coffee pot and the skillet on them - sort of like hot plates.

With that task done, Joe sat down on a log and opened one of the bottles of beer and took a long pull, empting half the bottle. Setting the half full bottle of beer aside, he emptied out the contents of the knapsack he bought from a man in Missouri for two dollars. The man had gotten a real job and no longer needed it and was happy to get the two dollars.

Said knapsack was actually nothing more than a large flour sack containing the basic essentials - a skillet, a coffee pot, a tin pan for eating, a tin cup for drinking, one knife, fork and spoon. There was also a small bag of coffee grounds, a large towel for when he was able to get a bath, one pair of clean socks and one wool blanket with an army issue number on the corner. The razor he'd purchased separately. Not much, but a man on the run didn't need a lot of unnecessary gear weighing him down.

Joe heard William returning and looked up. Joe was surprised at the armload of dry wood he was carrying.

There were small, dry twigs along with a handful of dry grass that would help get the fire started and medium sized logs that would burn well. William laid the firewood in two neat stacks close to the circle of rocks and then without a word, began sweeping the area using a leafy branch like a broom.

Joe was impressed and showed it by raising one of the bottles of beer in Mister Bain's direction.

"Thank you, no. After my last bout with alcohol, I believe I'll be abstaining for quite some time," William said with a smile.

Having a problem with alcohol somehow didn't fit the image Joe had conjured up in his mind and for a brief moment, he was almost tempted to ask him about it. Instead, he moved to the pile of wood and started a fire.

Next, Joe dumped some coffee grounds into a pot of river water and set it on one of the flat rocks that was by now, getting hot. Next, Joe empted a jar of meat, along with a jar of potatoes and a jar of green beans into the skillet. To top things off he added a couple of dried peppers he'd found in the root cellar and then mixed everything together, creating a passable stew with a bite to it.

After setting the skillet on the other flat rock, Joe leaned back and lit a cigarette, took a sip of beer and waited for everything to heat. Somewhere in the woods an owl hooted.

When the food was ready, Joe allowed William the use of the tin plate and a fork, while he used the spoon and ate his supper out of the skillet. Joe had also given William one of the Mason jars so he would have something to put his coffee in and by this time was beginning to feel like a nursemaid, but reasoned in his mind, somewhat reluctantly, they were sharing a camp and the man had collected a good load of firewood and made the camp presentable. Plus, it was only for one night. Tomorrow morning they would go their separate ways. Besides, out here things were different, he told himself. It was the common thing for men to share

Jared McVay

what they had and if you had nothing, there were other ways of earning your meal; like cleaning up the camp or gathering firewood. And they believed in safety in numbers.

In every camp he'd been in so far the men eyed him suspiciously at first, but welcomed him once they realized he wasn't an unwanted, a troublemaker, railroad spy or a slacker. At first Joe was puzzled by how they could know so quickly until he learned about the grapevine - a system that seemed to be faster than the telegraph. Within a few minutes of arriving at a camp you were either accepted or rejected. And if you were unwanted someone would hand you a match, which meant you had to leave and light your fire somewhere else.

After less than a week Joe learned they had a language all their own; not only in words but in other ways too. Small paper or cardboard signs attached to trees, posts or any other place where they would be seen indicated what you could expect. The outline of a cat tacked on a gatepost meant, nice lady lives here; a rectangle with a dot in the middle meant danger; a circle with a large X over it meant a good handout, but if you saw a plain circle with no other marks meant no reason to stay here. These and a whole list of other signs were left here and there by the hobos who had passed that way, giving information or directions without the locals knowing their meaning. It was just another finger of the grapevine.

The meal was consumed without conversation and when they finished, without being asked, William took everything down to the river and washed it, then set all the eating utensils on pieces of bark near the fire to dry.

The fire was small and gave off very little smoke, but emitted good heat that would keep them warm during the night as long as someone added more wood from time to time. What little smoke there was rose into the trees and disappeared while the fire's light was hidden from prying eyes by the boulder. William looked around the camp and decided the man had chosen well as he took his Mason jar of coffee and sat down, leaning against a nearby tree. As he sipped his coffee he checked his bruises and decided the bulls had not caused any serious damage thanks to the man who had yet to tell him his name or accept his gratitude.

Joe sat with his back against the boulder and pretended to read from a western book he carried in his knapsack. Each time he took a sip of his coffee he secretly studied Mister William Conrad Bains. The man looked and dressed like a city dweller, yet there was more to him than met the eye; such as knowing the kind of firewood to get and how to make everything clean and tidy. Maybe he'd been a boy scout, Joe thought. He figured the man would fit in well at most any Hooverville camp where keeping a clean camp was one of their priorities.

Suddenly, he felt a knot in his stomach. He wasn't comfortable with all this buddy, buddy crap and just the thought of the responsibilities was giving him a bellyache. Just looking after himself was a full time job without any excess baggage and this piece of baggage looked mighty heavy to him.

The sun had disappeared below the tops of the trees but it's glow still lighted the western sky while the cold stare of a full moon crept higher in the eastern horizon as it's emperor of the night. And with the coming of darkness the temperature dropped rapidly, as a wall of fog north of their camp floated just above the water making it's way down the river in the direction of the bridge. Several birds flew in and out of the fog bank as the sound of fish jumping and the splash of water could be clearly heard. And from the other direction, below the bridge, the sound of frogs croaking their night songs came drifting across the air.

Spreading his blanket on the ground near the fire, Joe rolled up in it and placed his knapsack under his head for a pillow and immediately went to sleep.

William however, had no blanket to cover himself with but knew enough to gather a pile of leaves and place them within the small area of heat, then burrowed his way down into the pile and drifted into a deep sleep.

For the weary travelers the night was at last, quiet and serene - at least for the moment.

Chapter 3

And a Texan makes three

Mister William Conrad Bains jumped like a frightened cat as the shrill sound of a train whistle filled the night air, bringing both men wide awake. Glancing across the fire, Joe noticed the look of fear in William's eyes and saw him begin to tremble.

"Relax, that's just ah train headin' outta town and since we ain't hitchin' ah ride on that train, we ain't got nuthin' to worry about. We'll be safe here for the night. Now go back to sleep," Joe grumbled as he pulled the blanket over his head.

"Easier said than done," William mumbled under his breath. He hadn't been the one they were beating and kicking; nor was he the one lying on the ground thinking he was about to die. No, not him, he was tough. He wasn't afraid of anything. Why else would he have done what he had done, rushing out there, challenging two large men with clubs; men who had been hired to beat up on people for hitching a ride in an empty boxcar on a smelly ole freight train. It took a brave man to go up against the likes of them.

He had always wanted to be brave and tough like some of the boys he'd known, but he wasn't - never had been and probably never would be. As a boy he'd shied away from trouble by staying after school and doing his homework in the library until the bullies were gone and the streets were clear.

This had been his first and only physical confrontation and he didn't feel at all proud of his performance. Instead of standing up to them like a man, he had acted like the coward he was, whimpering like a whipped dog and crying out for help.

But this man, a total stranger, had heard his cry and came to his rescue. From where, he didn't know, or why, only that he had appeared out of nowhere, rushing in like a warrior, slewing the foe. If not for this strange man he might be an item at the bottom of some obituary column in tomorrow's paper. 'Bum found dead along railroad tracks just outside of town. No identification; buried in the county graveyard with no head stone.'

He felt he owed his life to a man that didn't want his gratitude or his friendship which did nothing to help solve his problem of how to repay the man. But even if he had to follow along in silence, somehow, he would find a way to repay the man for what he'd done. Maybe he would do some act of bravery that would allow him to redeem himself in the man's eyes.

William had always been a bit of a dreamer and now as he closed his eyes he saw himself dressed in shining armor, astride a big white horse, charging into battle, facing untold numbers of railroad bulls, smiting the enemy as if they were nothing.

William opened his eyes as he felt himself redden. He sometimes had the tendency to be a bit melodramatic. As he laid there watching the fog drift down the river, a different picture crept into his mind, causing him to smile. Biting that railroad man on the leg was the wildest thing he'd ever done in his entire life. What a rush of excitement that had been! He wasn't sure what caused him to do such a thing, but he was glad he had.

Looking back it seemed like something out of a movie. And as scary as it had been, this had been the most exciting day of his life. He had nothing in his past to compare it to.

Taking several deep breaths to calm his nerves, William stretched out on his soft bed of leaves, telling himself there was nothing to be so jumpy about.

At that moment the train came slowly rattling onto the rock and steel bridge. Above the noise of the engine and the rattle of the cars, the sound of men yelling filled the air, bringing both Joe and William into an upright position.

"Get the filthy little maggot," a voice yelled.

"I'm tryin'!" a second voice echoed.

"I think he broke my foot!" a third voice screamed.

Both Joe and William scrambled to their feet and peeked around the edge of the boulder. From their hiding place they had a good view of the train, although the wall of fog was about to engulf the bridge and train. All they could see in the moonlight was the silhouette of several men scuffling on top of one of the boxcars. It appeared to be three against one.

The wall of fog engulfed the bridge and the train and the silhouettes disappeared into the mist like a scene from one of those horror movies. From that point on, only sounds of the fight could be heard as both William and Joe strained to hear what was happening.

Suddenly from inside the fog, they heard, "Noooooooooo,"

Next came the loud splat of something or someone hitting the water as the train passed on down the tracks. Joe and William looked at each other, then with Joe leading the way they left their hiding place and cautiously waded into the river.

It was William who found the body - spread eagle; face down in the water with no sign of life. William grabbed a handful of the man's jacket from the back and pulled his face out of the water.

"Over here," William called softly into the dense fog.

Joe waded over just as the man began to cough - water spewing from his mouth, turning the river red with his blood. The clatter of the train wheels grew faint in the distance as William and Joe hauled the man out of the river to the rocky bank where he spent several minutes on his hands and knees, coughing and gasping, trying to get his wind back. Drops of blood splattered on the rocks beneath the man as the night air brought life back into his lungs.

Even in the dense fog, Joe could tell that Mister William Conrad Bains was badly shaken by this whole occurrence but he was reluctant to say or do anything directly that might give William the wrong impression.

Even so, Joe mumbled under his breath, "Just another day where you can be beaten half to death by the bulls just for riding on a ratty ole freight train. We thank you very much President Hoover."

Joe walked back to their camp and got the last remaining bottle of beer out of his sack. He was disgruntled with the men who had allowed this depression happen to this country. He was no politician and had never wanted to be one, but there had to be men who could run this country far better than Hoover and his bunch. He sure hoped this Roosevelt guy would be the one who would put this country back on its feet.

After a couple of minutes the man raised his head and looked around to try and get his bearings. William helped him to his feet and supported him to a place near the fire so he could rest his back against a nearby tree and still get the heat from the fire.

Stepping back, William shook his head slowly. The man's face was badly beaten. Blood oozed from three nasty looking gashes in the man's head, making red lines down the man's face.

Both eyes were swollen nearly shut; he had no more than slits for him to barely see through and starting to turn an ugly color. And his lips were swollen and bleeding, too. The fact that the man's hands were cut and also bleeding showed he'd fought back which gained him a lot of respect as far as William was concerned. Even with three to one odds the man defended himself far better than he had with only two to one odds.

William wondered if two of the three bulls had been the ones who had beaten on him or had they been three new men. Either way, William hoped that before being thrown from the train this man had done more damage to them than they'd done to him. And if two of them were the ones who had beaten up on him, he hoped they had gotten their rightful due.

Feeling the pain of his own injuries, William felt a strong kinship towards this man. Both of them had survived the brutality of the railroad bulls and walked away, not totally unscathed to be sure, but walking under their own power nonetheless. To William it was like wearing a badge of honor.

Joe sat next to the fire nursing his last bottle of beer and watched as William fussed over the man like an old mother hen, wondering what he'd gotten himself into.

After recovering from the initial shock, William ripped off the lower part of his own shirt and soaked it in the river water and then gently wiped the man's head, face and hands. It took several trips back and forth to the river where each time the blood soaked pieces of cloth tainted the water, red. But finally, after many trips and cold compresses, the bleeding slowed and began to coagulate.

During the entire process, the man sat still and stared at the fire, saying nothing. His only movements were his eyes, which were barely noticeable behind the puffy slits as they watched Joe walk over and set a Mason jar of coffee within his reach. As Joe moved back to his spot near the fire, the man's eyes returned to the flame.

As they settled down for the night, except for the night sounds, all was quiet once again. Beyond the light of the fire the fog settled over the land, enveloping everything in a cocoon of mist.

With his back against the boulder, Joe sipped his beer and did some calculating in his head - like adding the height of the bridge and the height of the train. Added together the fall had to be close to thirty feet and the water was no more than waist deep at the spot where he landed - with a rocky bottom. The man would have to have landed spread eagle to survive the fall. Even so, he would have hit the rocks pretty hard and the way he figured it, this guy was lucky to be alive.

Jared McVay

And from the bloody cuts on the man's knuckles, this guy had made a good account of himself against three of them. By his reckoning it had not been an easy feat. What little of the fight he'd seen before the fog rolled in, of the four men, this man seemed to be the smallest in size, but there could be no doubt, this guy was a scrapper.

Joe guessed the man to be of medium height, maybe five-eight, possibly a hundred sixty pounds, and by the way he was dressed; run down cowboy boots, Levis pants, a plain shirt and a Levis jacket, but no hat, which was probably lost in the fight - Joe would bet the man was from Texas. And it wasn't altogether because of the way he was dressed, either, which helped some, but mainly it was because of all those stories he'd heard about Texans.

It seemed size meant very little when it came to the fighting abilities of Texans in a good ole knuckle buster. It was more like pride or somethin'. Plus, he'd heard on more than one occasion how Texans all liked a good rough and tumble.

Once, a few years back he'd heard this fella in a bar describing his first time in Texas and the scrapes he'd been in. The man had said, "Whippin' ah Texan is like tryin' ta stick ah wet noodle up ah wildcat's hind end, not an easy thing ta do."

Watching this new member of their group slowly reach out and take the Mason jar in his swollen hands and take a sip of coffee, his beady eyes barely visible but ever alert behind the puffiness, gave Joe more to think about. The man looked to be about thirty years old, with a shaggy mop of hair, redder than the blood he'd spilled earlier.

"No wonder he's a scrapper," Joe mumbled to himself. "On top of bein' a Texan, he's got some Irish in him, too."

Joe allowed himself a glimmer of a smile as he thought back to his days at the home for wayward boys and the scraps he'd had with that Irish kid named O'Banion.

What a scrapper he'd been. Last he'd heard about O'Banion was he'd become a police sergeant in Brooklyn.

Joe looked across at both William and this new guy and his mood sobered. What kind of trick were the gods playing on him? It just occurred to him that he now might be stuck with two dependents - Mister William Conrad Bains, sir, who was afraid of his own shadow and now this new guy who seemed to be man enough, but at this moment was unable to fend for himself.

Here he was, out here to disappear, become invisible, hide from the authorities and the mob, and somehow he'd become a babysitter and he wasn't sure how it had happened. But there was one thing he did know, he didn't like it one bit.

Dropping down on his blanket next to the fire, Joe decided not to worry himself sick over the situation. He needed a good night's sleep. Come morning he would head off on his own. He'd been a boy scout long enough. And with that, he closed his eyes and went to sleep.

After staying awake long into the night, checking on the man from time to time, William finally could stay awake no longer and drifted off into a deep sleep.

It seemed like he'd barely closed his eyes when the aroma of coffee awakened him. The morning sun was just barely showing it's light above the trees to the east. William looked around and first sighted the man, who was standing down next to the river, drinking coffee and staring in the direction of town. William grunted as he hefted himself to his feet. His whole body was stiff and aching from yesterday's ordeal.

The redheaded man was also awake and stared at both William and Joe through a black and blue swollen face, but made no effort to get up.

Lifting his Mason jar, William called out to Joe, "May we?"

Joe nodded and both men moved toward the coffee pot.

Jared McVay

Both Joe and William were amazed that the redheaded man could move at all as William poured coffee for both of them, then raised the pot in Joe's direction, indicating there was still some left. Joe walked over and accepted more, then turned and walked back down to the river without speaking to either William or the red-haired man.

The red-haired man sat his coffee next to the tree where he'd been sitting, then hobbled down to the river and after gingerly taking his clothes off, waded into the icy water, submerging himself for a few seconds, which was all he could tolerate. The icy water was a shock to his body, but especially to his hands and face. It felt like a whole swarm of bees were stinging him all at the same time, but it also invigorated him like it was causing new life to flow through his aching body.

Shivering from his dunk in the icy river water, the red-haired man got redressed as fast as he could and hurried back and lifted his jar of coffee in both hands, feeling it's warmth as he went to the fire, then sipped his coffee slowly while the camp fire did it's magic. The coffee warmed his inside while the fire stopped his shivering and he began to feel human again. While all of this was taking place, he quietly analyzed the situation, trying to put the events of last night in some kind of order he could understand.

He'd been making his way along the tops of the boxcars when the bulls had seen him and had come at him from both directions and began beating on him with clubs. As well as he could remember there had been three of them and he had fought back the best he could with only his fists and a few well-placed kicks. He was pretty sure two of them had lost teeth and at least one; maybe two of them had broken noses. He also recalled feeling bones crunch when he stomped down hard on one of the bull's foot with the heel of his cowboy boot. All in all, he felt like he'd given a good account of himself. Each of them would carry scars to remember him by.

But even so, in the end, they had over powered him and had thrown him off the top of the moving boxcar. From that point on things seemed a little bit hazy.

He remembered the air being very wet, like he was falling through a cloud, but he wasn't sure what that was all about.

Next, he remembered slamming into something hard that brought immense pain throughout his entire body, then nothing, just darkness. The next thing he remembered was being on his hands and knees, gagging and gasping for air as he spit blood onto the ground.

Then someone was helping him walk and he vaguely remembered his head, face and hands being wiped with a cold, wet rag. He could only vaguely remember the images of two men and wondering why he was having trouble focusing his eyes. And had someone given him a cup of coffee? He thought so, but wasn't sure.

After some rest and now in the light of day, he understood about his injuries and realized these two men must have dragged him out of the river and tended to him. As he was standing there thinking about things, the short, fat guy walked over and began speaking to the big guy.

"Yesterday was a very trying day for all of us, but for me, it was like staring into the face of death. I guess you might say I've lived a sheltered life. Nothing even remotely close to what happened has ever happened to me before. And if you had not appeared when you did, I don't know what would have happened to me. It staggers my mind to even think about it. So, I would like to take this opportunity to express to you my sincerest gratitude and hope I can somehow repay your kindness and generosity."

Joe stared down at William with a total look of confusion on his face. He'd never before been spoken to like that by anyone and he wasn't sure how to respond. What was with this guy? Repay him for his kindness and generosity? What kind of hogwash was that? If he'd harbored any doubts about them going their separate ways, he didn't anymore, not after that little speech.

William stood nervously trying to read something in the big man's eyes, some ray of hope that there could be a friendship between them. It had taken a lot of courage for him to speak his feelings to this man and if they were to travel together there needed to be a certain amount of communication between them, but the man remained silent and just stood there, staring at him.

The red-haired man felt the tension in the air, saw the look in the big man's eyes; a cross between confusion and anger and it didn't take long to size this guy up. He was one of those guys who built an invisible shell around himself and let no one in. He was definitely a loner and this William guy had little to no chance of breaking through the invisible wall.

With that, the red-haired man turned his attention to the little fat man who was standing there with a whipped hound dog look on his face, waiting to be patted on the head by his master. By the way he was dressed and spoke, the man definitely didn't belong out here. He belonged in a store or an office or maybe even a bank, but not out here riding freight trains. Here was a man who was used to a structured life and three squares a day, cooked by a woman who ruled the roost and didn't allow dirty shoes on her clean floors. No doubt about it, this guy was way out of his element out here.

"I reckon I owe some thanks to both you boys for pullin' my fat outta the fire. You know what I mean, haulin' me outta the river. More'n likely the fish and turtles would be chewin' on my dead carcass by now if'n you hadn't been here," the red-haired man said, hoping to break the tension.

Both men looked in his direction, but it was William who spoke.

"Well, we certainly couldn't allow that to happen, could we? Out here we all have to stick together, don't we? You know, like that old saying, safety in numbers," William said, sneaking a peek at the big man to see his reaction, but there was none.

William sighed and stepped toward the red-haired man and stuck out his hand. "My name is William Conrad Bains, but my friends call me William or sometimes, just, Willy."

The red-haired man tried to smile through his swollen lips and said, "And my name is Jonathan 'Red' Walker. Most folks just call me, Red, or Johnny Red."

He looked at William's out stretched hand and then down to his own swollen knuckles and fingers, then back up at William. "Maybe we can shake later, after the swellin' goes down."

They both laughed as William leaned in close to Red and nodded in Joe's direction.

"I don't know his name. We only met yesterday. He's a very nice man, but he's just not very talkative. You see, yesterday two of those railroad bulls saw me getting off the train and attacked me. They were beating and kicking me. I was afraid for my life, I can tell you that."

Glancing in the direction of the big man, Red noticed he was scowling.

"Then out of nowhere," William continued, "this man charged in and beat the tar out of both of them." Embarrassed, William looked down at his feet. "I guess I did help a little bit when I bit one of them on the leg."

Red couldn't help himself and laughed out loud as he lifted his jar in a salute to both Joe and William.

Joe had heard all of what had been said and anger grew inside until he could stand no more, like a pot of water about to boil over.

"That's it! Don't say anymore! Just shut up and leave me alone," Joe yelled.

Both William and Red looked in his direction, startled with the look on his face and the intensity of his anger. Neither of them said anything as Joe headed for his gear, mumbling under his breath.

Jared McVay

"I've got to get outta here. The next thing I know, they'll be wantin' me to claim them as dependents."

Joe picked up his knapsack, which he'd packed earlier while William and the other guy were still sleeping. His final piece of business was to rinse out his cup and the coffee pot and then stuff them into his knapsack. When this was completed, Joe swung the knapsack over his shoulder without a word or a backward glance and headed north along the riverbank.

That last bit of jabber jawing had made up his mind for him. He wouldn't wait for a train because they'd probably want to tag along and that wasn't going to happen, not now, not later, not anytime.

While Joe was washing his cup and the coffee pot, William had an urge that took him into the woods for relief and by the time he returned, Joe had gone. As William walked out of the woods, he noticed the big man was nowhere in sight. Thinking the man had also slipped into the woods for the call of nature, William looked at Red, who not wanting to get involved in their quarrel, just shrugged his shoulders and said, "I think your friend decided to go it alone. While you were out there in the woods he picked up his stuff and left without ah word. You sure were right; he's definitely a man of few words. I knew ah feller like that back in Texas. He was the..."

Red's words were just drifting off into empty space because William was rushing up the riverbank, searching for sight of the big man as panic rushed over him like a huge tidal wave. At the sight of the big man's back, the panic attack passed and William began to walk faster - almost a trot. The big man was setting a good pace as though he was in a hurry. While keeping his eyes on the big man, William called over his shoulder,

"Put out the fire, and be quick about it. Pour some water on it or kick some dirt over it, anything. We have to go with him! I'll try and have him wait on you if he will. Hurry!"

The Legend of Joe, Willy & Red

Before Red had a chance to reply, William was hotfooting it in the big man's direction, stumbling along trying not to lose his balance on the uneven rocky shoreline.

Indecision pressed heavily on Red's mind. 'Should I rest here a while longer, or should I go chasin' after them?' he wondered. He sure didn't feel up to runnin' around chasin' after some guy that had made it clear he didn't want their company.

Or was that just the way he was and he'd expected them to follow after him like some ole hound dog followin' his lord and master? No, he thought to himself. Not this guy. The man had meant what he'd said. He'd seen the anger and embarrassment on the man's face when William had bragged about what a hero the guy was.

What to do, what to do? Red wondered again. Was that panic he'd detected in William's voice and if it had been, why? Was there something he didn't know about? And if so, what was it? Or was it that William was just a meek little sheep needing a sheepherder's protection? He'd known people like that, too.

He looked down at his swollen hands and could feel the puffiness in his face. He was in no condition to be hoppin' ah freight train on his own, especially if he ran into more railroad bulls. In his condition he doubted he could out run them and he was sure he was in no shape to be brawlin' with ah bunch of thugs that wore brass knuckles and carried Billy-clubs. And on top of everything else, he had no food, nothing, not even a blanket.

What was that old saying, 'Never saw on a limb that's supporting you unless you're being hung from it,' and right now those two men were the branches that was supportin' him and he had to do what he had to do to survive.

Red kicked dirt over the smoldering coals and extinguished the fire, and then he hurried off along the riverbank in pursuit of the two men who had dragged him out of the river and doctored his wounds. For a few days he could be a sheep if he had to; at least until they got to a town where he could rest up and look for a job.

High overhead a hawk soared, gliding majestically on a wind current, looking down at the forest, searching the ground for his breakfast. He didn't seem happy as he screeched at the three intruders moving along the riverbank, invading his domain and scaring off any critters that might serve as a meal. He continued to circle, waiting patiently for them to leave.

Chapter 4

Tracking Joe

Red chuckled to himself as he trotted to catch up. Mister William Conrad Bains was still a short distance ahead of him and a vision popped into Red's head. In his mind he pictured a basketball with short arms and legs, dressed in a suit, bouncing along the riverbank at a awkward hop, jump motion over the rocks.

The sound of William's huffing and puffing carried along on the wind causing Joe to turn around. At the sight of William approaching, Joe's face pulled into a scowl, his eyes grew hard and angry and his fists knotted into balls at the end of his arms.

"Just where do you two think you're goin'?" he yelled as William hobbled up to him, followed by Red a few steps behind.

Red swung his look from the big man to William, clearly expecting him to be the one to speak. After all, William was the one who wanted to come chasin' after this guy, not him. It was just like his ole pappy used to say, "All quarrels are private - outsiders ain't welcome."

Feeling intimidated by Joe's harsh words, William sucked in a big breath and looked down at his feet, saying, "I assumed we'd be going with you. You know, security in numbers."

"Well, you assumed wrong," Joe said, grinding his teeth. "I travel alone and I don't want or need anybody taggin' along on my shirt-tail. And I'm for sure not gonna play nursemaid to the two of you! Who do you think I am, Florence Nightingale? Now just turn around and go back down the river and quit followin' me! End of discussion!"

As Joe turned and headed on up the riverbank he had a small pang of regret. He hoped it wouldn't come to this. That's why he'd left without a word, hoping they would take the hint. But no, they had to follow him, forcing the issue. When would he learn to mind his own business and not allow himself to get involved with people's problems?

Red could plainly see that William was shaken and it was apparent that ole Willy boy was takin' this 'I owe you a debt,' thing ah whole lot more serious than was needed. The big guy had made his feelings clear by what he'd just said. His turnin' and walkin' away was like puttin' up a big stop sign, as far as he was concerned.

Like an unconscious reaction, William squared his shoulders and tried to follow Joe once more, but Red reached out and grabbed him by the shoulder, forcing William to stop.

"Whoa, good buddy, I do believe he made it real clear he wants ta travel all by his-self, so lets you and me just head on back down to the camp and make some plans of our own. What'ya say? The truth is, we don't need that guy."

"No! Let go of me!" William said stubbornly with a look between fear and anger growing on his face. "You just can't get it through your thick head, can you? Where he goes, I go, at least for now. Maybe where you're from debts don't mean much, but to me they do and I have a debt to repay. I was hoping you'd come along too; but if not, I can't wait, I have to go now before he gets too far ahead and I lose track of him."

Red stood looking into the eyes of a man who'd made his decision and would not be talked out of it. He knew what William was going through because he also, felt an obligation to both these men for saving his life. And he could also understand where the big guy was coming from. But the bottom line was, feeling obligated to someone who'd saved your life was just as strong down in Texas where he was from as it was anywhere else. Back home, they called it Texas pride.

Releasing his grip on William's shoulder, Red nodded, showing that he not only understood, but respected William's decision.

"I understand," Red said with a sigh.

A large smile appeared on William's face as he tried one last time. "I really would appreciate it if you would come along. Please. We all need each other, especially at this time. This is not a good time for any of us to be alone out here."

When Red shrugged his shoulders and looked down at his feet, William's smile disappeared and was replaced by a look of disappointment. After a moment, William turned and headed up the riverbank at a slow trot.

Red stood watching him with mixed feelings tugging at him. The sun felt warm against his back and a fish jumped out of the water, making a big splash as the hunter high above soared in a wide circle waiting for the interlopers to leave.

Red looked up at the hawk and said, "What am I supposed to do? On one hand the big guy made it clear that he wants to be left alone; while on the other hand, Mister William Conrad Bains for some reason wants us to all be together like we're longtime buddies or somethin'. I feel like I'm between ah rock and ah hard place."

The honest fact was, he was indebted to then both for pullin' him out of the river, but it seemed that neither of them were concerned about that. Why was that? Did his life mean so little to them? Why did things have to be so complicated?

Red spit into his hand, then slapped his palm with his other hand and looked to see which way the spittle went. It went up river. He shook his head and started off at a trot. As he trotted along, he reasoned with himself; even with his swollen hands and face, he was still in better condition to travel than William was, plus William would more than likely need his help.

Catching up wasn't the problem. It was the big guy himself Red was worried about. He was afraid if William pushed him too far, the big guy might get physical and from what William had said, he was not looking forward to a confrontation if it came to that.

Joe had glanced over his shoulder a few times and knew William was still following him and decided to take a different tact. Taking a last glance, he saw not only William, but the Texan as well. As he turned back, he saw what he was looking for. Just ahead the river curved to the left and would put him out of sight for a short time, giving him the opportunity to loose them once and for all. Encouraged by the thought, Joe increased his pace.

Once he rounded the curve, Joe looked behind him and they were no longer in sight. Joe smiled and headed into the trees and began to run, knowing from yesterday's experience William could not run fast or far, which would also slow down the Texan.

William saw Joe disappear around the curve but thought nothing of it until he rounded the curve and realized Joe could no longer be seen. Panic seized him and he began to jitter step all around like a nervous racehorse, trying to figure out where Joe had gone. His breathing became erratic and he began to sweat.

As Red came trotting around the curve he saw William dancing around like he was standing barefoot on an ant hill, talking to himself. Red looked around and saw the big guy had disappeared.

"Headed into the woods, did he?" Red said. It really wasn't a question, but an observation that anyone could figure out.

William looked at Red like he'd just asked him to explain the theory of relativity.

"How would I know where he went? One minute he was right in front of me and the next he was gone, poof, just like that," William said with a snap of his fingers. "I guess he could've gone off into the forest, but I don't know where or why? He knew I was trying to catch up."

"Could be that's why. He did tell us not to tag along after him. He made that pretty clear to me. You did hear that, didn't you?"

The Legend of Joe, Willy & Red

William settled down and finally stood still, staring at Red. "Yes, I heard him, but I didn't believe he really meant it, and I still don't. I don't think he's used to having friends, so he doesn't know how to deal with it; plus, I think he's afraid to try."

Red could see that turning back was still out of the question - it was not an option they could even discuss. Red also knew William was going to need his help, because without it, Mister William Conrad Bains would wind up running around in circles and get himself totally lost, maybe even hurt, or worse. Red hated to think what would happen if William ran into a bear or a mountain lion.

Scouting back, Red slowly checked the ground along the tree line above the rocky shore, figuring if it was him wantin to get away, he would take the first opportunity to head into the forest. Sure enough, just beyond the curve he found where Joe had headed into the forest.

"Hey, Willy boy, come over here and look at this. I found his footprint. He went into the trees right here," Red called out, pointing to a small indention in the grass.

Excitedly, William hurried over and stared down to where Red was pointing.

"What? I don't see anything," he said as he looked up at Red's smiling face.

"You have to know what you're lookin' for. Look right here, the grass has been stepped on, leavin' ah depression." Pointing, Red said, "The rounded area back here is where the heel of his shoe came down hard. And up here," he said, moving his finger, "This is where the toe of his shoe dug in a little deeper, like he was startin' ta run. I think he'll be easy enough ta track as long as he keeps runnin'."

To say the least, William was dumbfounded. Looking down to where Red was pointing, he only saw some grass that was slightly bent over.

"That's amazing. Where did you learn to do that? " William asked.

~ 41 ~

Jared McVay

Red's grin got even bigger as he rubbed his nose and said, "Ya see I'm only half Irish. The other half is Comanche Indian. And my grandfather on the Indian side taught me ta hunt and fish and track. Some folks say we're descendents of Quanah Parker who was the son of the famous Cynthia Ann Parker who was taken as a young girl by the Comanche back in the early eighteen hundreds. There's been a book written about her. Anyway, it ain't any different with animals or humans, ah footprint is ah footprint."

Red might not think it was a big deal, but William did. He was very impressed. It was a wondrous thing, the people you met at your time of need, and right out here in the middle of nowhere.

William waved his arm, pointing toward the trees, "Lead on oh great white hunter, we've big game to catch," he said laughing at his little joke.

Red moved into the forest with William a few paces behind.

At first the tracks were clear and easy to read. Joe was a big man and running left deep, easy tracks to follow. Red considered this and figured Joe doubted if he could be followed just by looking at his tracks. Besides, he was in a hurry to put distance between them and the quickest way to do that was to run.

The farther into the woods they got, the tougher the tracking became. The forest grew thicker, the trees were taller, their limbs intertwining with the tree next to it, like giants with their arms around each other's shoulders, blocking out the sun. It became a giant canopy that made it dark and hard to see. Pine needles covered the ground in this area, deep and thick, making a cushion that didn't leave tracks.

Red had to slow down. His skills were put to the test. He now had to look for a bent twig, a bent piece of grass when he could find one, or a broken limb where the man had run into it. It was slow, tedious work.

The Legend of Joe, Willy & Red

As the day wore on, Williams's endurance dwindled rapidly. He was tired, hungry
and his whole body ached. His feet were killing him and he was confused.

"Why haven't we caught up with him, yet? Are we lost? Can you still see his trail? You said he would be easy to track. Can't we go faster, I'm hungry and I need to rest."

Red was about to tell William to do the tracking himself, when they exited the forest and stood looking at a beautiful green valley three quarters of a mile long and a half a mile wide with a narrow creek cutting right through the middle. The small channel of water was no more than ten feet across and a bit less than knee deep, but the water ran cold and clear.

After zigzagging back and forth Red finally found a deep depression where Joe had knelt to drink. They followed Joe's tracks to a place just inside the tree line where a ring of boulders formed a nice camp that wasn't far from the stream. Here they found Joe's knapsack and a small pile of firewood, but Joe was nowhere to be seen, which seemed to upset William.

"Where could he have gone? There's no place to go. It isn't like there's a grocery store close by or anything."

After a short search, Red found Joe's tracks heading northwest into the forest. This time Joe was walking and they had little trouble following him. After a short way they topped over a small rise over looking a valley and a well kept looking farm with a white farmhouse, a red barn, a chicken house and several out buildings, plus a good sized coral where four work horses were milling around.

Red noticed a movement far to his right and when he realized what it was, he nudged William and pointed.

Joe was methodically making his way down the hill in the direction of the chicken pen. He was in plain sight for Red and William to see, but not from the farmhouse. Joe entered the chicken pen, stepping easily, making sure he

~ 43 ~

didn't disturb the chickens that were pecking the ground and entered the chicken house.

Chapter 5
The Chicken Pen Incident

Inside the chicken house there were thirty-five nests, but only twenty of them had hens sitting on them. Quickly and quietly Joe went down the row, checking under each hen for eggs, his ears alert for any sound of the farmer approaching, but the only sound he could hear was chickens clucking and scratching.

With six eggs in his coat pockets, Joe crept back toward the entryway. Near the door he decided a chicken might taste good and picked up a hen, cradling it in his arm.

Outside, Joe cautiously tiptoed toward the gate, nervously looking around for the farmer when he should have been concerned with the Road Island Red rooster eyeing him from a place not far from the henhouse. He was a big fella with bright feathers and small, beady eyes and was scratching the ground like a mad bull about to charge. This was his territory and intruders were not allowed. He was the lord and master of this yard and he ruled with a vengeance.

Even the farmer had to carry a broom to keep the big rooster at bay when he came in to collect eggs and that wasn't always enough to keep him from getting scars on his legs from where the rooster pecked and spurred him, but Joe wasn't privy to this information and was totally unaware of what was about to happen.

Joe was halfway to the gate when the rooster's top feathers stood straight up as he puffed out his chest, crowed, flapped his wings and launched his attack, causing Joe to run for the gate. Being too interested in the attacking rooster, Joe didn't see the metal feeder and tripped over it. Off balance and juggling the hen, Joe stumbled head first out through the gate and landed face down in the dirt, breaking the eggs in his pockets. The hen leaped away, running to join

~ 45 ~

the other hens that were fleeing the pen as they rushed past him, flapping their wings and cackling loudly.

Before Joe realized what was happening, the angry rooster jumped on top of his head, flapped his wings in triumph, crowed his victory song, pecked Joe on top of the head, then defecated on his neck.

Joe made a vicious swipe at him, but the rooster was too fast as he leaped away, then turned back to face Joe, his beady little eyes spitting fire, his wings arched, neck stuck out, ready to launch another attack if this intruder tried to bother his harem again.

Hidden among the trees, William and Red watched the show and were laughing so hard their stomachs hurt. William was making funny little croaking noises, trying to regain his breath and Red was leaning against a tree, wiping tears from his eyes. After all the hardships they'd endured, their laughter was uncontrollable. Both men covered their mouths, trying to keep their laughter from being heard.

As Joe got to his feet, the rooster suddenly turned and ran toward his flock as the sound of a barking dog presented new danger.

Joe looked around and saw a very large mongrel come charging out from under the farmhouse, headed in his direction. He was huge, black and ugly looking; a monster with long white trails of gooey slobbers sliding between his large, bared teeth.

It took Joe no time at all to figure out that he would be in a world of trouble if he didn't light a shuck, right now, so he took off, sprinting hard for the woods with the dog not far behind.

Joe had taken only a few steps when the farmer came charging out of the back door of the farmhouse with a shotgun in his hands.

Pandemonium greeted him. Chickens were running helter-skelter all over the yard, cackling at the top of their lungs, causing a big commotion, herded by an indignant rooster flapping his wings and crowing loudly. His dog was

The Legend of Joe, Willy & Red

barking and slobbering, hot on the heels of a strange man running toward the woods and the gate to the chicken pen lay in the yard, ripped off its hinges.

More from reaction than conscious thought, the farmer raised his shotgun and fired. Joe heard the roar of the shotgun and the buzzing of pellets as they ripped the air above his head. Luckily for both Joe and the dog the farmer's aim was as bad as his eyesight. Feeling a wave of relief, Joe pushed himself to run even faster, hoping he wouldn't wind up forfeiting his life for some broken eggs and a hen he couldn't even hang onto. If he died today it would be that rooster's fault!

Shoving another shell into the barrel of the shotgun, the farmer lit out on the run, hoping his dog Sampson would catch the guy before he reached the woods.

To the astonishment of both Red and William, Joe was headed straight in their direction as though a magnet had drawn him. Red made a motion and they moved back into the woods, looking for concealment where they wouldn't be seen, but still be able to watch what was happening.

Joe was running flat out, arms swinging, legs pumping and heart pounding, as the angry farmer fell farther and farther behind. While that was good, the slobbering dog was gaining on Joe by leaps and bounds.

Near the trees, Joe looked over his shoulder and saw the dog not twenty feet behind him! The dog's lips were pulled back in what looked like an evil grin with those large, vicious teeth bared, ready to rip Joe into small pieces.

Both fear and adrenalin washed over Joe like a huge tidal wave as he turned his head back to look for a tree he could climb. He figured he could deal with the farmer but not with some mongrel dog almost as big as he was, ready to make a meal out of him. He could almost feel those canines ripping and tearing his flesh.

As Joe's head came around his eyes went wide. A large tree was directly in his path, not more than half a stride in front of him and he was running full out. He dodged to his left to miss colliding with the tree but couldn't duck the fat stub of a limb sticking out, head high and right in front of him.

There was a loud thwack as Joe's head smacked into the limb, which gave off a reverberating sound that echoed throughout the forest like the crack of the bat against a baseball when the mighty Babe Ruth hit a homerun.

Joe had one quick stab of pain as his feet went into the air and then he came down, hard, flat on his back, lost in a sea of darkness.

Both Red and William felt helpless as the big mongrel dog ran up and straddled Joe's chest, teeth bared, ears back, growling and snarling as his slobbers dripped onto Joe's face.

The farmer came lumbering up the hill, yelling at the dog, "Hold him Sampson! Hold him boy! I'm ah comin'! "

Not knowing what else to do, William and Red did nothing but watch as the over weight farmer clambered onto the scene, sucking wind like a fish out of water gasping for air. He was a big man with a long gray, stringy gray beard that showed dark brown tobacco stains. The man was definitely not used to running. He removed his hat and wiped his balding head with a rag from the back pocket of his overalls. His eyes were gray and bloodshot. Both his hands and his face had a brown tint to them from working outside a lot. His bib overalls were patched and work stained and his shoes were in need of repair. Overall, he appeared to be somewhere in his late sixties.

The farmer stood for some time propping his arm against a tree, trying to regain control of his breathing as he stared down at Joe with a very unfriendly look on his face. Sampson, the dog, remained standing astride the unconscious man.

For a while, both Red and William thought the farmer might have ideas about shooting Joe, but fortunately didn't and seemed to relax after catching his breath, which also

The Legend of Joe, Willy & Red

allowed Red and William to relax, too. They remained deadly quiet least the farmer or his dog learn of their whereabouts. They wanted no part of the dog or the shotgun.

After what seemed an eternity, Joe's eyes began to flutter. He moved slightly, then went rigid. Somewhere in the recesses of his brain, Joe remembered the big dog that was now snarling with bared teeth close to his throat. He felt large globs of hot sticky stuff landing on his face.

Some of the worst fear Joe had ever known jumped to the conscious part of his brain. To be torn apart by an angry dog would be a terrible way to die. If push came to shove, he knew he would do what he could to defend himself but he also knew at this point, he wouldn't be able to do much. An intense pain akin to huge lightning bolts were striking his brain and war drums thundered loud in his ears, plus, he could barely see.

From somewhere down near his feet, over the sound of the war drums, came the sound of a gruff voice.

"Easy Sampson, easy boy. Good dog."

Joe watched through the tiny slits of his swollen face as a hand reached in and pulled the dog off of him, only to be replaced by the business end of a shotgun. It was then he remembered the farmer who had been shooting at him as he ran for the safety of the trees. Had he been shot? That would account for the terrible pain in his head. But there was also a flash in his brain of a tree. He wasn't sure what that was all about and before he could sort things out, he heard that gruff voice again.

"You thevin', low down, no good tramp, give me one good reason why I shouldn't blow your head off and feed your carcass to the crows. You tore off the gate to my chicken pen and scattered my chickens from here to Denver and morn' likely stole some eggs. I could kill you right here and now and nobody would be the wiser."

~ 49 ~

Jared McVay

When Joe didn't respond, the farmer poked Joe with the barrel of his shotgun and said, "Sit up mister and explain to me why I shouldn't do just that."

William had seen and heard enough. Fear mixed with a force he couldn't explain started his feet moving and before Red could stop him William ran into the clearing and stopped less than ten feet from where Joe lay on his back.

Sampson turned to face him, slobbering, growling and baring his teeth, ready to attack as soon as his master gave the word.

Startled by William's sudden appearance, the big farmer pointed his shotgun in William's direction. To William it looked like a cannon pointing at him. His throat went dry and his mouth felt like it was full of cotton and his knees were straining to hold him up. He looked at the dog, then up to the farmer, down to Joe and finally back to the farmer again.

Chapter 6
The birth of Willy the Con

"Thank god you've found him! I've been running around in circles," William said, as though a weight had been lifted off his shoulders. "You can't imagine what I've been through. And now at last, all the worrying has been lifted from my mind. Thank you, thank you."

The farmer stared at the short, fat man in a three-piece suit and was confused. He put his hand on Sampson's back to quiet him until he could get this figured out, as he glanced down at Joe, then back to William.

"What'ya mean, thank God I've found him? Who in God's name is this guy? And who are you?" the farmer asked, raising the barrel of his shotgun slightly just in case some kind of funny business was going on.

All the while, Sampson eyed William menacingly with a look that made William feel weak and sick to his stomach. Suddenly, fear and adrenaline rushed throughout his body, as his heart began to beat out of control. He had chest pains and his stomach was trying to turn upside down.

Then, as quickly as the feelings had come, they disappeared and a miracle of sorts happened. All of his nervousness disappeared like smoke in the wind. A calmness like he'd never experienced before flowed smoothly through his veins

Putting his first finger to his lips, William whispered, "Shhh," while motioning for the farmer to come closer.

The farmer stood his ground while he mulled things over in his confused state. As he stood there, his eyes scanned the forest behind William to see if there were any more people who might suddenly rush out, but there was no movement that he could see other than the leaves swaying in the gentle breeze.

The farmer swung his attention back to the short, fat man. He was wearing the clothes of a city fella and appeared to be alone. And by the looks of him, he didn't look threatening. He was portly, with a friendly, round face and body.

Finally, he looked down at Sampson and said, "Stay."

With slow, deliberate steps, the farmer walked toward William, still holding the shotgun at the ready. The farmer wasn't worried about the guy lying on the ground for several reasons. First, he was in no condition to do anything but lie there. And if by some miracle he was able to get to his feet, he still had to deal with Sampson.

It was his curiosity about the fat man in a dirty three-piece suit that intrigued him and moved him forward. He seemed to have some big secret to tell and he wanted to know what it was. Living out here all alone with no one but the animals to talk to had it's drawbacks. Even his radio had called it quits a couple of weeks ago and he hadn't had time to go into town and buy a new one. Thinking about it, he realized he hadn't been to town in over a month. He'd go tomorrow.

Red wasn't sure what William's plan was because he'd run out there without a word. Red wasn't sure William even had a plan and was just acting on impulse or some urge to help. Whatever it was, Red was sure it had something to do with that obligation to help the big guy and repay his debt.

With that in mind, Red decided to just sit tight and watch. There was no reason to expose his-self if he didn't have to. And if things didn't go right, he could always start ah diversion of some kind, like hollerin' or somethin'. But his gut told him that wouldn't be necessary. Call it an intuition, or whatever name you put to these sort of feelings, Red just knew that somehow, some way, William was gonna get the big guy out of trouble.

As Red sat there watching an idea began to form and when he was sure William and the big guy would be all right, he slowly inched his way back into the forest.

The Legend of Joe, Willy & Red

Joe turned his head slightly as the farmer moved away, following him with his eyes as he walked toward; William? How did William get here? This wasn't possible. William and that red haired guy from Texas were supposed to be wandering around somewhere in the woods. He figured this must be hallucination, his brain playing tricks on him and he looked away, blinking his eyes to focus them better.

Yet when he looked again, there stood William, big as life, babbling away with the farmer. His eyes were wide and he was making wild jesters with his arms. And even though William was acting like a crazy man, he was speaking very quietly, almost at a whisper and he wasn't able to hear what William was saying.

From time to time the farmer would glance in his direction, then shake his head and make little, tsk, tsk, tsk, noises. It was all very confusing.

Joe closed his eyes, hoping the pain in his head would go away. He was about to drift off to sleep when he heard the farmer call to his dog.

"Here, Sampson, here boy; com'on, let's go."

Joe opened his eyes and watched as the big mongrel dog ran off, chasing some unknown foe.

With William's help, Joe was able to sit up, scoot over and lean his back against the tree, his head throbbing and spinning with every movement. From where he sat he could see the farmer walking down the hill, noticing that with a weary look on his face, the farmer would look back over his shoulder from time to time and shake his head from side to side, then continue on for another ten to twenty steps before he would do it all over again. Near the bottom of the hill, the farmer stopped and turned back to stare at Joe for a long moment while he pulled an old rag from his back pocket and blew his nose and wiped tears from his eyes. Then with a farewell wave, the farmer turned and walked slowly back to his farm.

Jared McVay

"What in blue blazes did you tell that farmer to make him call off his dog and walk away? And why is he acting like that? What have you been up to?" Joe asked in a voice that needed answers. In a matter of minutes his world had been turned upside down.

"Well, if you really want to know," William said, grinning like some little boy who'd done something mischievous. "I told him you were my retarded cousin and you weren't responsible for your actions. I told him that you had been kicked in the head by a mule a few weeks back, leaving you with severe brain damage and you only had a few weeks to live."

"You're the one who is retarded!" Joe said. "How in the world did you ever come up with a hair-brained story like that?"

Still grinning, William said, "The clincher was when I told him about your folks getting killed in a car wreck while they were bringing you home from the hospital so you could die in your own bed."

Joe couldn't believe what he was hearing. "You didn't actually tell him that, did you?"

William beamed. "I sure did. And I told him you must have been thrown from the car, somehow, and being retarded and scared, and probably confused, we figured you ran away. I told him I've been searching for you for the better part of a week. I also told him I was eternally grateful for him not shooting you or letting his dog chew you up. He seemed touched by the whole thing and was definitely sympathetic."

"Sympathetic? Are you tryin' ta tell me that old man bought that cock-ah-mammi story?"

William nodded his head. "Certainly, He had no reason not to. I have to admit, I did come off sounding very convincing and sincere. There was even tears in my eyes, and that really got to him."

Leaning back against the tree, Joe closed his eyes, praying this absurd dream would end. It wasn't real. It

The Legend of Joe, Willy & Red

couldn't be. None of this could really have happened and after a minute he opened his eyes. Nothing had changed. The farmer and his dog were still headed down the hillside, William was still hovering over him and he still had a bad headache.

Looking up at William, Joe said, "There's still one thing driving me crazy. How did you get here? How did you find me? You're supposed to still be wanderin' around back in the woods or back down at that camp we stayed in last night."

"Oh that," William said. "As it turned out, Red is half Indian and his grandfather on the Indian side taught him how to track things. So, we just followed your tracks. Then we found your camp up close to the creek, then followed you here."

Pointing in the general direction of where he and Red had been hiding, he said,

"We got up there just as you were crossing the field down there and watched the whole thing. When the farmer and his dog started chasing you, we moved back up the hill and hid behind some bushes."

"I see," Joe said, shaking his head in wonderment. "Is that when you got the bright idea to play boy-scout and save me with that outrageous story?"

"I'm not really sure," William said. "I guess something inside me snapped when I heard that farmer talking about shooting you and dragging your body into the woods for the critters to feast on, because the next thing I knew, I was running out here, telling him that story. I can't explain it. Honestly, I've never done anything like that before."

Joe glanced down the hill and grinned when he saw the farmer get close to the chicken pen where the chickens were still running around wildly, making a ruckus. And that ole rooster was still protecting his ladies because he flapped his wings and crowed loudly, challenging the farmer just like he had done him. But the farmer would have none of it and reached down and picked up a hand full of dirt and threw it right in the rooster's face, which caused the rooster to prance around the yard crowing and flapping his wings like he'd been insulted.

Watching the scene caused Joe to recall his own run-in with the lord of the hens. That must have been quite a sight, he thought. And when the dog and the farmer came chasing after him, well, that would have been the grand finale to the show.

Joe looked up at William and said, "Well, I guess that makes us even. Yesterday I pulled you out of harm's way and today you saved me from getting chewed up by that ole mongrel dog or shot by that farmer. Now you don't owe me anything and I don't owe you anything. We're all squared up. You can go your way and I can go mine. Right?"

"Oh I don't know if that's such a good thing. I think you'll need some doctoring for a while."

"No!" Joe said sternly. "I don't want or need ah nursemaid!"

"I didn't mean it like that," William hastened to say.

"I don't care how you meant it. I go my own way. You're probably a decent guy and all that, but I'm a loner, always have been and always will be. So try to get that through that thick skull of yours. I travel alone."

Joe leaned his head back against the tree; his head was beginning to feel like it was going to split open with all this talk. He felt like he might pass out again.

William hung his head, slowly toeing the grass in a circular motion with his shoe, looking like a young boy who'd just been reprimanded.

By now the farmer had enticed the chickens and the rooster back into the pen by dropping a trail of corn and by the time Joe looked in that direction again, the farmer was re-hanging the gate.

Joe turned back to William and said, "I guess we'd better get out of here before he has a chance to think about what you said and realizes he'd been hoodwinked and gets

The Legend of Joe, Willy & Red

mad all over again. I definitely don't want you to have to come up with another one of those outrageous stories on my account. God only knows what you'd come up with this time."

As William helped Joe to his feet, Joe asked, "By the way, I don't see that other guy. Where is this famous tracker from Texas?"

William had forgotten about Red and looked up to the spot where they'd been hiding and called out, "Hey, Red, Red, are you still up there?"

When there was no answer, William said, "That's where he was when I came running out here. I can't imagine where he is now."

"Did you consider that he had more sense that to tangle with a mean dog and a man with a shotgun?" Joe said with a bit of testiness in his voice.

William looked at the sky and said, "No. Actually we didn't discuss it. I just came running out on my own."

"Well, no matter. I need to get back to my camp," Joe said as he turned to head up the hill and would have fallen if William hadn't taken his arm.

Tramping through the forest in his condition made Joe almost helpless. Not only could he not see well enough to navigate on his own because of the puffiness around his eyes, he also had great difficulty keeping his balance. The terrain was uneven and the world kept spinning, forcing him to stop frequently to let his vision clear.

While all of that was bad enough, the part that made him angry enough to grind his teeth was having to hold onto William like a crutch and letting William lead him like he was a blind man.

On the other side of the coin, William was happy that Joe needed his help, but a little nervous about having to lead the way. Red was much better at this sort of thing.

Try as he might, he couldn't understand where Red had disappeared to, or why. Adding to his worry was the fact that it was getting darker by the minute and somewhere far away a wolf's lonely cry pierced the mountain air, causing goose bumps to pop up on the back of William's neck.

Aside from his immediate problem, getting them back to camp safely, William felt proud of himself, rushing out there like that, telling that big whooper and making that ole farmer believe it. And best of all was saving the big guy from being chewed to death by that vicious dog or blown apart by that angry farmer, who would have left him lying there for the wolves to finish off.

He was an honest to goodness hero; yes-sir, a full-fledged hero! In his mind he could see the newspaper headline: Former bank teller, William Conrad Bains took a dangerous situation and turned it around. In fact he turned it into something laughable while at the same time saving a man's life and repaying a debt he never thought he would be able to repay. Thank you Mister Bains.

The next time they had to stop and let Joe's head clear, Joe leaned against a tree and sulked. Letting this city guy lead him through the forest like a helpless child was against his nature. He hated depending on anyone, especially that Mister William Conrad Bains, but through some eerie twist of fate, here he was, out here in the middle of no where, hardly able to stand on his feet and harboring the most horrendous headache he'd ever had, stumbling along behind a man who couldn't find his way across the street let alone through the woods.

And to make matters worse, yesterday, this same man had been curled up in a ball, lying on the ground, screaming for help. But today he had appeared out of thin air and snatched him from the jaws of death by telling some far-fetched tale that only an idiot would believe, and now was acting like some boy scout earning his merit badge for helping an old lady across the street.

Even though he couldn't read the man's mind, William knew he wasn't the best of guides. All the trees

The Legend of Joe, Willy & Red

looked the same to him and if anyone had asked him, he'd have to admit he was lost most of the time.

The moon was shining brightly when they finally emerged from the dark forest near the creek. The contrast was startling for a moment. One minute you could barely see your hand in front of your face and the next it almost seemed like daylight. William halted, as he stared at the campfire in the distance with hope in his heart and a prayer on his lips.

He hoped and prayed it was Joe's camp and Red would be there waiting for them to show up, because if it wasn't they might be in big trouble. What would he do if it were somebody else's camp? Or what if somebody else had found Joe's camp and had taken it over as their own?

"What's the matter? Why have we stopped? I don't need a rest yet." Joe said.

Joe heard the sound of water running and guessed they weren't far from where he'd made his camp. At least he hoped that was the case. With Mister William Conrad Bains leading the way, who could be sure?

They had gone only a short distance when William uttered a sigh of relief as he saw Red in the glow of the firelight and no one else.

Joe sniffed the air and said, "I smell coffee and bacon."

"That's what it smells like to me, too," William exclaimed.

But whose coffee and bacon is it, William wondered? The coffee might be Joe's, but he couldn't recall the big guy having any bacon and for sure neither he nor Red had any when they arrived at the camp earlier that afternoon.

Nearing the campsite, William saw Red squatting next to the campfire with a cup of coffee in his hand and heard the sound of bacon frying in a skillet. A wonderful aroma filled the air and made William's mouth water.

He could hardly believe they'd actually made it back to the camp. His reaction was mixed with confusion over

~ 59 ~

seeing Red here in the camp. What made him run off like that, William wondered?

As they approached, Red raised his cup in a salute. "Well, it's about time you two showed up. I was just beginning to think I was gonna have ta eat all this food by myself. The coffee's fresh. Pour yourselves ah cup from those mugs there," Red said, pointing to two big, brown coffee cups sitting close to the coffee pot. "Rest yourselves while I fry up some eggs and taters and burn some toast ta go along with the bacon. It'll only take a couple of minutes," he said as he noticed Joe's dependency on William for help.

William stared around the camp, completely flabbergasted. Not only were there three coffee mugs, but also there were plates and eating utensils. And not far from the fire, three blankets were laid out, with pillows!

"Where did you get all of this?" William asked, waving his arm around the camp.

Red moved the skillet to one side so the bacon wouldn't burn and stood up. "Well sir, after you ran out there ta parlay with that farmer and his dog, and seein' how you and him was getting tighter'n ah couple of love birds, I didn't see any need for me ta stick around cause an idea was kickin' around in my head. I reckoned it might be a good time ta have ah look see at that ole farmer's house - you know, see if there might be ah few things he could spare that would make our livin' out here in the open ah bit more comfortable. The only thing I had ta keep an eye out for was that killer rooster."

For no more than a moment Red and William stared at each other before filling the air with laughter, remembering the hilarious incident between Joe and the big Road Island Red, ruler of the chicken yard.

Joe made his way to a spot near one of the boulders near the fire where he could sit and rest, and remember that cantankerous ole rooster, but not finding it humorous in any way. The broken eggs still lay crushed in his pockets and were beginning to give off a bit of an odor.

The Legend of Joe, Willy & Red

As they were finishing their meal, a question popped into William's head and he looked over at Red and asked, "When you decided to go down to that farmer's house, did it occur to you that he might have a wife and she just might get a mite upset with you for barging in and, you know, borrowing all this food, along with the blankets and pillows and other stuff?"

"Sure," Red answered. "But during all that ruckus that was goin' on, with them chickens ah squawking', the dog ah barkin' and that farmer shootin' off his shotgun, well doncha' think if there was ah woman about, wouldn't she be checkin' on things and out there tryin' ta get them chickens back in the pen? But ain't nobody even looked out of ah window. So, I reckoned the coast was clear. And it was, too. And from the way the place was all cluttered up, that inside ain't seen ah woman's touch in quite ah spell. Besides, he won't miss what I took cause he had plenty and then some."

William grinned at Red and said, "Well, I can't remember when bacon and eggs ever tasted this good." And with that, William nodded his head in Red's direction while raising his coffee mug and said, "My thanks to our benefactor and my compliments to the chef. And to show my appreciation, I'll do the dishes."

Red raised his coffee mug and said, "Friend William, you are a gentleman and a scholar. I accept your most generous offer."

While William was preparing everything to take down to the creek and wash, Red studied Joe as he cleaned up his plate. He was a strange one. The man had not uttered a single word since getting back, not one word. Red wondered if this guy had bothered to thank William for what he'd done for him, or how much courage it had taken for him to do it; probably not. What made the man so standoffish, Red wondered, as he stretched out on his blanket?

Even though Joe wouldn't admit it to them, he was glad they had come along when they did and knew he should say something, but he just couldn't bring himself to do it. Instead, he got to his feet and made his way down to the creek where he washed his own dishes, then cleaned the broken eggs out of his jacket pockets and soaked his towel in the cold creek water.

Back at the camp, Joe placed everything near the fire to dry, then lay down on his blanket and put the cold towel over his swollen face.

After banking the fire, William also curled up in his blanket and dropped his head onto the pillow. It had been a long day.

Shortly, the sound of snoring from both William and Red mixed with the crooning of frogs filled the air. Joe got up and made his way down to the creek again, where he re-wet his towel, then went back to the camp and sat down close to the fire, which was in need of fuel. After adding more wood he lit a cigarette and leaned back against one of the boulders, then placed the cold, wet towel over his eyes and sighed. It felt good. As he smoked his cigarette and let his body relax, thoughts of the past week ran through his mind. When at last he climbed back under his blanket, Joe wondered how he was going to deal with the days ahead.

Laying his head on the pillow and closing his eyes, Joe decided he'd wait for morning to make a decision.

Chapter 7
Gone Again

A fish jumped in the creek, then a blue jay squawked loudly and a woodpecker tapped reveille on the trunk of a nearby pine tree as shafts of sunlight weaved their way through the trees. One shaft in particular found its way onto William's face, causing his eyelids to flutter. Gradually, William opened his eyes and looked around as the robust aroma of coffee filled his nostrils.

William sat up and pulled the blanket around his shoulders, shivering in the cold morning as he looked around, trying to orientate himself.

"Mornin'," Red said as he poured more coffee into his mug. "Glad ta see you're finally awake. For a while there I was beginning ta think you were gonna sleep the day away. Plenty of coffee left. Get yourself some while I put on some bacon."

William's eyes swept the camp, down along the creek, then back to the camp.

"Where's our friend?" William asked, climbing to his feet.

"He's gone again," Red said. "And he's not our friend."

"Well why didn't you wake me? We have to go after him. He shouldn't travel on his own in the condition he's in," William shouted nervously. "Come on, help me break camp. We've got to find him."

"No. Let him go. The man doesn't want us hangin' around. He keeps tellin' you, but you don't listen."

Red felt sorry for William, but he had to come to terms with how things were.

William was rolling up his blanket when Red offered him a mug of coffee. "Here, at least drink this before you leave. And like I said, I ain't trackin' him no more. You can do what you want," Red said, trying to keep his voice calm.

Jared McVay

"When I got up just before daylight, he was already gone. Now what does that tell ya? Paints ah clear picture to me and it should to you, too."

Reality is sometimes a hard pill to swallow, but William had to admit Red was right as he walked off into the forest to do his morning business. Any debt he might have felt toward Joe had been paid in full, yesterday. Their association was over and done with, and as sorry as he felt, he might as well accept it.

Even though Joe had stated several times that he was a loner and didn't want anyone tagging along after him, he had never truly believed him, and he felt a sense of loss that he couldn't quite understand.

Back at the camp he sat down on a nearby log to drink his coffee and think.

"I wonder what makes a man act like that? Why can't he just accept us as friends which would be the normal thing to do," William asked to no one in particular.

Red thought for a minute, trying to find a way to explain it to William so he would understand.

"That's somethin' only he can answer. Ever think that maybe he doesn't know either? Each of us is how we are and I doubt if many of us try figuring out why. I know I haven't. I heard ah man up in Dallas couple years ago say folks are products of their environments and the genes of their parents, whatever that's supposed ta mean."

Red turned the bacon so it wouldn't burn, then stuck slices of bread onto sticks and held them over the fire, turning them slowly so they would toast evenly.

"Strange, ain't it, how we don't think much on things like that. We discuss folks and all their good or bad points, but we don't look too hard at ourselves," Red said as he took the bacon off the fire and set it to one side. "Can you honestly tell me why you're the way you are?"

William stared into his coffee mug, shaking his head, "No, not really. I suppose my upbringing and education had something to do with it, and maybe the genes as well, I guess. I've been told I have my father's look and my mother's temperament. But I also know of people who are nothing like their parents. What about murderers and thieves and rapists? They don't all come from a poor environment, or have terrible parents."

As William ate his breakfast, he pondered over what kind of environment the big guy had been raised in, and what his parents had been like.

Jared McVay

Chapter 8

Josiah Nathaniel Wilson

Standing in the darkness and away from the light coming through the back door, Joe handed two nickels to the man with a dirty apron. The cook handed Joe a bowl of stew and a cup of coffee.

"Just leave the bowl and cup here on the back porch when you're done and give ah knock on the door so I can pick'em up afore the boss has ah chance ta find'em," the cook said, nervously as he pocketed the two nickels. "This is the most I can do."

Joe would have gone into the café in Haden, Colorado, to eat, but he didn't want people staring at him, or asking questions. So, he went to the back door where the cook was glad to get the ten cents for himself.

The swelling on his forehead and around Joes eyes had gone down considerably but his face was still black and blue; and people being what they were would be curious, or he might run into a policeman who would definitely want to know why he looked like he'd just gone ten rounds with Jack Dempsey.

As Joe sat in the darkness of the back stoop, eating a large bowl of stew, dipping his bread in the juices so as not to waste any, he allowed his mind to dwell on a mixture of things.

Both William and Red were in deep sleep when he'd crept silently from the camp, just before daybreak. Part of him felt bad about leaving like that. They were decent guys who only wanted his friendship, but they didn't understand. He wasn't able to have close friends.

Twenty-eight years ago, his parents had split on him. One day they were there and the next, they were gone. Just like that he'd become an eight year old boy roaming the streets of New York City, alone, with no place to go.

The Legend of Joe, Willy & Red

Evicted for non-payment of rent, his parents had left him a note saying they could no longer take care of him. That was it. The note didn't say anything about why, or that they were sorry, or offer any suggestions about where he should go - possibly a relative or something. Nothing. They hadn't even signed the note.

Joe remembered feeling confused, deserted and scared. And why shouldn't he be, after all he was only eight years old.

At least the landlady had said she was sorry for him when she saw him leaving; and that he was probably better off since his parents were both alcoholics who cared more for their habit than their only child. That was also the day Josiah Nathaniel Wilson became a loner. From that day on he depended on no one but himself.

For several months he'd roamed the alleyways, eating out of trashcans behind restaurants and sleeping in cardboard boxes or anywhere else he could get in out of the weather.

His first job had been setting pins in a bowling alley for a penny a line. With his wages and a tip now and then, he was able to get by for almost a year; until some old, fat waitress at the bowling alley found out he was living in a metal container in the alley back of the bowling alley and put in a call to the juvenile authorities.

The juvenile authorities sent this holier than thou young woman, who with the aid of the police, hauled him away to the county orphanage, while she ranted and raved at him about the injustices of the poor, misbegotten children of the world. In between her ranting, she pointed to the bible she carried and quoted this or that scripture to prove her point.

Joe learned very quickly that orphanages take away your freedom. But on the other side, he did get a roof over his head, a bed to sleep in and three squares a day, such as they were. There was mush for breakfast, mush and block cheese for lunch and mush and a few vegetables for supper.

~ 67 ~

On Sunday when people were around, they had stew and hardtack bread.

At first, he'd tried to make friends but quickly learned that none of them could be trusted. A big, Irish kid named O'Banion had come the closest, but in the end, after a couple of fights, Joe excluded even him.

The infamous Miss Hatch, a large, brute of a woman, was the head administrator and lorded over the home with an iron fist and a leather strap. For some reason, Miss Hatch had taken an instant dislike to him and seemed to delight in punishing him for this or that minor infraction; most of which he'd never heard of. Even so, he'd never cried or offered any excuses to keep from getting punished, which irritated her even more.

"Cry, damn you!" she'd shout.

But he would only stare at her with cold, young eyes that held no tears.

Once the other kids found out about this, they used it to keep themselves out of trouble by blaming Joe for their misdeeds until he figured out what they were doing and caught each one alone and made them wish they had taken their own punishment.

After that, word got around and they shunned him like the plague, which was fine with him. At least now he wasn't getting as many whippings.

Headmistress Hatch had two female aids that were almost as cruel as the head mistress herself. One in particular would make Joe drop his pants when Miss Hatch gave her permission to give him a strapping. She knew the humility he would suffer because none of the boys wore underwear. Sometimes Miss Hatch would stay to watch and make jesters.

By the time Joe was thirteen, he was bigger than any of the other boys except the O'Banion kid, who was taller than Joe by an inch and outweighed him by ten pounds or so.

On occasions, Joe caught the female aids spying on him when they could catch him in the shower, alone. And Miss Augustine made it clear on more than one occasion that she would go easy on him if he would do certain sexual favors for her. After turning her down on each occasion, she made it her business to see that Joe was first in line on her punishment list.

As time went by, Joe began to notice that hardly any of the girls and a couple of the young boys, ever got punished. And it was about this same time Joe also began to believe the rumors that the head mistress gave special treatment to anyone who did certain favors for the gentlemen who dropped by from time to time.

The headmistress didn't believe in wasting their time on education, either. As far as she was concerned, it would be a waste of time since none of them would profit from it.

Prostitutes and common laborers was the best they could expect.

While working off a detention by cleaning the basement, Joe discovered several boxes of schoolbooks furnished by the state of New York.

Next, Joe learned that the night watchman had a habit of coming to work half in the bag, so it took no great effort on Joe's part to sneak down into the basement each night where he studied from the books.

This went on until he was sixteen and by then, he was within two inches of his present height of six feet. Along with his height, Joe worked out and had filled out nicely.

And after careful planning, one rainy night as the night watchman, who had come to work with a snoot full, sat bent over with his head lying on his desk, snoring loudly, Joe had simply walked out the door, climbed the fence and was gone.

At first, work was not easy to come by, but on the third day, Joe found a place where his size counted more than his age when he landed a job on the docks, working as a roustabout, loading and unloading ships. He was a good worker and the pay was decent. But instead of going to the bars like many of his fellow workers did, Joe spent his free time at the city library, reading books on every subject that caught his eye, One day, while reading a newspaper, he read an ad that he decided to follow up on.

He was eighteen by then and with the hard work on the docks, along with a diet of good food, he'd not only grown big and strong, but had developed a fondness for a good scrap now and then, which was easy to find. There was always someone looking to mix it up.

The ad had said he could make cash money working as a sparring partner for the professional prizefighters at a gym not far from the boarding house where he lived. Joe tore out the ad and headed for the gym.

Boxing seemed to come naturally to him and he quickly earned a reputation as a good sparring partner. From time to time there were offers to fight as a professional, but he turned them down. He hadn't decided what he wanted to do with his life, but getting his head bashed on constantly, definitely wasn't it.

When the war broke out he'd joined the army and soon found himself in France as a member of the one hundred seventy five thousand men attached to the American Expeditionary Force, then on the line as a foot soldier in the Allied section near Belford where he was promoted to sergeant for bravery and leadership.

The truth was, he was just trying to stay alive when a bunch of Germans got in his way. The other soldiers, the officers and the army, had blown the whole thing way out of proportion. But he soon found out, such was the way of the war.

By the time World War One ended, he'd seen enough of France and Germany and was sick of it all. He'd survived, but thousands and thousands of men hadn't. Far too many of the men under his command would never see their families again, or would go home a cripple, wondering how they would make a living.

Joe sighed as he sat the empty bowl and coffee cup on the porch near the door and then rolled himself a smoke as his thoughts returned to the present. Two days had gone by since he'd left William and Red sleeping. They hadn't caught up with him yet, which he hoped was a good sign.

When a train whistle pierced the night, Joe banged on the back door as he stood up and headed for a place where he could hopefully board the train without being seen.

His next stop, if the cook could be believed, would be Craig, Colorado. Just west of town there was supposed to be a decent hobo camp where he could catch some rest and hide out for a while.

Joe crouched near the water tower, watching as a fat man in bib overalls walked along, glancing inside and under each boxcar in a nonchalant manner as he headed for the front of the train. The man didn't seem too worried about anyone boarding the train here, inside the town limits. At least, Joe hoped that was the case.

A few minutes later, while the railroad men had their backs turned to him and laughing at some joke one of them had told, Joe ran the short distance and quietly climbed aboard an empty boxcar.

As the train headed west, Joe relaxed inside the empty boxcar and allowed a chuckle to escape his lips for the first time since that fiasco with the rooster and the farmer.

"That William," he said to himself, "may not be much of a fighter, but if he ever gets the chance to talk..."

Chapter 9

Following the same trail

On the third day after Joe's disappearance William and Red found themselves in Hayden, Colorado, eating at the same restaurant Joe had frequented the night before, only they were eating inside, not on the back porch.

Unlike most men riding the rails, Joe, William and Red each had a little money on their person the day their lifestyle had been turned upside down. By no means were any of them rich, but each man had just enough to appreciate that they weren't destitute and could afford a decent meal now and then.

Their first day after Joe had left had been very slow. Instead of attempting to hop a freight train, which had been their first option, they decided to try hitchhiking, which turned out to be not so enjoyable.

The only person to offer them a ride was an old man who made them ride in the back of his truck with the livestock: two old mossy backed cows who dropped big piles of dung everywhere and eyed them with hostility.

The second day turned out to be worse than the first. By late afternoon, no one had offered them a ride and they were worn to a frazzle from walking all day. That night they camped on the bank of a small creek and ate the last of their food.

On the third day they abandoned the hitchhiking idea and climbed aboard a slow moving freight train that delivered them to their present location, Hayden, Colorado. It was early evening when they jumped from the train just outside of town without incident.

It had been no more than dumb luck for them to board a train that had a railroad bull, if you could call him that, who was a man that firmly believed in live and let live; and any sort of physical labor was beneath his caste in life.

The Legend of Joe, Willy & Red

Yelling loudly at someone seemed to him to be quite sufficient to justify his job title.

Besides, he was not a well man, most of the time, and even a big man such as himself could get hurt in an all out fisticuff situation with someone he didn't know, nor care about. That made absolutely no sense to him. Some of these hobos could be quite mean. At least that's what he'd heard.

He liked his job. A distant cousin had been instrumental in helping him attain this position that not only paid well, but also kept him far away from the constant belittling of a woman he sorely detested; his wife.

Red and William had debarked the train and were walking in the direction of the restaurant when by chance coming up just behind the bull and the engineer heading for the same restaurant and happened to over hear their conversation. The bull was asking,

"How long before we pull out?"

"Bout an hour. Just long enough to get a bite to eat," the portly engineer said, patting his stomach.

All four men walked into the restaurant and Red and William purposely sat nearby so they could overhear the bull and engineer's conversation.

"I've got stomach cramps and the forty yard trots," the bull stated, grimacing and rubbing his belly.

This illness came as no surprise, nor did he believe the bull was really sick, not with the big meal he was putting away. It wasn't the first time he'd faked being sick in this same town. Gossip had it that there was a friendly widow in town who welcomed his visits. Pleasure before duty. Some guys had all the luck, and even if he knew of some willing lady to keep company with, in some remote town, who would keep the train on schedule?

"No problem," the engineer said, "this is just a turn around. I can pick you up on the way back. Can you find a place to stay for a couple of days?" He knew the answer without asking, but this was part of the game.

Jared McVay

"Yea, sure. I got an aunt that lives here. Are you sure it'll be okay? I don't like leaving the caboose empty like that, or you bein' shorthanded," the bull said, trying to sound sincere.

"Hey, who's gonna know? This is the middle of nowhere and I ain't seen no bums hanging around," the engineer said, waving his arm in a wide arc. "Now you go on and get outta here. I'll see ya when I come back through."

As the bull hurried out of the restaurant, the engineer felt a twinge of jealously. It had been six years since his wife died and in all that time, there had been no woman in his life. She'd meant the world to him and no one could ever take her place. He'd tried several times when he felt a need, but guilt would overcome him and he would not seek out female companionship.

All of a sudden his appetite was gone and he left without finishing his meal.

Shortly thereafter, Red and William found themselves riding west in the caboose of the train; sitting in seats with a table between them, just like at the restaurant. Not only were they comfortable, they also found things in the cabinets to snack on - cookies, apples, peanuts and a few staples they would take with them when they got off the train.

William was as happy as a kid at Christmas time as he packed, eggs, coffee, bacon and bread into a sack.

Thoughts of reuniting with Joe were temporarily placed on the back burner of their minds. And the fact that they were stealing from the railroad didn't seem to bother their conscience one little whit.

Actually, it seemed appropriate after the abuse each of them had suffered at the hands of the bulls. William had only one concern.

"I hope what we're doing won't make it tougher for the other men who ride this train. I mean, I wouldn't want to get anyone in trouble because of what we're doing.

Red looked up and grinned. "Don't worry about it. I doubt they'll even miss it. And if somebody does, he'll think one of the other guys took it. Besides, nobody knows we're on this train."

Red laid a checkerboard he'd found on the table and said, "Black or red?"

William nodded and gave what they were doing no more thought as he began to place the red ones on the board in their proper order.

Grinning, William said, "I hope you know you don't stand a chance," As Red put the black checkers on his side of the board.

After two games with each man winning one game, the train began to slow down. Their comfortable ride had lasted less than an hour. Red pulled the curtain back just as they were passing a sign that read, Craig, Colorado, Elevation 6168 feet.

To their surprise, there was no forest to run to or hide in. They had entered the city limits and all they could see were a lot of buildings facing them. Grabbing their gear they headed for the back door of the caboose with Red in the lead.

On the back stoop of the caboose Red looked around as best he could without being seen. A lumberyard stood on one side of the tracks and warehouses on the other. He gave a sigh of relief. They hadn't gotten to the rail yard yet.

Knowing they had to get off the train, now, before it got to the yard or suffer the consequences, Red motioned to William to follow him, then leaped from the train on a fast run. William followed, doing his best to keep up and not fall down.

The coal stoker just happened to be looking back and saw the two men leap from the train. "Hey, you there," he yelled as the two men ran out of sight behind a building. And that was as far as he took the matter. Chasing a couple of bums behind a building where he might get hurt wasn't his job. Where the devil was that lazy bull when you needed him, he wondered. Not that he ever did anything, anyway.

The engineer turned his head in the stoker's direction and yelled, "Who are you yellin' at?"

The stoker thought for a moment, and then said, "Nobody, just a couple of kids who were throwin' rocks at the train."

Neither Red nor William knew who had yelled, only that someone had spotted them, and from past experience, that meant trouble associated with pain and both men felt they had had more than their fair share lately.

For several blocks they ran up and down alleyways, making them hard to catch. Red finally called a halt, saying, "Whoa, good buddy. I think we're in the clear. If there was anybody chasin' us, they ain't now," as he put his hands on his hips and blew hard to get his wind back.

With eyes wide and nostrils flaring, William hauled up and stood, bent over with his hands on his knees, sucking in air like a sump pump sucks in water.

"Are you sure?" William asked between breaths, his eyes wide with fear.

"Yea, I'm sure," Red said.

Keeping mainly to the alleys, they zigzagged back and forth checking out the town and found that even the main street had very little activity.

When they finally reached the far side of town they stopped next to a building whose front faced the highway, giving them a clear view in both directions. Oil derricks dotted the landscape, but most of them were idle.

"I reckon the hardships of this-here depression reaches far and wide, even to Craig, Colorado," Red said as they looked out across the giant oil field.

The building next to where they stood was empty, but across the highway was a gasoline station, with the old man who ran it, sitting quietly out front in an old rocking chair, smoking his pipe.

Red turned to William and said, "Wait here while I go over to the gas station and get us ah soda pop and maybe pick up a bit of information. What kind do you want?"

"Oh, any kind. Thank you," William said.

As Red started across the highway, William yelled after him, "Orange, if they have it."

Red didn't bother to look back, but his arm went up in the air, waving with his hand to signal he'd heard William's request as William sat down in the shade of the building to rest.

Shortly, Red came running back across the highway with two, cold bottles of soda pop; an orange for William and a cream soda for himself.

"The old man said there's ah small hobo camp not far out of town. He gave me directions and I picked up a few things I need. I got me ah razor, ah tooth brush and ah clean shirt that I'll put on if I can get a bath at that there camp."

This was good news. A camp meant they could rest up and talk with other men and maybe pick up some information or tips about upcoming work. You could even find out what bulls were guarding what trains. Sometimes you even ran into guys you knew from some other camp.

So, without much conversation, they drank their sodas, took the bottles back to the station where Red collected a penny apiece for each bottle.

As they headed off down the highway, their spirits were high as they laughed and joked about riding in the caboose and the story it would make in the camp tonight.

Stories were a big part of camp life and the more adventurous it was, the better they liked it. Sometimes some real whoppers were born during storytelling time.

Information about the beatings they'd taken would also be important news, along with the number of the train they'd ridden.

"The camp should be right over there," Red informed William.

William looked around as far as he could see and saw nothing but open range land, rolling hills and a small cluster of trees, but not much else.

William sighed. The beauty of the mountains and the forest was behind them. Out here it was miles and miles of nothing but miles and miles as far as the eye could see.

"I think I'm going to miss the mountains and the forests with their streams running through them," William said.

While it was true, Craig, Colorado didn't sit in the middle of a big forest, it wasn't exactly beyond the mountain range, either. Craig, Colorado was at an elevation of over six thousand feet and still part of the great mountain range known as the Rockies. And not far in any direction there were places that rose to considerably higher elevations, such as Yellow Jacket pass to the south which rose to over seven thousand feet. While to the north, both Mount Welba and Steamboat Lake, were each well over ten thousand feet.

What this part of the country didn't have was trees. High rolling hills and broad valleys claimed this part of the mountain range. Tall grass swayed in the breeze, which reminded a person of ocean waves. This was big country; cattle, horses, oil and big ranches, but not densely populated.

Less than fifty miles to the west from where they stood, the remains of a dinosaur had been found. And from there to beyond the border, well into Utah was considered by many scientists to be one of the largest graveyards ever found of these giant beasts that roamed freely over the land more than sixty million years ago. What other artifacts would be found of the past was still a mystery as they continued to search.

Although no one can state it for a fact, it is believed by many, that as the great Rocky Mountain chain grew to its present height; it had been responsible for the great beasts extinction, along with the end of an era.

But to William who was used to the beauty of Minnesota, it seemed to be nothing more than a barren, foreboding land with a lot of wind that made him feel small and vulnerable. He would be glad to get to the camp and surround himself with other people.

Jared McVay

Chapter 10
Bad Press

  Darkness had settled over the land by the time they found the camp that was located in a small clump of trees with a small creek running through it. Some thought had gone into this place before starting a camp here, Red thought to himself; far enough away from the town and the highway that it kept them out of sight and sound of people, yet not so far to catch or jump off a train leaving town in either direction.
  Between the directions the man at the gas station had given them, the brightness of the moon and the smell of coffee drifting through the trees, the camp had not been hard to find. When they could see the glow of firelight, they stepped up their pace.
  The noise of their hurried walking and twigs breaking under foot carried some distance ahead of them and alerted the camp several minutes before their arrival. But the people of the camp weren't overly concerned. Earlier, one of the men from the camp had been gathering firewood and had spotted them leaving the highway and heading in their direction.
  "Hello in the camp, we'd like permission to come in," Red called out as they got close.
  "Come ahead," a raspy voice called back.
  William and Red entered the circle of light and stopped. For a long moment they stared at a small group of men who stared back at them. A yellowish, red glow from the campfire caused shadows to dance like ghosts across the faces of the men; but only for a moment, then vanished as quickly as they came.
  From the middle of the group a small, grizzled old man with bushy, uncombed hair, a gaping mouth that

showed no teeth, beady eyes and several days of stubble on his face, slowly limped up to them and said,

"Howdy, I'm Sammy and you might say this is my camp. I started it and built the buildings you see," he said, pointing to several lean-to shacks built out of pieces of tin and any old pieces of lumber he could find.

Right away, William sensed the man was proud of his accomplishments and decided a compliment might be in order.

"Well, I'd say you did yourself right proud, Mister Sammy. You have a real nice place here. We would be honored if you'd allow us to stay the night."

Sammy beamed with pride and said, "Thank you, thank you. Sure, you boys can spend the night, and welcome. We don't have much but we'll share what we got. You don't by chance have ah little something ta contribute, do ya?" Sammy asked, eying the sack hanging over Red's shoulder.

Red swung the pack off his back and handed it to Sammy. "You'll find some eggs and bacon, a little coffee and ah bag of ginger snap cookies in there. We're willin' ta share all of it with ya. The other stuff is just my personals."

"Ginger snap cookies! My, my, that's just fine, just fine indeed," Sammy, said as he swung his hand in the direction of the fire. "Come on over by the fire and make your selves ta home. The coffee, when we have some is always on, so have ah cup and get yourselves ah bowl of stew from that big pot hangin' over the fire."

While William and Red got themselves a cup of coffee, Sammy was busy giving out ginger snap cookies to any who wanted one.

William leaned in close to the large cauldron containing the stew and sniffed. The sweet aroma of spices and chicken filled his nostrils, causing his stomach to grumble even though it had only been a few hours since they'd eaten back in Hayden, Colorado and then some snacks on the train. William had never been one to shy away from food and since he'd been on the road, it had been awhile since he'd had his fill. William stood up and raised his cup to the group of men waiting for a cookie.

"My compliments to the chef or chefs," he said. "This smells wonderful and I'm sure, tastes as good as it smells."

Only one man had not gotten in line to get a cookie and it wasn't because he did not like cookies, because he did, but there was something a whole lot more important on his mind at the moment. He remained sitting with his back resting against a tree as he leafed through the newspaper he'd been reading. Watery eyes surrounded by a pudgy face and a sour look stared intently between the newspaper and the new men standing next to the fire.

Their arrival had triggered something in his memory, which caused him to look hard at Red several times before searching through the newspaper for an article he'd recently read.

A small framed man with thinning hair and a friendly smile walked up to William and said, "Thanks," holding up an uneaten portion of cookie. "I ain't seen a cookie in ah month of Sundays. "

He stuck out his hand and said, "Most folks just call me, Bones. I don't believe I caught your name."

William grinned as he took the man's hand and shook it. "That would be because we haven't introduced ourselves, yet. I'm very glad to make your acquaintance, Mister Bones. My name is William Conrad Bains."

Sammy chuckled as he turned toward them and said, "Well now, we ain't all that fancy out here; nicknames, mostly." He rubbed his chin, and then said, "Why don't we just call you, Willy. That might be ah bit easier for people to remember."

Several men standing nearby grinned and nodded their heads in agreement.

Turning to face Red, Sammy asked, "How about you, boy? What name do you go by?"

Before Red had a chance to answer, the surly man with newspaper stood up and said, "His name's Johnny

The Legend of Joe, Willy & Red

Walker, but mostly he goes by, Johnny Red, or just Red. He's from down Texas way. Aren't you, boy?"

Everyone, including William and Red were taken by surprise at the man's bold statement. Everyone stared back and forth between them to see if they knew each other but saw no sign of recognition or friendship between them.

Red stared at the man, searching his memory, trying to recall ever seeing this man before, but nothing came to him. Then a cold chill swept over him as the man eyed him and raised the newspaper and Red knew right then his worst nightmare was about to become a reality.

"At least that's what this here newspaper says. It goes on to say that some folks down in Texas want this ole boy on charges of rape and murder. It even has a picture of him, and that's him standin' right there, no doubt about it," the surly man said, raising the paper so everyone could get a good look at the picture.

Red started backing away from the fire in hopes of finding a chance to escape, but before he'd gotten far, three men grabbed him and one of them had a knife.

Now that the surly man had everyone's attention, he walked up next to the fire, shaking the newspaper in Sammy's direction and motioned to the other men to gather around, then waited, taking a long, pregnant pause for effect before lowering the boom with his final announcement.

"It also says here," he said in a loud voice so as to be heard by everyone, "that some ole boy down there in Texas is mighty anxious ta have old Johnny back, cause he's offerin' up ah ten thousand dollar cash reward for his capture and return. And we gott'em right here! We're rich boys! He's like ah gift sent from heaven! Yes-sir, no doubt about it, ah gift from heaven!"

By now his voice had risen several octaves as the other men became caught up in the excitement and promise of more cash money than any of them had ever seen all at one time.

"Somebody get ah rope! We'll tie him to that tree, yonder, so he can't get away," Sammy yelled as one of the men ran to find a rope.

Two of the men slammed Red against the tree and held him there until the man with the rope came running back.

They pulled Red's arms backward around the tree and tied his wrists together, securely, to the cheers of the other men.

While Red was being tied to the tree, the surly man, now full of bravado stepped close and yelled in Red's face, "You wandered into the wrong camp, boy. We don't have no truck with rapists and murderers around here. And we're gonna be happy ta see you get what's coming to ya."

Sammy, who had been doing some figuring, raised his hands and said, "We just made ourselves over eight hundred dollars apiece!"

At that news, they all began to shout and congratulate each other, shaking hands and slapping each other on the back to celebrate their good fortune. Not only were they doing what was right and just, but also making rich men of themselves at the same time.

Red could see these men were getting out of hand and he knew a mob could be talked into doing things they might not otherwise do. He could wind up swinging from a tree instead of being tied to one.

"Hey," Red yelled, "don't I get ah chance ta tell my side of the story? The paper says, accused, not tried and found guilty."

The men stopped their shouting and the camp got quiet for a moment, but only for a moment, because the surly man wasn't about to let his hour of triumph slip away so easily. Stepping up close to Red, he cuffed him along side the head with the palm of his hand and yelled in his face.

"You shut your mouth, boy! We ain't interested in hearin' no pack of lies."

Sammy, who was caught up in the thought of all that money, sided with the surly man. "Yea, you'd probably say most anything about now to get set loose."

At this point, any remembrance of food or cookies he'd brought to the camp had gone by the wayside.

During all the excitement, William had been forgotten, but now as he fought his way to the front of the crowd, found his weight of use when it came to a shoving match. Always the gentleman, he pushed men out of his way while still trying to be polite.

"Excuse me," he said to one of the men. "Please let me get through," he said to another. When they paid him no attention, his hackles flared and he began shoving men out of his way as he shouted, "Get the hell out of my way! There is something needs to be said and I mean to say it!"

A space opened for him and William marched straight to the front of the crowd before turning to face them, having no idea what he was going to say.

"Gentlemen, gentlemen," he said, raising his arms. "Is this still America, where you are innocent until proven guilty?"

From somewhere near the rear of the crowd a man said, "That's true, it is, but I don't think they would print it in the newspaper and offer a big reward, just on a hunch."

Another man chimed in, "Yea, don't cha think they'd have to have some mighty powerful evidence against him to offer that much cash money?"

And then a third man voiced his opinion. "I'd bet they even have a witness or two to back up their claim."

"Wait a minute, wait a minute," William shouted, trying to buy himself some time to come up with a rebuttal, but was drawing a blank. He glanced over at Red. Could the story be true? He desperately wanted to believe it wasn't.

Sammy stepped up to William and said, "They're right you know. It all points to him bein' guilty and unless you know something we don't, I reckon we'd be better off turning him over to the law and let them figure it out. What

~ 85 ~

about it? Can you prove to us he's innocent of the charges in that story in the paper?"

Red swallowed hard, wondering if William was going to come up with another of his outrageous stories like the one he'd told that farmer, but he doubted it. The truth was this was a whole different situation and he doubted if they would even believe the truth, let alone some wild concoction William might come up with. No, Red decided, William couldn't help, this time.

At that very moment, William was recalling his own situation that had put him at odds with the law and was shocked to realize some people would lie, or create false documents that pointed directly at an innocent person, making you look guilty even though you weren't.

What an empty feeling that had been, filling him with fear of trusting anyone ever again. Especially the people you thought were your friends because any of them were capable of making you their scapegoat.

William turned and looked at Red, again, trying to read something in his eyes, any tiny spark of hope, but he saw nothing. He'd known Red for such a short time and the man had not talked about his past, so he knew very little about him - only what he'd seen of him in their short time together. Personally, it was difficult to believe Red was capable of rape or murder. But what he believed wouldn't be enough to convince these men to go against the story in the newspaper.

Suddenly, William realized he was looking at this whole thing wrong. It was Red they should be listening to, not him! He had to convince them to listen to Red and let him tell his story. William raised his hands once more.

"Maybe he's guilty and maybe he's not. I don't know and it's not for me to say any more than it is for you. But there is one thing I do know and that is, just because a man is accused of a crime, doesn't automatically make him guilty. Think about it. Is there any one of you here who's never been accused of something he didn't do? And how many of you could prove your innocence when the evidence was stacked against you? All I'm trying to say is have the decency and the courtesy to give the man the benefit of the doubt and allow him to tell his side of the story."

There was a long silence while everyone mulled over William's words. A slight breeze flowed through the camp, carrying with it the tapping of a woodpecker as each man reached back into his bag of memories of being accused falsely and with some of them, being wrongly punished for a deed they had nothing to do with. And for just an instant, each man had second thoughts about Red, except one - the surly man.

"Don't be taken by this, con man. Remember, they showed up together. As far as we know, they might be partners," the surly man yelled as he stepped to the front of the crowd. "What was it you called him, Sammy? Willy? Well I say he should have a new title. I say we call him, Willy the con, because he's tryin' ta con us, right now."

Leaning against the doorway of one of the shacks toward the back of the camp, Joe rolled and lit a cigarette. The sound of voices, two in particular, had awakened him. And after going to the door to make sure, Joe had seen and heard enough to know for certain it was them and they were in trouble. Joe gritted his teeth and shook his head as he ground the cigarette butt into the ground with the toe of his shoe.

He should grab his sack and just walk away. He could slip out the backside of the camp and no one would see him. Yea, that's what he should do, just keep out of it and mind his own business.

"They didn't need my help getting into trouble, so why should they need my help getting out," Joe said to himself. Besides, rape and murder were serious charges. There was even a picture of him in the newspaper.

Joe watched the heavyset guy with the newspaper turn a bunch of decent guys into a mob. And he didn't know if Red was guilty or not, but remembering his own story, he knew a man should at least have the right to vindicate himself by telling his side of it. Maybe it would change their minds and maybe it wouldn't, but in this country a man had the right to say his piece.

Joe wondered what would have happened if he would've hung around and told his side of the story. Would anyone have believed him? He reckoned not, not with the mob controlling the attorneys and judges.

Joe ran his fingers through his hair. How much did he really know about either one of these guys? Even though they may have spent a couple of days together, none of them knew anything about each other. Hell, they didn't even know his name, and yet, William had risked his own safety to help him. Maybe the guy was just trying to repay a debt, but he sure as the world was there when the chips were down.

Okay, Joe wondered, so what did he know about this guy from Texas? He was a good tracker, he'd kept his wits about him when he swiped that stuff from the farmer and he wasn't afraid to duke it up when he was cornered.

And as Joe reasoned to himself, the guy could have killed somebody accidentally in a fight, but it was hard to believe Red was the kind of man who would rape a woman. Somehow it just didn't feel right in his gut, and over the years, he'd learned to rely on his gut instincts.

He didn't believe either one of these guys were hardened criminals, but that still didn't make him their wet nurse.

He chuckled as he listened to William talk about rights. If he wasn't a lawyer, he should be, Joe thought. The man did have the gift of gab. Maybe he was some sort of con man, but Joe didn't believe that, either. He believed William Conrad Bains was just a guy who believed in helping his friends and with that mind set, was always seeking new people to be friends with. The problem with that was, once he befriended you, he would always be there defending you like some ole hound dog protecting what was his.

The Legend of Joe, Willy & Red

Joe had smoked a second cigarette and now it was time to make a decision.

"Let him speak his piece," Joe yelled, dropping the stub of his cigarette to the ground and stepping on it before he headed for the crowd of men.

At the sound of Joe's voice, as a whole, the group of men turned and watched in silence as he approached. The mere sight of Joe heading in their direction made them quiet down and step back.

Even though Joe had been on the rails barely a week, he had already built a reputation as a man to give a wide berth. There was something about the confident way he carried himself and the commanding way he had of saying things. Plus, the look in his eyes when he stared at you was enough to make most men fearful and cautious.

Their attitude about him was not lost, nor was it something new. He'd seen this before. Even the kids at the orphanage had backed off when he'd look at them in that certain way. He wasn't sure what that was or how he did it, but it amused him to know that he had a certain power over people. And as the years had gone by, he'd learned to temper his vanity and not let it get out of hand, although, from time to time, like now, it came in handy.

Joe looked neither left nor right as he walked straight as an arrow to where Red was tied to the tree. Stopping in front of the surly bum, Joe looked at him and said,

"Untie him."

The man swallowed, trying to keep his composure, not wanting to lose what little control he'd gained over the men. He started to say something, but the message in the big guy's eyes told him to keep his mouth shut and do as he was told. But something kept him thinking about all that money. And like the rest of the men, he'd heard stories about the big guy and what a tough guy he was. And there was the story about him ridin ole #106 and getting away with it. You had to have cajones to do that.

But the big guy wasn't the only one with a reputation; he had one too, although his was more in the line of being called a bully than a tough guy - basically it meant the same thing as far as he was concerned. Plus, the thought of all that money made the bravado in him swell up. Greed was a strong motivator.

"Butt out, Joe. This don't concern you. Besides, what do you care? You'll get your share."

Joe glanced at both Red and William, who stood there staring at him with their jaws hanging open. They were in total shock by his sudden appearance, plus the fact that he was standing up for them.

The surly man never saw it coming. There was only the loud crack of Joe's open palm slapping the man alongside his face with such a force that it lifted him off his feet.

The man landed flat on his back with a stunned look on his face and his eyes watering.

Action first, talk later had always been Joe's motto. Over the years he'd found it to be an effective way to cut down on the banter over trivial nonsense that didn't amount to a hill of beans, anyway.

"I'm not in the habit of explaining myself," Joe said, "I told you to untie him, now. I want to hear his side of the story. You got any objections to that?"

"No, I reckon not," the surly bum said, rubbing his stinging cheek and wiping the tears from his eyes.

He felt ashamed of his own weakness as he stood up and untied the man called, Johnny Red.

Looking around, Joe pointed at a man standing close to the tree. "You, help him."

The man had no desire to tangle with the big man and rushed to do as he'd been told.

While Red was being untied, Joe headed for the coffee pot and after pouring a cup, Joe found a comfortable place to sit and waited as Red, William and the rest of the men crowded around.

Joe noticed the surly bum stayed by the tree where Red had been tied, staring at Joe with hatred in his eyes, but keeping his mouth shut.

Red stopped near the fire and nodded at Joe. He'd never been gladder to see anyone in his entire life. "Thanks," was the only thing he could think of to say.

Joe nodded without any hint of recognition. "Just tell your version and don't leave anything out."

William's heart was beating like the lead horse in the Kentucky Derby and had been ever since Joe had mysteriously shown up; once again, like a gladiator to save the day. No matter what he says or how he acts, William thought, there is a bond between the three of us, even if he does continue to deny it.

But this was not the time to let that piece of information be known. No, if the men knew the three of them had traveled together they would definitely take it the wrong way and that surly bum would make a big issue about it.

William stood to the side, just out of the attention area, but still close enough to hear and hoped and prayed Red's story was one that would set him free.

Jared McVay

Chapter 11
The Truth Shall Set You Free

Red looked over the crowd of men and saw all their eyes were on him, waiting for him to begin. Should he make up some wild, crazy lie, or tell the truth? He was troubled because he wasn't sure they would believe the truth, but on the other hand, he wasn't good at lying.

Who was it that said, "The truth shall set you free." No one he knew, that was for sure, but he sure hoped whoever said it knew what he or she was talkin' about. He took a deep breath and began.

"Part of what's in the newspaper is true. They got my name right and that is my picture, but that's the only part that's true. I've never raped a woman in my life and I for damn sure have never killed anybody."

Having gotten some feeling back in his jaw and still thinking about the money he might lose, the surly bum called out, "If you ain't guilty, then why are they lookin for you so hard, with ah picture of you in the newspaper and that story and ah big reward?" His eyes going straight to Joe, who only stared back at him.

Red thought for a moment and then said, "Because of the fickle finger of fate," he said at last.

Sammy shook his head and said, "The fickle finger of fate? What kind of answer is that? If you're tryin' ta give us some kind of flim-flam talk, we ain't havin' none of it."

An outbreak of heads nodding and mumbling broke out among the others and before things could get out of hand, Joe took charge, again.

"Everybody just shut up! What he means is, the gods, or fate, or whatever played a cruel joke on him."

Joe turned to Red and said, "Now, I think it would be better for all of us if you go back to the beginning and tell us in good old plain English what this ironic twist of fate is all

~ 92 ~

The Legend of Joe, Willy & Red

about. And remember, all we want is the plain and simple truth, nothing else."

Red blew out a breath of air and tried to decide where the beginning was. When was it exactly that his world had been turned upside down? He wanted to tell the story so it wouldn't sound like some, crazy pipe dream. Finally, he decided to tell it just like it had happened and let them judge for themselves.

"Until five days ago I was just ah guy with no real problems ta speak of. I lived in ah small town down in southern Texas where folks all knew each other. I had ah decent job at the gas station, ah small apartment and the companionship of ah young lady ah couple ah times ah week. She worked as ah waitress over to the Horseshoe Inn. We had kind of an understandin', you might say."

"Was she ah looker?" one of the men in the back called out.

"Yea. I reckon she was the purtiest gal in town."

William handed Red a cup of coffee. He took a sip and then continued.

"Like I was tellin' ya, life was treatin' me fine, that is until Paul Roland, the meter reader for the electric company come ah runnin' up, actin' all nervous like.

"I'd just finished doin' ah lube and oil on Freda Boyle's big ole Buick. She's the wider lady who's one of our regulars. She began tradin' with us ah few years ago, just shortly after her husband got his-self run over by ah thrashin' machine. Anyway, like I said, Paul Roland was ah huffin' and ah puffin' and yellin' that I gotta get my butt outta town in ah big hurry. Well, I told him I had no idea what he was ah talkin' about. And I had no reason ta get outta town cause I hadn't done nuthin' to nobody. Then he starts telling me there's ah mob formin' down at the Horseshoe and I asked him what that had ta do with me? And he yelled, it was me they was plannin' on hangin'! Well, I thought he musta' gone crazy or had misunderstood - you know, got the names mixed up or somethin'."

Red took a pause and had another sip of coffee, then continued.

"About that time he started lookin' around and said maybe we ought ta go inside cause he didn't want anybody ta see him talkin' ta me. So, inside the station we went, where he tole me, Joe-Bob and Big John McNally were in the back room of the Horse- shoe right now, buyin' drinks for everbody and gett'em all riled up ta hang me."

Red held his hands up, palms forward.

"I know sellin' liquor is agin' the law, but like most towns, the Horseshoe had ah back room where you could get somethin' stronger than coffee."

Taking another sip of coffee, Red looked over the rim of his cup and saw that he had their attention.

"Now, I'd known these ole boys most of my life and we'd had ah friendly scrap or two over the years; especially when we'd had ah bit too much john-barley corn, but not anything ah body would hold ah grudge about and for sure, nuthin' that would get me hung. The fact was, just ah few nights before, we'd all hoisted ah few together.

"Thinkin' this might be some kind of ah joke, I went to the front door and looked all around ta see if they was out there, waitin' ta rib me, but Paul assured me this was not ah joke. He said they was serious as ah heart attack. Well, as you can imagine, about now it was beginnin' ta sink in that he wasn't jokin' and I begun ta get ah tad bit nervous even though I couldn't for the life of me figure out what I'd done - and believe me, ever little transgression I ever committed flashed through my head.

"Well sir, since I couldn't think of nuthin', I turned and looked Paul square in the eyes and asked him what it was I was supposed to have done that Joe-Bob and Big John would want me hanged for. And he said the boys were down there tellin' everbody that I had raped their mama and she'd been too ashamed to say anything until she found out she was pregnant."

Red took a long pull from his coffee cup while he let this bit of information and it's implications sink in. Some of the men were shaking their heads, in deep thought, while others sat there with a dumbstruck look on their face. Red knew each man of them was wondering what he would do if something like that happened to him.

Red blew his nose and then took another sip of coffee, which by now was getting cold.

"Pregnant? How in the world could she be telling folks that I had got her pregnant when I hardly knew the snooty ole holier than thou heifer, except maybe ta say good day to and even then she hardly ever returned my greetin'.

"Ya see, ah workin' class fella like me was beneath her stature and I only spoke ta her ta be polite like cause I knew her boys - you know what I'm sayin'?

"You half'ta understand - Sarah McNally was one of them southern Texas bible thumpers who looked down her nose at half the town. I expect you all know of her kind, always thinkin' she's better'n everbody else. And even if they are the richest family in town, that don't give her the right ta be so all fired uppity and high and mighty."

Now that he had everybody agreeing with him, he continued with new assurance.

"Paul said, Big John was goin' on and on about keepin' the streets safe for all the women and children and church abidin' folks.

"In my confused state I was only pickin' up bits and pieces of what he was sayin' until finally he said somethin' that made me take notice, and I asked him ta repeat what he'd just said. And he told me he knew I wasn't the one who did it."

"How did he know that?" Sammy asked.

"That's what I asked him. And he said, because he knew who did."

"Did he tell who it was?" another man piped in.

"When I asked him to tell me who it was, he said, no."

"And just what did you say to that?" William asked.

Jared McVay

"Well now, Paul and I had been friends for some time, but I was in no mood ta be toyed with, so I grabbed him and threw him against the wall and then shook my fist in his face and told him that if he didn't tell me, I was gonna beat it outta him.

"That made him even more nervous and he said okay, but I had ta promise him I wouldn't tell anybody where I got the information. He didn't want to get in trouble with the McNally's. So I agreed not to tell and when I let go of him he was shakin' so bad he stumbled over and flopped down in ah chair and just stared at me.

"After a while I said, 'Well, who did it?' and he looked up at me and said his throat was awful dry, so I went over to the pop cooler and grabbed ah bottle of soda pop and started ta hand it to him when he asked if I would open it for him. So I opened it for him and tried ta hand it to him again and he started ta take it, but pulled his hand back and told me that wasn't the kind he liked.

"By then I was about ta blow my top and I yelled at him ta drink it anyway and he did, but he took his own sweet time about doin' it. And by the time he'd finished the soda his hands had stopped shakin' and finally he told me she hadn't been raped at all. He said she'd been foolin' around on her husband and got herself in the family way."

Isn't that just like a woman, William thought to himself, but didn't voice his opinion like several of the other men did.

When the muttering finally settled down, Red continued.

"At this point I asked him what the man's name was and told him I didn't want any more stallin' and he looked me straight in the eyes and told me I wouldn't believe him - nobody would.

"I told him to try me, and he said high and mighty Sarah McNally had been havin' an affair with none other than that ladies man, Reverend Phillips.

"Well, he sure was right, I had ah hard time believin' that pious, self-righteous bastard had the guts ta be havin' an affair with anybody, let alone the juice to knock her up. I asked Paul flat out if he was sure and he said, yes, he knew it for ah fact."

From over by the tree, the surly bum's voice came grumbling through the quiet of the evening. "How long's this story gonna take? At this rate we'll all be dead and buried before you get finished."

Several of the men booed and threw rocks at him. This was a hum-dinger of a story and they wanted to hear the rest of it.

Joe stood up and took a couple of steps in the surly bum's direction and said,

"Nobody's forcing you to listen. You can always leave, but if you decide to stay, keep your mouth shut until he's finished."

The surly bum nodded his head in agreement and Red smiled.

"I'll try not to take all night, but there are several facts that are kinda important for you ta be able ta understand the whole situation and how they tie together to put me on the run."

"Please continue. We're all listening," William said.

Everyone got quiet again as William poured fresh coffee into Red's cup and gave it to him and then moved to a spot where he could sit down, as Joe and a few others also filled their cups and resumed their seats.

Red took a sip of coffee and then continued with his story. "About now my mind was in a state of confusion. If it was the preacher, why did she accuse me? It made no sense. But on the other hand, Paul wasn't the kind ta spread rumors nor make things up just ta cause trouble - no-sir he just wasn't that kind of guy.

"So I focused my thoughts on that no account preacher who was always attendin' ladies meetin's. Oh he was ah soft talkin' man who could get'em all riled up over one cause or another. One of his big issues was ta get the Horseshoe Inn closed down. He called it ah den of iniquity or some such thing.

"And as I thought about it I realized he was in ah perfect position ta take his leave with some of the women if he had ah mind to. I never did like him or his holier than thou attitude.

"I was so upset that I walked over to the pop cooler and got me ah bottle of beer that was hidden on the bottom. That seemed ta calm my nerves down ah bit and then I asked Paul how he was so sure it was the reverend that did it. I was sure he was tellin' the truth, but I wanted ta hear his story just in case it might be that whoever told him had got the story wrong. You know how gossip can get all blown outta proportion.

"Paul said it wasn't gossip and no one had told him anything. He said he was at the back of the reverend's house the other day, readin' his electric meter and the meter just happened ta be on the back wall next to the reverend's bedroom window and the window was open just enough for him to hear what was goin' on inside.

"He said it sounded like ah quarrel and before he knew it he was caught up in what they was ah quarralin' about; which he was quick ta add, wasn't his regular habit.

"He said that normally he would have walked away, but not this time, because he recognized Sarah McNally's voice and he was shocked by what she was ah sayin'. He said she was madder than ah wet hen and worried at the same time. He said she was tellin' the reverend about goin' up ta Dallas ta see this here doctor who'd examined her and told her she was gonna have ah baby."

"And what did this here, Paul fella do then?" Sammy asked.

"I sure know what I'd ah done," another piped in.

"He said by then he was curious as some gossipy ole telephone operator - so he inched his way over closer ta the open window ta try and see inside. He said the crack was wide enough that he could see the whole room.

"Paul told me Sarah was standin' in the middle of the room with her hand on her hip, glarin' at the reverend while he paced back and forth like ah caged coyote and then, after ah bit he stopped and asked her what she was gonna do about it. Pall said Sarah got all red in the face and asked him what he meant by that. He was the father - what was he going to do? 'You're the one responsible for this,' she said as she pointed to her stomach.

"Paul said the reverend just stood there, staring at his shoes and finally asked, 'Are you sure it's mine?'

"Sarah informed him that she hadn't had sex with her husband since his accident four years ago, so there was no way she could claim it was his. She went on to tell the reverend that he was the only man she'd had sex with outside of her husband so there was no way he could claim it wasn't his. And when he just stood there, she cursed and berated him for all his loving sweet talk and how she'd believed him and now it broke her heart to find out he was nothing more than a liar and had whispered all those sweet things just to get in her pants.

"Paul said by now she was clinching and unclenching her fists and started askin' him how many other women he was sweet-talkin inta sleepin' with him and what was he gonna do if some of them was pregnant too. And then she started laughin' hysterically.

"Paul went on ta say, the reverend was so rattled he didn't seem ta hear anything Sarah was ah sayin'. He was too busy wavin' his arms in the air and lookin' up at the ceiling, callin' out ta God, beseechin' him ta forgive him for fallin' under the spell of this low down jezebel who was sent by Satan ta ruin his life.

"Paul said, after ah minute or so, when the reverend dropped ta his knees and began prayin, Sarah shook her head and said something about figurin' things out for herself and then turned and walked out of the room.

Jared McVay

"He figured the preacher didn't even know she'd gone.

"Paul told me he believed that's why she came up with that rape story; ta get both of them off the hook.

"After thinkin' about it for ah minute, I come ta believe he might be right. But I still didn't understand why she used me as the scapegoat. It didn't make any sense."

Suddenly, one of the men jumped up and yelled, "Hold on just a minute!" and ran into the woods.

The man returned shortly, looking kinda sheepish as he took his place again and waved his hand in the air for Red to continue. There were several chuckles as the man sat down.

"I had ta find some way ta prove my innocence and didn't figure Paul would be any help, as scared as he was of the McNally's. Mister McNally was a rich and powerful man in that part of the country and wouldn't take lightly to Paul callin' his wife ah liar and ah adulteress.

"No, I had ta go ta the weak link in the chain, which was the reverend. I told Paul not ta worry, I wouldn't tell anybody about him comin' ta warn me or sayin' anything and thanked him. Then I ushered him ta the back door so no one would see him leave and he skedaddled down the alley like some ole convict tryin' ta out run ah pack of blood hounds.

"I knew what I had ta do and as soon as Paul was out of sight, I headed straight for the reverend's house, usin' the alleys ta get there. Like I said before, it's ah small town, so it didn't take me long ta get over ta his place.

"And right here and now, I admit that if push come ta shove, I planned ta rough him up ah mite if I had to ta get him ta fess up. But I knew in my mind, threaten' him would do the trick. The reverend had no backbone."

Red took a moment to drink the last of his coffee and rub the back of his neck to smooth out a kink and then resumed his story. It was getting close to the end and he wanted to be done with it.

"When I got there, I beat on the door pretty loud, but nobody answered, so I tried the door and it opened. So I stepped inside, real cautious like ah callin' out for him, but I wasn't prepared for what I come face ta face with."

At this point, Red paused again and saw that every man there was on pins and needles, waiting; no one was saying a word.

Red coughed and blew his nose, then said, "Right in front of me was this circular stairway leadin' to the upstairs and danglin' from the upper part with ah rope around his neck hung the reverend, his eyes all bugged and his tongue stickin' out and it looked like he'd soiled himself.

"I froze right there in my tracks, sweat ah poppin' out all over and I was shakin' and beginnin' ta feel sick ta my stomach. I ain't never seen nobody hung before and believe me I don't ever want ta see it again. My heart was poundin' like ah jackhammer and I was suckin' air worse than if I'd run ten miles.

"God only knows what goes through ah mans mind ta cause him ta do somethin' like that. I reckon it was ta keep from havin' ta face everbody, but I do believe I would have looked for some different choices, but that's just me.

"His hangin' his self didn't help my situation none and I knew I needed ta get outta there before anybody saw me"

Just thinking about it again caused Red to start shaking and William offered him his cup of coffee to help calm his nerves, which didn't go unnoticed by the men.

Red squared his shoulders and continued. "Maybe I should'a gone out the back door, I don't know, but I do know I wasn't thinkin' none too straight about then. Anyway, as I come out the front door, around the corner comes Big John, Joe-Bob and ah bunch of liquored up men, maybe ten or twelve, I don't know, I didn't take time ta count. Some of'em were staggerin' and talkin' loud."

"Did they see ya?" one of the men up close, blurted out.

Jared McVay

Red looked down at him and said, "Yea. About the same time I saw them, they saw me. Ah couple of'em started yellin', so I took off like ah scared rabbit. I ran down alleys, across back yards, jumped fences, anything I could do ta get away. I was scared and all liquored up like they was, I figured I was ah dead man if they caught me. They'd hang me from the closest tree and not care ah twit about it til they sobered up.

"Somehow, I wound up down at the railroad yard and saw ah train just pullin out. And the next thing I knew, I could see the town disappearin' behind me."

"And not one day has gone by since that I haven't thought about what it's gonna take ta prove I didn't do any of those things they wrote in the paper. I called Paul ah few nights ago and he said ta never show my face down there again. He said ta change my name and my looks cause the McNally's had the town convinced I was guilty. He said ole man McNally, himself, personally swore ta see me hanged."

Red rubbed his face with his hands and said, "Well, that's about it, boys. I guess what happens next is in your hands."

Without a word, the men rose and went to the places where they slept. William, Red and Joe were the only ones left near the fire.

The surly bum who'd gotten everybody all worked up in the first place, walked over and stuck out his hand.

"I guess I kinda got carried away. All that money. Makes a man do crazy things."

Red shook his hand and smiled. "I don't reckon I can blame ya none. If the shoe had been on the other foot, I might'a done the same thing."

The man nodded and turned and walked away. When he had gone, Red turned to William and Joe.

"When I talked ta Paul the other night, just ah couple of hours before you boys dragged me outta the river, I tried ta get him ta talk ta the old man in private, but he said he was afraid ta get involved, besides, he didn't think the old man would believe him and then the old man would do something ta get him discredited so nobody else would believe him, either. He thought he might wind up losing his job. So I told him to forget it and hopped that west bound freight and you know the rest."

Joe stared at Red, but said nothing. He couldn't because he knew exactly what the man was going through. Even though his circumstances were different, the end result was the same. Ironic, wasn't it, Joe thought.

What was going on here, William wondered as he thought about his own reasons for being here, feeling this kinship with these two men. And what was that look in Joe's eyes? Was it compassion? Another page in the book of Joe's mystery.

Joe threw down his cigarette butt and ground it out with the heel of his shoe.

"It's been a long day," he said and turned and walked away, headed for the shack he'd come out of earlier.

William and Red gathered up their pillows and blankets and ran to catch up.

Chapter 12

The Look Alike

It was not yet daylight as Joe, William and Red sat shivering from the cold, hiding in the tall weeds not far from the railroad tracks leading west. Adding to their discomfort the fog was so thick they could barely see each other even though they were less than a foot apart.

William's teeth chattered like hail on a tin roof as he sat with his arms wrapped around his upper body. "If a train doesn't come by soon," he said, "I'm going to build a fire."

"Why not just stick a sign next to the tracks saying, three men waiting to board your train?" Joe whispered.

Joe's voice was filled with the same irritation William and Red had heard before. Red smiled to himself, knowing the denseness of the fog would hide his grin. For some reason it felt good for the three of them to be together, again.

But William was not in the greatest of moods this morning. He hadn't slept well and they hadn't eaten anything before they left the camp. A retort to Joe's comment was forming on his lips when the sound of a train engine filtered through the fog. It was still a ways off, but the laborious way the engine was working they knew it would not pick up a great deal of speed by the time it reached their location. And with the fog as thick as it was, they should be able to get on board without any trouble being seen.

Shortly, the ground began to vibrate and the air was filled with coal smoke and loud engine noise as the heavily loaded freight train crawled toward them at a snail's pace; and when the open doorway of an empty freight car finally appeared, Joe sprinted toward the train and dove head first through the open door.

The Legend of Joe, Willy & Red

An instant later, Red landed next to Joe and immediately reversed himself to help William. It was all he could do to see William through heavy fog and coal smoke.

"Run!" Red called out in a loud whisper.

William was not the sprinter the other two were. He was struggling hard to run on the rocky track bed as the open doorway of the freight car and Red's outstretched arm was little by little disappearing into the smoke and fog.

"I'm trying!" William called with a gasping voice. Pain shot through his cold, stiff legs. He felt like he was running with concrete blocks tied to his feet.

What was he doing here? He wasn't cut out for this kind of life and he wasn't built for running on loose rocks, or chasing freight trains.

William's problem at this point was, his friends were in that boxcar and he didn't want to be left behind and he guessed that was reason enough, so he pushed himself to run faster.

Red braced himself with his right arm against the inside wall of the boxcar and reached out to William with his other arm.

As William came within range, he out reached for Red's outstretched hand and

just as their two hands clasped, William stumbled and almost jerked Red out the door.

"Joe, grab my feet," Red called over his shoulder.

Instead, Joe jumped off the train and between Red pulling and Joe pushing, they finally got William aboard and then Joe easily dove back into the boxcar before it picked up too much speed.

William was a nervous wreck as he lay sucking in great gasps of air; still unable to believe he'd actually made it.

Two things made the realization complete. First, was Red's laughter along with a couple of chuckles from Joe, but most importantly was the pain in his belly caused by a large splinter from the rough wooden floor, which kept stabbing him with each vibration of the train wheels as they rolled along the tracks.

Sitting up, William felt the flush that rushed to his face and looked down to hide his embarrassment, As he pulled the sliver of wood from his belly, his face twisted in a grimace as it came free, which caused another burst of laughter from Red.

Tossing the splinter aside, William climbed to his feet with as much dignity as he could and said, "Thank you," wondering to himself if he could survive out here, alone. He knew he couldn't, and right then and there, he determined to never let that happen.

"Hey, old buddy, helpin' each other is what friends are for," Red said. "If it wasn't for you guys I'd more than likely drowned in that river or be on the way to the hoosegow about now."

Joe was turning to find a place to sit down, but Red's next words caught him in mid-stride, causing him to turn back.

"What's that at the far end of the car?" Red asked as he pointed at a vague form they could barely make out.

In the darkness, all they could see was a lump near the end wall and whatever it was, hadn't moved with all the noise they'd made.

Spreading out, the boys made their way closer for a better look and as they came near, they saw a woman lying next to the end wall like she'd been dumped there without regard to how she landed.

Both William and Red knelt next to her, but it was William who touched her throat in search of a pulse.

"Well, she's alive," William, said. "Joe, will you spread a blanket close to the door. I need more light so I can check her over."

Joe made a pallet near the door and Red and William gently placed her on it and as William kneeled down to examine her injuries, his heart almost stopped. He had to swallow the sound that caught in his throat. He began to tremble and his breathing was irregular. William bent down closer to the woman to try and hide his reactions from Joe and Red.

The woman on the pallet looked so much like his wife, Brenda; at first he thought it was her. But on closer inspection, he realized it wasn't, although she could easily pass as her twin sister.

Even though William tried to hide it, both Joe and Red noticed William's reaction, but each misinterpreted his actions, thinking William was nervous because he was not only looking at, but also touching her so intimately.

Ugly, purple bruises were wide spread over her entire body as though she'd been beaten and kicked, then handled roughly.

After getting over the shock of this woman reminding him of his wife, William was able to concentrate on the examination, touching her gently while praying there were no internal damages.

"She gonna be okay?" Red asked, almost reverently.

William looked up. "I don't know," he said, and looked back down at the woman. "Someone beat her very badly. The only thing we can do is to try and keep her warm and see if she wakes up. She needs to be looked at by a doctor and maybe have some x-rays taken to see if she has any internal injuries."

"Right, sure, and while you're at it, maybe you can find her a dentist too, just in case she has a toothache," Joe said as he lit a cigarette and blew the smoke into a rag.

It wasn't that he felt unsympathetic toward the woman, but a woman would throw a monkey wrench into an already complicated situation, especially one who needed to be in a hospital, which from the looks of her, she did.

Some time during the night they were awakened by loud noises coming from the woman as though she was fighting off some evil predator and had kicked her blanket off which left her legs bare, almost to the crotch.

William hurried to her side, stroking her forehead gently and offering soothing words, "It's okay. You're safe. No one is going to hurt you. Just try and get some rest," he told her as he pulled her dress down and recovered her with the blanket.

Red had moved up next to William to observe as William's gentle words calmed the woman. If the bruises and dried blood was gone, she'd be ah good lookin' filly, Red thought. She's got ah good figure and ah pretty face.

He too was concerned; not only for her safety, but also for the attachment Willy boy seemed to have towards her, and so quickly, too. Somethin' was goin' on that he couldn't quite put his finger on - the way his eyes lit up when he looked at her and the soft words he always used when he talked to her, or about her, like ah lover would talk. It wasn't anything he could put his finger on, exactly, but for sure, somethin' was goin' on. His gut told him so and his gut never lied to him.

"She needs nourishment and medical attention," William whispered, almost as much to himself as to Red.

Just then, the boxcar lurched as the train began to slow down. William turned to the woman and checked her, but she hadn't stirred.

William looked at Joe and Red. "Guys?" he said pleadingly.

"Alright, already," Joe said as he got to his feet and went to investigate. Peeking around the edge of the open door, Joe could see the outline of buildings in the distance just ahead, which looked to be a small town. In his mind, Joe quickly calculated their traveling time and guessed they were now in Utah. He wasn't sure just where, but that didn't make much difference, a town was a town. Maybe they could find some way to get rid of the woman, maybe leave her on the doorway of the hospital or doctor's office. It didn't matter as long as they got rid of her and weren't involved.

"You better wake her up. There's a town up ahead," Joe said over his shoulder. "If you're bound and determined to play wet nurse we have to get her off the train before it stops. Or, we could just leave her here and let the railroad people deal with her."

"No! I mean, what if they don't find her, or what if there isn't a doctor or a hospital in this town? She could die, or maybe the bulls might try to take advantage of her. In her weakened condition, she wouldn't be able to fight back!"

"Before we know it, we'll be taking in stray cats and dogs, too," Joe mumbled to himself as William stared up at him with a hound dog look on his face.

"I don't know, maybe it would be better if we took her with us, at least until we can find somebody ta treat her wounds," Red said.

Joe took a deep breath and shook his head. "I'll get off first and keep a lookout while you two get her off the train. I saw a shack back behind us a ways. We can take her there until we figure out what to do with her," Joe said.

Without waiting for an argument, Joe dropped onto the ground, motioning for Red and William to get the woman off the train.

By now the train was moving very slowly, which enabled Red and William to lift her out the door, using the blanket like a liter.

Once she was safely off the train Joe led them back along the tracks and into the safety of some nearby trees. Fortunately it was still several hours before daylight and not many people were up and about yet. Storm clouds were drifting across the sky and partly covered the moon, making them mere shadows as they moved away from the train.

Less than half a mile from town, Joe approached what seemed to be an empty shack. Using great stealth, Joe eased along a sidewall and tried looking through a dirty window but he couldn't see anything. Straining his ears to hear any sounds, he detected none, not even snoring or breathing. Still moving quietly, Joe went to the front door and tried the knob. The door opened with a slight creak. Joe entered and then immediately stepped sideways and pressed his back against the wall. He stood there for a minute, listening for movement as he allowed his eyes to adjust. Finally, Joe decided the shack was uninhabited and called for William and Red to bring the woman inside.

"I can't see a thing," William protested. "Could somebody turn on a light?"

"Be quiet. Even if there is a light we can't take a chance on somebody seeing it. Just put the woman on the floor. It'll be daylight soon and then we can decide what to do," Joe said.

William wasn't happy about it, but he did as he was told. Once she was on the floor, William sat down next to her to wait for the coming of the dawn.

"While it's still dark, I'm gonna do ah little sight seein'; get the lay of the land so ta speak. I won't be gone long," Red said from the doorway.

Joe didn't try to stop him. In fact, he thought it might be a good idea. Maybe he'd find a doctor or a hospital. The sooner they got rid of the woman, the better.

"Thank you, " William called out as Red closed the door. He hoped Red would be able to find the woman some help.

Feeling a need to relieve himself, Joe moved out of the shack and quietly crept into the woods behind the shed.

On his way back, Joe stopped near the backside of the shack where he rolled a cigarette and briefly struck a match, keeping the lit end cupped between his hands so the glow would be difficult to see. Joe took a deep puff and let the smoke drift lazily into the air where it disappeared among the trees, while he considered their situation.

Chapter 13
A Ghost Town Full of Booty

  A sliver of light, barely a shaft no larger than a piece of pencil lead forced it's way through a minute spot on the dirty window of the shack and found it's way onto William's right eye causing the eyelid to flicker ever so slightly, then with a jerking motion brought William wide awake. He sat up, looking around, confused at first, until he realized where he was and figured out he had dozed off for a short while.
  The sound of someone stirring close by drew his attention and he looked over to see the woman moving around and moaning incoherently in her sleep. The blanket had been kicked aside again and her skirt was hiked up nearly to her waist, revealing very sheer pink panties.
  Embarrassed, but also mesmerized, William gazed down at her for a long time. Without the bruises she reminded him so much of his wife that it was difficult to keep himself from taking her in his arms and holding her close.
  This woman also had the same shapely legs and hips that caused men to turn and stare, and her stomach had that same slight roundness to it, while her voluptuous breasts looked to be the same size and fullness as they rose and fell with her breathing.
  Before pulling her skirt down and drawing the blanket back up over her, William had to come to grips with himself. This was not his wife, Brenda. Brenda was gone forever. She would not be coming back to him.
  Glancing around, he noticed, save for a kerosene lamp and a pot bellied stove, the room was bare - not a stick of furniture and there were no decorations or pictures - even Joe and Red were still gone.

Clamoring to his feet slowly, William went to the door and peeked out, but could see or hear nothing but a fat crow being chased across the sky by several sparrows.

Easing the door shut, he turned back to inspect the interior more closely. It was small, approximately fifteen feet by fifteen feet, square, with a wooden floor and bare walls. The windows were so dirty that hardly any light was able to get through and a thin layer of dust covered everything.

The creaking of the door caused William to spin around. Red was standing in the doorway, grinning. "Scarred ya, huh?" Red said as he entered the shack.

William shook his head and said, "Yes. I guessed I dozed off for a while. Did Joe go with you?"

Red looked around and said, "No. He was still here when I left." Then he nodded toward the woman and said, "I'm sorry, there ain't no doctor or hospital. This place is ah ghost town."

William was shocked by the news. "You mean there's no one here? What about all those buildings? Are you saying they're just sitting there, empty?"

Red hung his head. He was truly sorry he wasn't able to find help for the woman.

"This used ta be ah minin' town, but my guess is they only use the warehouses now ta store minin' tools and other equipment and they have three men who guard the place, at least as far as I can tell and they all carry guns, so obviously I didn't stop for ah chat or try ta introduce myself and ask where the nearest hospital was."

Red felt sorry for William who was standing there looking like a man who had just lost everything he had. Both men were silent, not knowing what else to say.

This time it was Red who jumped when he heard the door making that creaking sound as Joe came in with a half full gunnysack over his shoulder.

"She awake, yet?" Joe asked.

The Legend of Joe, Willy & Red

"She stirred once and a couple of times she mumbled something incoherent, but that's all," William answered.

Joe nodded his head and set the gunnysack on the floor and began to pull out coffee, cigarettes, cigars, clothes, canned soup, pots, a skillet and even some medical supplies.

"Where'd you git all this stuff?" Red asked, mystified.

Immediately, William began checking the medical supplies. He was, after all, the nursemaid of the group - at least that's what Joe had referred to him as.

William found bandages and other assorted things that come in a typical medical kit. He could use the gauze to wrap around her if she had any broken ribs, but until she woke up, they wouldn't know.

Joe lit a cigarette and said, "Let's just say it's a little contribution from the National Mining Company and let it go at that." He turned to Red, " Here, have a cigar."

Red accepted the cigar, but didn't ask any more questions. It was the chicken house thing all over again, without the rooster.

Rather than attract the attention of the guards with smoke coming from the pot bellied stove, Joe went behind the shed and built a small, smokeless fire in a round hole he dug in the ground, and soon had coffee and soup for everyone.

After they ate, Joe and Red were enjoying cigars while William knelt next to the woman, stroking her hair, gently. Next to him was a bowl of soup, cooling down so it wouldn't burn her swollen lips if she woke up soon enough to eat it.

"Don't worry, pretty lady. I'm right here and I'll take care of you," William said in a low, soft voice.

Whether it was the smell of the soup, cigar smoke or the gentle stroking of her hair that woke her up, she wasn't sure, but all of a sudden her eyes popped wide open. The sight of a man sitting next to her caused her to sit upright, ready to defend herself.

Jared McVay

Sharp pains radiated throughout her bruised and battered body and raced to her brain. Wild eyed she scooted away from William and stared at the three men who stared back at her.

William remained where he sat as she scooted against the back wall, but when he spoke, his words were soft and reassuring. "Easy, lady. We're not going to hurt you. We found you in a freight train boxcar. You were hurt and unconscious. We took you off the train and brought you here. We're trying to find a doctor for you."

Picking up the bowl of soup, William slowly extended it in her direction. "Have some soup. Joe, here," he said, nodding toward Joe, "he fixed the soup and coffee. It's really very good. Do you think you can eat something? You really need to try. You can have both; the soup and the coffee, I mean."

As the woman looked around the room she scrutinized the three men as her nerves began to quiet down, a little. Something in the way they sat, quietly looking at her and the gentleness in the fat guy's voice told her they posed no threat. The aroma of the coffee and soup caused her stomach to grumble. She nodded her head, yes, and the portly man leaned over and handed her a bowl of soup and a spoon.

"I'll get you some coffee and there's more soup if you want it," he said, gently.

As she reached for the bowl, their hands touched, briefly. She noticed his hand trembling, slightly. His eyes held what could only be perceived as love and kindness, the way her father used to smile at her mother. It was the kind of smile she'd always hoped for from a man, but as of yet, had never to her memory, ever received.

For a moment she stared at William, trying to remember. Did she know this man? Had they ever had a relationship? She didn't think so, but she couldn't remember - a fact that startled her. It was strange. She couldn't even remember her own name, or anything about herself, except quick visions popping into her head of several men beating on her; but she couldn't remember why. And the fat man had said they found her in a boxcar? What was she doing in a boxcar? Had someone put her there? Her stomach grumbled and she decided to eat first and get answers later.

When she put the spoon to her lips, she found they were swollen and sore, along with her other pains. Suddenly she felt like she might faint.

William had turned to look at Joe and Red. He was feeling very proud of himself.

"How about that, she's awake and eating some soup. I think she's going to be all right," he said.

But the look on Red's face was far from the jubilation William hoped to see.

Red leaned in toward William and whispered, "I don't think she's outta the woods yet."

William swung his attention back to the woman and found her pale looking and shaking. With great effort, she set the bowl of soup on the floor, spilling some of it in the process. Her hands went to her face and she began to cry.

Slowly, William scooted close to her and gently put his arm around her shoulders as he stroked her hair soothingly.

"Please, don't cry, it's okay now. No one is going to hurt you anymore," William whispered close to her ear.

For some unknown reason she didn't shy away from him. His closeness and soft words seemed to have a calming effect on her and she allowed herself to lean her head against his shoulder as tears streamed down her cheeks. He was like some, big, cuddly teddy bear; soft and warm, which made her feel safe and protected.

After a few minutes she was able to stop crying and sat up, drying her tears on a handkerchief offered to her by the man with the loving eyes and kind voice. He was giving her that look, again.

"Thank you," she said as she returned his handkerchief. "I feel like such a fool, crying like some addlebrained school girl, when I should be trying to get a grip on myself like and adult."

Red moved slowly toward her and squatted down a few feet away and said, "Hey, I don't know what happened to you, or why. But from the looks of things, I reckon you got ah right ta cry."

Lowering her head, embarrassed, she said, "That's the problem, I don't know, either. In fact, I can't seem to remember anything at all, except a few images of some men beating on me."

"Are you telling us you have no memory at all? Not even your name?" William asked.

She shook her head and looked at both William and Red and said, "I'm sorry, but the only thing I can remember are some men beating and kicking me. And even that is blurry."

William reached over and picked up the bowl of soup and extended it toward her.

"Here, try and eat this before it gets cold. It'll make you feel better."

Feeling calmer, she took the bowl of soup and began eating with a relish. It was chicken noodle; her favorite and she could feel its warmth going all the way down into her stomach.

Joe had been standing next to the partly open door, making sure no one sneaked up on them. Blowing his cigar smoke into the room, he said, "Well, memory or not, we need to be clearing out of here before those guards come snooping around."

William jumped to his feet and approached Joe, speaking in a nervous whisper, "We can't ask her to travel in her condition. She's still very weak."

Joe took William by the arm and escorted him outside, ushering him away from the shack.

After being in the dimly lit shack, the bright sunlight hurt William's eyes and he shielded them with his hand.

The Legend of Joe, Willy & Red

Joe stopped in the shade of a tree and said, "Her coming along wasn't part of the plan."

Defiance welled up in William like a roaring hurricane. "Well we're sure not going to leave her here! Especially not in her condition!" William said, hands on his hips and glaring defiantly at Joe.

William expected Joe to give him an argument and was ready for it, but he didn't and after a moment, to William's surprise, shrugged his shoulders and headed back to the shack.

William was stunned. He'd readied himself for a fight that didn't happen and was thrown off balance. This wasn't like Joe. He never gave in this easy.

The truth was, Joe wasn't sure what might happen if those men in the warehouse found her; and find her they would. As much as he wanted to be rid of her, he knew she would be better off with them, although he wasn't about to admit that to anyone.

Back at the shack, Joe walked over to Red, while William went to attend to the woman, who had just finished her bowl of soup.

Joe looked at Red and asked, "You have any idea where we are?"

Red was busy packing their gear and looked up and said, "Yea, actually I do. I saw ah map of the state on the wall in one of them abandoned stores. It showed a mark that was this place, here. There ain't much between here and Salt Lake City but ah lot of miles, maybe ah hundred and fifty of'em. There was ah couple of towns some miles off the track line; but Salt Lake looks like our best bet."

Joe nodded his head as he rolled things around in his mind. A hundred and fifty miles was a long way on a freight train and he'd said there was a couple of towns, but not close to the tracks. So it looked like Salt Lake was their only option. At least Salt Lake would have doctors and hospitals.

Red interrupted Joe's thoughts. "It's not all that far and it's purty much ah straight line trip. Plus, I reckon there's help for the woman ta be found," Red said, trying to help Joe make up his mind.

Joe took his time; lighting a cigarette and letting the smoke curl up around his head, thinking about all the pros and cons of her going with them - knowing of course that Red and William were right, it wouldn't be safe for her to stay here, alone. Joe blew out a long stream of smoke, feeling like he'd lost control over his own destiny, which irritated him to no end.

"Okay," Joe heard himself say. "I must be crazy, too. Let's get outta here before those guards figure out they're missing a few items. Maybe we can find another place to hide until the next train comes through."

"I think I know of ah place," Red said with enthusiasm.

While her future was being decided, the woman sat with her back against the wall, admiring the tall, rugged looking man who made her insides feel all funny. Why she was attracted to this man, she wasn't sure, but attracted to him she definitely was. Even with all her aches and pains and her weakened condition, uncontrolled fantasies danced through her mind in vivid color that made her blush.

What kind of woman am I, she wondered. I shouldn't even be thinking things like that, especially in my condition; or even when I'm healthy for that matter; or should I?

The woman tried to concentrate on her past, who she was, where she was from and what kind of life she'd lived to cause men to beat her up and leave her for dead on a freight train. But try as she might, her mind would not reveal her past.

It was all so confusing. While praying that her memory would soon return, she also hoped her past wouldn't be too devastating, like maybe killing someone.

Oh God, she hoped that wasn't it. Or, what if she'd done something so horrible, so horrendous that her mind had blanked it out forever. What if her memory never came back? Was that possible, she wondered?

"Oh God, I hope not," she blurted out.

"What was that?" William asked, turning in her direction.

"Nothing," she said, turning her face away, not wanting to give away anything through her eyes. The eyes are the windows of the soul. At least, that's what she'd heard one time, she thought, but couldn't remember where or when.

Jared McVay

Chapter 14

Over here, boys, I think I've found him

Meanwhile, not far away, a tall, bony man resembling a weasel with beady eyes, hooknose, no chin and yellow stained teeth, noticed a window open on the backside of one of the warehouses. Flattening his stomach against the wall, his breath coming in short gasps, he inched his way to the edge of the window and with great caution peeked in the window and gave a huge sigh of relief when he saw no one.

Once his breath became normal again and his nerves calmed down enough to move, the weasel hurried back in the direction he came from, glancing from time to time over his shoulder.

When the weasel burst into the guard office, Buck, the head guard was pouring booze into his coffee. As the door came crashing open, Buck almost spilled his precious whiskey. And when he saw who it was, his eyes became ablaze with anger.

Buck was a short, very stocky man with unruly hair and red veins showing on his cheeks and nose from too much who-shot-john. He was a drinking man and proud of it which constituted for his normal temperament which reminded you of a polecat with a toothache. But when he had a hangover, like this morning, he was more like a wounded grizzly bear.

"What in the double D hell do you think yer doin'? Have you gone plumb crazy?" Buck yelled, with his pistol in his hand, pointing at the idiot who burst into his office and nearly scared the wits out of him and almost made him spill his morning pick-me-up.

Rafe, the tall bony man who resembled a weasel, stood looking down the barrel of Buck's pistol, which from his point of view reminded him of a cannon. He was not only horrified, but also about to wet himself.

The Legend of Joe, Willy & Red

"Well, speak up, man! Don't jest stand there like the idiot you are! Why'd you come ah runnin' in here like ah swarm of bees was after ya? Well, say somethin'!" Buck roared as he lowered the pistol.

Rafe swallowed hard to keep from throwing up his breakfast and then swallowed a large gulp of air to bring his heart rate back to normal. "They's ah winder open on the back wall of warehouse number eleven, like somebody had crawled in. I looked through the winder but I didn't see nobody. And I looked real good, too, Buck. You would'a been proud of me cause I was brave. Huh Buck?"

Buck gave a grunt and a nod. Rafe was always seein' things that weren't there so he wasn't too concerned. What he needed right now was ah good stiff drink to make his headache go away.

"There was tracks outside the winder on the ground. I see'd'um clear, Buck. But there weren't nobody inside the warehouse. Where do ya think he went, Buck?"

Buck stood up and rubbed his nose on his shirtsleeve and then took a long drink from his coffee cup that had been laced with a strong dose of moonshine. He supposed he'd best go check it out and a few other places as well. After all, that's what they were payin' him for.

"Rafe, go check that old shack down by the tracks. See if any of them bums has been stayin' there," Buck said as he set his coffee mug on the desk.

Turning to a third guard, George, who had followed Rafe in and had heard what Rafe had said, was already loading two Winchester rifles.

Buck said, "George, you check the town while I check the warehouses."

George was more non-descript than the other two guards; brown hair, brown eyes, medium height, medium build - nothing outstanding that would attract anyone's attention, but in truth was the most stable of the three.

George handed one of the rifles to Rafe and then nodded as he shoved Rafe out the door ahead of him.

~ 121 ~

Jared McVay

"You see anybody, you bring him back here, alive, you hear? You have ta shoot somebody, shoot him in the foot!" Buck yelled as the two men left his office.

When the two guards had gone, Buck took a long pull straight from the bottle of moonshine, smacked his lips, then took a cigar from his shirt pocket, lighting it as he left his office to stand on the front stoop of the building, his bloodshot eyes surveying the compound as an evil grin spread across his face.

First, he would strip the man naked to humiliate him and then chain him by the ankle to the tree out back. And, if the man protested, like they always did, he'd have ta introduce'em to the whip - let him know what he could expect whenever he felt like complainin'.

This time he might even set ah bowl of food and ah jug of water on the ground just beyond the man's reach. Yea, that might be interestin' ta watch the man strainin' ta try and get to the food and water and fightin' off any critters that might come ta steal it. It gets so borin' out here that ah man has ta figure out ways ta entertain himself. Maybe this one would be tough and last longer than the other four had. At least that last one had done pretty good. He had to admit that. Five days chained stark naked to that ole tree out back with no food or water was ah long time. The only thing was, after that first taste of the whip, the man hadn't uttered another word.

Buck looked up at the sky and thought, the weather turning cold wouldn't help none. That one feller was stiff as ah board when they'd dumped his body in that ole well out back, Buck remembered.

Glancing toward the warehouses, Buck decided not to bother checking them. He figured whoever had broken in wasn't stupid enough to hang around after he'd gotten what he wanted. Besides, that bottle of whiskey was sittin' there on his desk, unguarded and anybody could make off with it if they was a mind to.

Red swung the burlap with all their supplies over his shoulder as Joe and William walked over to where the woman was sitting propped against the back wall.

"We need to be leaving. Do you feel strong enough to walk?" William asked.

"I don't know, but I'll try," she said as she attempted to stand. She seemed to be in a lot of pain and a bit wobbly. William took her by the arm and helped her to stand up. She stood there quietly for a moment and then said, "I think I'm going to faint."

With that, her eyes closed and she fell toward Joe. It was purely a reflex that caused Joe to catch her.

"Women," he said as he scooped her into his arms.

William got a strange look in his eyes and Red was grinning as they started for the door. Joe glanced over and said, "What are you two lookin' at? Ain't you ever seen a woman faint before?"

Red chuckled and Joe said, "Let's just get outta here!"

With the woman in his arms, Joe hurried out the door with a need to leave this place pressing heavily on his mind. It was like a sixth sense or something that told him trouble was on the way.

With the gunnysack over his shoulder, Red hurried after Joe. William brought up the rear because he took the time to close the door to the shack tightly before hurrying to catch up, mumbling to himself as he ran. "Why couldn't she have fallen into my arms when she fainted? I would have been happy to carry her. But no, she had to fall in the big tough guy's direction. And he doesn't even like her, or does he?"

Red was just a few steps behind Joe and the woman and just happened to look up in time to see the woman's eyes open slightly and look up at Joe as a small smile creased her lips. Then, with what appeared to be an unconscious motion draped her arms around Joe's neck and snuggled closer to him. It was a smooth motion and Joe, in his hurry to get away, didn't seem to notice.

Jared McVay

Red glanced over his shoulder to see if William had noticed the woman's actions, but William's head was down and he was mumbling something to himself, too caught up in his own emotions to notice.

Red sighed and said to himself, "I got ah bad feelin' about this," as he hurried to catch up and possibly take the lead sometime soon, since he was the only one who actually knew where they were going.

Fear of actually confronting someone all by himself caused Rafe to move slowly and cautiously through the woods as he headed for the old shack. In his reasoning he figured if he didn't hurry, hopefully whoever might have been there would be gone by the time he got there. He would be happy to let Buck and George deal with whoever had broken into the warehouse.

He wasn't a brave man and he knew it. So, when he walked around a large out crop boulder and came face to face with a large man carrying a woman in his arms, he almost had a heart attack. And behind the man, Rafe could see two more men!

His breathing became labored as he stepped in front of the man carrying the woman. Only his greater fear of Buck kept Rafe from bolting. His mouth felt dry even though white foamy saliva drooled down over the corners of his mouth, coating the dark stubble of whiskers on his chin. He looked down at his violently shaking hands and tried to point the rifle in their direction.

"Hold..... hold it.. rrrright there," Rafe heard himself say in a squeaky voice. His knees were shaking so hard he wasn't sure they would hold him up.

The man carrying the woman and the other two men stopped and stood staring at him, waiting for him to say something more, but Rafe couldn't think of anything else to say.

Finally, the man carrying the woman shook his head as though he was disgusted and turned and handed the woman to the fat one. And before Rafe realized what had happened, the big man had walked over and snatched the rifle out of his hands, yelling at him, "Give me that thing before you hurt somebody!"

A large cloud passed across the sun and blacked it out momentarily, and when it passed on, shafts of sunlight streamed through the trees, and Rafe, in his panic, was sure God was sending the angel of death to claim him and take him home. Wild eyed with terror, Rafe turned and began to run, knowing that at any moment there would be a bullet in his back that would end his life here on earth, and he would be dragged down into the pits of hell because of all the sins he'd committed.

Rafe screamed and yelled at the top of his lungs as he ran through the brush that tore at his face and body. "Help! Help! Buck! George! Come quick! Help me!"

Joe turned to Red and William, "We've gotta get a move on before that idiot gets back with help. If the other two are as crazy as this one, they'll start shootin' as soon as they see us and dump our carcasses in a hole somewhere."

Buck heard Rafe's screaming well before he came charging into the clearing next to the office. Buck was already standing there with his pistol in his hand as Rafe came running up to him. He could see the terror in Rafe's eyes and tears running down his cheeks, along with a large wet spot in the front of his pants. And somewhere along the way, Rafe had lost his rifle.

If Rafe weren't kinfolk he'd have thrown him down the well with those others, long ago. Not only was Rafe dumber than a rock, he was also a coward. Buck looked at this loser he was ashamed to call his cousin and as calmly as he could, said, "Where's your rifle? I told you to shoot him in the foot, not drop your rifle and run."

Rafe danced back and forth from one foot to the other, a new fear sweeping over him. Buck could kill him right here and now and feel no sorrow about it. Ole Buck had ah mean streak in him ah mile wide. And he'd tell ma I had just run off, and never blink an eye about lying ta her, Rafe thought as he tried to come up with something to say.

"They's three men and ah woman," Rafe stammered. "They caught me unawares and surrounded me. The big fella, well he jest grabbed the gun right outta my hands. He was gonna shoot me. There weren't nuthin' else I could do but run as fast as I could and try ta get back here ta warn ya. It's ah wonder I weren't shot in the back!"

Rafe was drenched with sweat by the time he finished his partial lie. Rafe prayed to the almighty for Buck ta believe him.

Buck was glaring at this miserable, trembling excuse that called himself a man as George came running up to them and stopped short at the sight of Rafe.

"What in the world are you yellin' about? What happened?"

Before Rafe could tell his story again, Buck said, "Rafe! You stay here, and get yourself cleaned up! George, you come with me."

Buck chomped down on his cigar and started off at a dogtrot in the direction of the shack.

As Rafe watched Buck and George disappear into the woods, he looked skyward and said, "thank ye, Lord."

He felt powerful thankful he wasn't dead and laying in the bottom of that well with them others. It had been real close. He was glad George had showed up when he did.

During the day they hid in an empty building at the far side of town and twice they saw two men searching for them, but only one of the men was working very hard at it.

Red checked the rifle Joe had taken from Rafe and found it was fully loaded. He wasn't sure he could actually shoot somebody and crossed his fingers that he wouldn't be put to the test.

Around dusk, a freight train stopped to pick up two large crates that were setting on the dock.

The Legend of Joe, Willy & Red

As the train arrived, Buck, George and Rafe all approached the dock and Buck went up to the bull riding the train and spoke to him; then all four of them spread out and began patrolling the nearby area, along with searching each freight car while the stoker and the engineer loaded the two crates.

"Well, there goes our chance to ride this train. We'll never be able to get aboard with them out there watching for us," William whispered.

Red grinned and said, "Don't be so negative. When the time comes, get in that boxcar two cars up from here, the one with the open door. I'll be along, directly.

As Red picked up the rifle and turned to leave, Joe grabbed him by the arm.

"What are you plannin' on doin'?" he asked

Red winked at him and said, "Nuthin' you wouldn't ah done if you'd thought of it."

Joe had a puzzled look on his face as Red slipped out the back door, carrying the rifle.

Buck was standing less than twenty feet from where Joe, William and the woman were hiding, looking like he was going to enter the building, when a shot rang out down near the far end of the train.

"Who the hell fired that shot?" Buck yelled, as he began to shuffle off down along the train, with everyone following after him.

While they were all running down the dock, Joe, William and the woman sneaked aboard the boxcar Red had indicated, without being seen.

They had just gotten on board safely when another shot rang out from a different location and the guards and railroad men turned and ran into the town, each going in a different direction. And within a minute, they heard the engineer call out,

"Over here, boys, I think I've found him. Careful now, he's pointin' ah rifle in our direction. Don't do nuthin' foolish."

Jared McVay

In the darkness, all they could see was the silhouette of a man standing next to the corner of a building, pointing a rifle at them.

The engineer turned to Buck and said, "Well, we've done our part. You boys can take it from here. We ain't getting paid ta get shot at."

He turned to the stoker and the bull and said, "Com'on boys, we got ah schedule ta keep."

The train was almost to the edge of town when Red dove through the open door and looked up with a broad grin.

William ran over and helped Red to his feet. "From the sound of it, we thought they had you cornered."

"Na," Red said, "They just thought they did. I sure wish I could'a hung around and seen their faces when they found ah manikin propped up next ta that building with an empty rifle in his hands. I found him in one of the stores earlier and used him kinda like ah decoy."

Chapter 15

Rejected, again

As the train rumbled across the barren country on it's way to Salt Lake City, there was only desert and giant mesas of rock and dirt that had been pressured into existence millions of years ago when giant predators roamed the earth and soared across the sky.

It was lonely and desolate - yet it was grander than anything they'd ever seen. It had a magnificent beauty all it's own.

Joe and Red stood in the doorway of the boxcar and looked out, awed by what they were seeing. After a while Red turned to Joe and said, "Well, I reckon we're safe, I don't see any dinosaurs or pterodactyls, or whatever they're called."

Joe nodded his head as the two of them turned back into the car. Joe sat down with his back against the wall and lit a cigarette, while Red busied himself digging into the supply sack, trying to find his blanket and pillow so he could get some rest - it had been a long day.

William fussed over the woman, trying to cover her with his blanket to keep her warm, but she was having none of it.

"Please, I'm fine. Really, I'm not cold, honest," she said, trying not to offend the kindly man that hovered over her like a worried mother.

"You need to keep warm and rest," William said in a soothing tone. "We'll be in Salt Lake City before long and I'm sure we'll be able to find some help for you there."

"Really, I'm fine. I don't need a doctor," she said, testily as she got to her feet and went and sat down next to Joe.

Jared McVay

Enough was enough. He was like an old mother hen. Plus, it gave her an excuse to sit next to the big man who caused her to have certain feelings, inside.

Red had his back to them, arranging a pallet where he could lie down and hadn't seen the woman go over and sit down next to Joe, so when he made his comment, it was to where he thought she was.

"Don't kid yourself, or us, either. You do need a doctor. You're black and blue from head ta toe and you might have internal injuries we don't know about; plus, you can't even remember your own name or anything about yourself. Yea, I'd say you need ta see ah doctor and maybe even stay in the hospital for ah few days," Red said with a great deal of assurance.

It wasn't until he stretched out on his blanket that he saw the woman, sitting all snuggled up close to Joe that he realized he'd been speaking in the wrong direction. Oh boy, this is a bad omen if he ever saw one, he thought to himself.

Without being obvious, Red sneaked a peek at William to see his reaction to all this, even though he was pretty sure he knew what it would be.

William had the look of pure dejection on his face. There was hurt in his eyes and Red felt sorry for him, but what could he do, except keep his mouth shut. After all, when you got right down to it, he didn't want to get in the middle of a love triangle. In the end he could wind up the loser, with both of them mad at him.

His grandfather on the Indian side had said it best, 'There are many theories about how a woman thinks, and none of them work.'

As far as Red was concerned, his grandfather had always been a wise man that had always given him sound advice. He wished there had been time to talk to him about his situation before he'd hopped that freight train.

To say William was shocked and hurt by the woman's actions would put it mildly.

The Legend of Joe, Willy & Red

Once again, he'd been rejected and wasn't quite sure how he felt about it. Bad, that was for sure, but what could he do? Nothing. He had no claim on her and legally he was still a married man. And he'd never actually told her how he felt about her or that she was the spitting image of his wife.

And even if he had, how could he ever think she could be attracted to him over someone who looked like Joe. There was no contest. Joe was tall and ruggedly good looking, while he was short, fat and ordinary looking. Still, it grated him to see her sitting next to him, all googley-eyed, mooning over him like a schoolgirl.

She had sat down very close to Joe and was staring up at him with a look even a blind man could see, without seeming to care how it made him feel. William decided then and there, he would never understand women.

"It was very nice of you to carry me when I was too weak to walk," she whispered close to Joe's ear. "If there's ever anything I can do to repay you..."

She let the sentence go unfinished, but the meaning was loud and clear, as far as Joe was concerned.

This was all he needed, Joe thought. He'd known from the beginning she would be trouble and right here was the proof.

Joe lit another cigarette, trying to ignore the woman as his eyes flicked between Red and William.

From Red, he received a blank stare, showing nothing of his true feelings, which was about what he'd expected. Red wouldn't want to get involved and the best way to do that was to act unconcerned.

But William was a different story. He was hurt; hurt badly, and it showed on his face and in his eyes.

Joe's first reaction was to move away from her, or, simply tell her to get away from him; that he wanted nothing to do with her, but, before he did either, another thought entered his mind. If he just let things alone, maybe - just maybe it would be enough for Mister William Conrad

Bains, Sir, to get mad enough at him to call it quits with him. Now that was something to think about.

There was something about the woman that drew William to her and when she rejected him, he was visibly upset. He didn't know what that something was, nor did he care, as long as it provided a way for him to be on his own again, which in the end is what he wanted.

They should be in Salt Lake City in a few hours and by then he could figure out some way so they could go their separate ways. Maybe he could give the woman back to William so he could take her to a hospital and by the time they'd done that, he would be on another freight train and his own man, again. It would be easier on the little guy that way. He'd be able to play nursemaid, with no competition from him.

Joe might have thought his plan a good one, but the forces that be, didn't see it the same way.

Chapter 16

Mister William Conrad Bains, Dupe

William knew Joe hadn't encouraged her, but that didn't make things any easier and he tried to put the whole situation out of his mind. When they reached Salt Lake City, she would get the medical attention she needed and that would be the end of it.

Once again, it would be just the three of them and things would get back to the way they were. At least that was what he hoped would happen.

He had to admit to himself, the woman had created friction between them, just as Joe had predicted. He'd already been crushed by one woman and didn't need for it to happen a second time.

Red was rolled up in his blanket and snoring loudly. Joe was smoking a cigarette and staring idly at the passing landscape as the woman slept with her head against his shoulder.

William stretched out on his blanket and pulled the pillow under his head. There had been precious little time for rest or sleep since they had found the woman, so with the rumble of the wheels, the steady rocking motion of the train and his heavy eyelids, William slipped into a deep sleep.

The dream took him back to the day his troubles had begun. He was dressed in his brown suit, ready to leave for work. At the door, his lovely, blue-eyed wife, Brenda, stood waiting to send him off. She was dressed in her bathrobe and wore no makeup. Her soft blonde hair was still all rumpled from last night's sleep and she was wearing those big floppy house shoes he'd gotten her for Christmas, which in William's opinion, made her look adorable. Even looking her worst, as she would put it, to William she was the most beautiful girl in town.

Jared McVay

He leaned in to kiss her goodbye, but at the last minute she turned her cheek to him.

"My breath must smell awful," she said, "I haven't brushed my teeth yet, okay?"

William contented himself with giving her a peck on the cheek before he walked out the door, wondering what that was all about. She'd never done that before, whether she'd brushed her teeth or not. And he couldn't remember her breath ever smelling bad.

Maybe it was just her woman thing and shrugged it off as he got into their five-year-old car and fired up the engine.

"Have a pleasant day," she called as he backed out of the driveway.

William parked the car on a side street, next to the curb, a full block away from the Minneapolis State Bank where he worked as a teller. He always did that so as not to take a space near the bank that might interfere with customers who had business there.

With thousands of banks being closed because of the big crash, along with the unwise investments many of them had made and other reasons, William felt lucky to still have a job, even though they all had to take temporary pay cuts until times were good and the country was back on it's feet again.

Bill Davis, the bank manager, might be a donkey's rear end but he was smart. He had seen hard times coming and had planned for it. William wasn't sure just how, but he had, and somehow kept the small state bank solvent.

Bill hadn't gone along with many of the other banks that had invested heavily in the stock markets. He made investments for the banks patrons that had little or no risks because the bulk of their business came from several local area businesses and their employees, along with nearby farmers and other assorted tradesmen.

The Legend of Joe, Willy & Red

Somehow, Bill Davis had talked many of them into using less cash money, and going back to the barter system; trading with each other for food and goods, or services.

Standing at his teller station, counting his start up cash, William's mind wandered back to his wife and the incident this morning. Had they been drifting apart lately? When was the last time they had made love, he wondered? Not since she'd started taking that night cooking class. And she always seemed to get home late and a bit tipsy, which she said was from sampling the cooking sherry. William had accepted that, but now that he gave it a bit more thought, her hair and her clothes always seemed to be rumpled, like she'd been rolling around in them. And why did she always have to dress up to go to cooking school? And if she was learning all these fancy, new recipes, why hadn't she cooked any of them?

These and other thoughts were roaming around inside William's head when John Axel walked up to him.

John was spending his last day at the bank doing very little work and a great deal of making small talk with the female employees. According to John he'd had enough of the banking business and had given his notice two weeks ago.

"Bill Davis wants to see you in his office, muy pronto," John said with a smirk on his face.

John was one of those, tall, good-looking, smooth talking men that women were always chasing after. When he'd given his notice, he said he was going out to California and try his luck at being an actor in the movies.

William envied him and thought he had a good chance of making it. John always seemed to have it all together. Maybe he'd become another Errol Flynn.

Bill Davis met William at the door and ushered him in, which wasn't a good sign. He only did that when a person was in serious trouble. Bill also had a scowl on his face but that wasn't unusual, he always seemed to have a scowl on his face.

~ 135 ~

Jared McVay

William looked at the curtains on Bill's office window and saw they were open; a thing Bill did when he was dressing someone down for some infraction, but for the life of him, William couldn't think of anything he'd done wrong.

Maybe Bill Davis was just fooling with him and in the end he would congratulate him, and then give him John Axel's old job and a raise. Yes, that must be it, a promotion and a raise, William thought and felt his spirits rise.

As William entered the office he noticed another man standing somewhat off to the side, with a sinister look. And it wasn't just his appearance, although that would be enough in many cases. The man was short and thin, with beady eyes behind his small, rimless glasses that were perched on a curved, hawk like nose, which ended just above a pencil thin mustache. The lips were thin, drawn ever so slightly into a leering grin that wasn't a smile. It was more like he was about to do something bad and was enjoying the thought of doing it.

William felt a cold shiver run down his back as the grim faced Bill Davis walked behind his desk and sat down.

Bill took a cigar from a container on his desk and snipped off the end and then lit it with a lighter that looked like a fire breathing dragon. Bill took several puffs as he sat there and stared at William.

Finally, Bill Davis blew a long stream of cigar smoke in William's direction and said, "Mister Bains, I'll come right to the point. I've just heard some very disturbing news and I believe you know what I'm talking about."

During the long, pregnant pause that followed his statement, the bank manager looked at William and waited for a reaction, but when he got only one of confusion, he continued.

"This is Simon Elliott, the state auditor," Bill said, nodding toward the evil looking little man who had moved up next to Bill's desk. "He's just informed me the bank is short by one hundred thousand dollars."

The Legend of Joe, Willy & Red

William was totally confused now as he asked, "So. . . what does that have to do with me?" not knowing anything else to say.

"Do you know the meaning of the word embezzlement, Mister Bains?" the state auditor hissed at him.

William became shocked as the implication sank in. Once again a shiver rushed down his spine.

"Embezzlement? I'm sorry sir, but I don't understand. Are you implying?"

"Don't be coy," Simon Elliott butted in. "I've traced it to you, every last dollar and there is no doubt. I've checked and rechecked. And you weren't even clever about it."

William was dumbstruck. His mouth became as dry as desert sand in the middle of July. His legs began to tremble and his heart felt like it was about to burst. How could this be happening to him? This had to be some kind of a joke. With a voice not quite his own, he said,

"Gentlemen, please, I honestly don't know what you're talking about. I didn't steal any money from the bank; not even a penny from anyone in my entire life."

"What did you do with the money, Mister Bains?" the bank auditor asked.

"This has to be some kind of mistake," William answered, weakly.

For the first time William could ever remember, there was a hint of sympathy on Bill Davis's face.

"I'd like to believe that, Mister Bains, but Mister Elliott has assured me there is no mistake. Every transaction leads straight back to you."

William was too stunned for words. There was nothing he could say that would change their minds. He could only stand there, staring at his shoes, wondering how and why this was happening to him. If he was in a nightmare, he hoped he would wake up soon.

After another long silence, Bill Davis said, "You've had a good record up to now, William. And to save both, the bank and you a lot of embarrassment and bad publicity, I'm going to give you twenty-four hours to return the money, along with your letter of resignation, of course."

William heard Bill Davis speaking but it seemed to come from a long way off and from the time he left the bank until he walked into the front door of his house, it was like he was drifting along in a thick fog.

Upon entering the house, William headed straight for the bedroom without seeing Brenda, who was lying on the couch, reading a book.

"You're home early. Is there anything wrong?" she called out as he walked past.

"I don't feel well," he said without realizing he had responded to her question. "I'm going to lie down for awhile, maybe take a nap."

As she retreated behind her book, the hint of a smile crept across her mouth and slowly grew into a grin.

William didn't notice that, either, as he trudged his way toward the bedroom.

William flopped down on the bed without removing any of his clothing or taking off his shoes, which is something he'd never done before. For a long time he just laid there, staring at the ceiling, wondering what had happened. His life as he knew it was over.

How could he return a hundred thousand dollars when he didn't have it to begin with and never did have? He wondered how many years he would spend in prison for a crime he hadn't committed. One or fifty, it didn't matter. His life was finished. And what would Brenda do when she found out? He couldn't ask her to wait for him.

In his mind, he could only conclude that someone had set him up. Yes, that was it. They had stolen the money and made it look like it was him - but who would do such a thing?

He went over each employee at the bank carefully in his mind, but drew a blank. He couldn't think of even one person who might have a vendetta against him and would

The Legend of Joe, Willy & Red

do such a thing. He felt sure he got along with everybody, including the bank manager, Bill Davis.

His mind was like a whirlwind. All sorts of thoughts buzzed around in his brain at random, but none of them made any sense. He was even struggling with how he was going to tell Brenda. She would be devastated.

Suddenly, the phone rang and William almost had a heart attack. When it rang a second time, he rolled over and reached for it. When he put the receiver to his ear, he heard Brenda's voice.

"Hello," she said in that soft, sexy voice of hers.

"Hi, honey," came a man's voice that sounded familiar to William. "Have I got some news for you."

Brenda's voice now had a touch of panic in it. "John, you shouldn't be calling me at this time. William is home. He's in the bedroom taking a nap. He said he didn't feel well. Is it what I think it is?"

"It sure is, baby," John Axel said in that smooth tone of his. "I'll bet ole Willy boy is a nervous wreck about now. He's got twenty-four hours to come up with the money or go to the hoosegow," John said with a chuckle.

This time Brenda's voice had a worried note to it. 'Are you sure they can't trace the money to us?" she asked.

"No way, darlin'," John said confidently. "Old Willy is practically behind bars with the key thrown away. In a few days it'll be just you and me, baby. But in the meantime, I need to see you. I can hardly wait."

"Alright, darling," Brenda whispered huskily. "I need you, too. In the state he's in I doubt he'll even notice that I'm gone. I'll be at your place within an hour. I love you."

William waited until he heard both receivers click before he took his hand off the mouthpiece and set the phone back in its cradle.

Upon hearing Brenda's footsteps coming softly down the hallway, William rolled over on the bed and pretended to be asleep as the bedroom door opened slightly, then closed. William listened as her footsteps retreated back down the hallway.

Had she come over next to the bed, she might have noticed his trembling body, or the tears running down his cheeks.

Shortly thereafter, William heard the front door open, then close, followed by the sound of the car backing out of the driveway.

William's mind was still in a daze as he stumbled down the hallway and into the kitchen, where he found a note propped against a glass on the kitchen table. A lump formed in his throat as he slumped into one of the kitchen chairs and stared for a long time at the note before actually reaching for it.

*"Have gone to my cooking class.
I heard about the terrible thing
you did and I'm appalled.
I'll be spending the night with a girlfriend.
I want a divorce and I would appreciate it if you are
gone by the time I come home."
Brenda*

William walked to the cupboard and removed a bottle of whiskey from its hiding place and took a long drink, straight from the bottle, gagging as the raw alcohol tore at his throat. When he got his air back, he sat down at the table and began some serious drinking.

No wonder John had given his notice and made up that lie about going out to Hollywood, California to be an actor. He had all that money. The frame-up had worked perfectly. And, he had Brenda, while Mister William Conrad Bains, the stooge, was left holding the proverbial bag. And on top of that, John had done it all so skillfully that there was no way to prove he was innocent. Who would believe him based on an overheard phone conversation? All they had to do was deny the whole thing and he would look like an idiot

The Legend of Joe, Willy & Red

who had concocted the whole thing and was trying to pull a fast one. The judge would just say he was trying to shift the guilt.

John was a smart guy who knew all the ins and outs of the banking business. No, there would be no traces to him. The weasel bank examiner had made it clear that he had checked and rechecked the books and each time, all of the evidence pointed in a straight line to Mister William Conrad Bains, stooge extraordinaire.

John Axel had pretended to be his friend, while he was sleeping with his wife and stealing all that money, with him as the patsy.

William took another long pull from the bottle and felt his body begin to go numb.

"If the truth was known," William said out loud to the bottle with a slurred voice,

" It was probably Brenda's idea from the start. She made advances to that ladies man, Mister Errol Flynn look-alike, John Axel, and then set the whole thing up. She got rid of him without looking like a slut; and for the grand prize, she got a handsome lover and a big bag of money."

By the time he'd finished the bottle, not only was he not able to think clearly, he could hardly stand up.

"Maybe, I should kill them both," he said to no one in particular. But upon further reflection, decided that took more courage than he had and instead of just prison, he would be sent to the electric chair.

Disgusted with this whole situation, he threw the empty bottle against the kitchen wall, shattering it into small pieces, then staggered out the front door leaving it standing wide open.

William's next recollection was leaning over the railing of a bridge, staring at the cold, fast running water of the Mississippi River, with every intention of ending his life. But he was even too much of a wimp to do that.

He was not only stupid, but on top of that, he was also a coward and a weakling who couldn't even kill himself.

Jared McVay

As he stood there in his drunken stupor, he couldn't help thinking of his wife, his beautiful Brenda.

She appeared out of the fog, slowly, as though she were floating in his direction. And she was laughing at him.

Somewhere in the distance, a train whistle pierced the air.

Chapter 17

From Banker to Con Man

The sound of the train whistle jerked William out of his dream with a start and he sat up, looking around. He was disoriented and still lost in his dream world and what he saw, almost caused him to have a heart attack. Sitting right there in plain sight was his wife, Brenda, and she was with the man who had stolen her from him, John Axel!

The fact that she was leaning her head against his shoulder was bad enough, but the smile on her lips was too much for William to stand.

He leaped to his feet and raced across the boxcar, yelling, "Nooooo, you can't do this to me!"

At this point, William was so enraged and still living in his dream world that what happened next went beyond anyone's imagination.

William grabbed the woman he saw as Brenda and jerked her to her feet by her arm, then swung her so hard she went sailing out of the open boxcar door.

A high-pitched scream erupted from her throat as she flew, spread eagle into the air.

Fortunately for her, the train had slowed to a crawl and she landed in a ditch filled with muddy water, which more than likely saved her life.

Her screaming brought William back to his senses and brought both Joe and Red to their feet, racing to the open boxcar door, wondering what had happened.

What they saw was the woman lying face down in a ditch full of brown water.

The woman's luck was still holding because the train had just passed a railroad crossing where an elderly couple was sitting in their car waiting for the train to go by and when the woman came flying off the train, they jumped out

Jared McVay

of the car and ran along the ditch to the spot where she lay floating in the water.

While the man pulled the woman from the water, the woman stared intently at the men standing in the open doorway of the boxcar.

Joe grinned, then slapped William on the back, "Well, that's one way to get her some medical attention in a hurry," he said, thinking this couldn't have worked out better if he'd planned it. And to think, Willy boy had been the one to do it.

William hung his head in despair. "I didn't mean to do that. I was dreaming about something from my past."

Red was already stuffing their gear into the gunnysack. "Forget about the past. We got to think about the future and it ain't lookin' too good about now. We gotta get off this train in ah big hurry. Look out the door, we're already pulling into the rail yard!"

They jumped out of the boxcar door and landed on the run as soon as their feet touched the ground - and found themselves running straight toward a man carrying a big stick.

It was a railroad man who was checking cars for bums.

"Hey, you there. Stop!" he yelled.

With a quick about face and a sliding of feet, Joe, William and Red turned and began running in the opposite direction with the railroad man in hot pursuit,

"Hey, over here," he yelled. "I got three of'em on the run!"

Suddenly, the yard was full of railroad men who were yelling and waving clubs.

Joe was in the lead, dodging between railroad cars, searching for a way out of the railroad yard.

Red found the gunnysack too heavy and cumbersome for decent running - even William was ahead of him. He dropped the sack in front of a yardman who had come out between two of the cars close to him. The man stumbled and fell as Red pushed hard to catch up to his friends.

As they raced out of the rail yard and onto the city street, it was William who fell behind and saw Joe and Red turn into an alleyway up ahead. When he reached the same opening and turned into the alleyway, he found Joe and Red standing next to a dead-end board wall approximately eight feet high.

William immediately took stock of their surroundings. The alley was littered with trash and several large trash containers, some full, some partially full and some empty.

Looking at Red, Joe said, "Give me a hand."

Together, Joe and Red rolled a large barrel over close to the wall.

William's brain kicked into gear; immediately surmising there wouldn't be time for all three of them to get over the wall before the railroad men came charging down the alley. Plus, he wasn't sure he could get over the wall, even standing on top of the barrel. In fact, he wasn't sure there would be time for any of them to escape. He had to make a decision, now.

Looking around, William found a large trash container that was only half full and climbed inside and squatted down, pulling trash over his head. He was just finishing as he heard yelling and the sound of running feet.

Twelve railroad men came running into the dead-end alleyway and saw Joe and Red. Red was just starting to climb onto the barrel and Joe was giving him a hand.

The mob fell on them like a heavy blanket, smothering them to the ground, and after a short skirmish, Joe and Red realized they had no chance against twelve big men with clubs and called an end to it.

"We give up," Red yelled as he and Joe raised their arms in defeat.

The mob stepped back and allowed Joe and Red to get to their feet, then started pushing and shoving them toward the front end of the alley. They had only gone a short distance when one of the railroad men said, "Hey, where's the other guy, the fat one?"

Glancing around, Joe saw that William had somehow disappeared and grinned as he turned his head and nodded at the top of the board fence.

Just then a police car and paddy wagon screeched to a halt at the entryway to the alley and several policemen jumped out and came running down the alley.

After putting handcuffs on Joe and Red, one of the policemen said, "We heard there were three of'em. Where's the other one?"

One of the railroad men pointed at the top of the board fence and said, "He must have gotten over the wall before we got here. There were only these two when we got here and the red haired one was climbing onto that barrel over there. He was gonna be next."

The policemen nodded and loaded Joe and Red into the paddy wagon.

Down at the station, Joe and Red were put into a lineup with several other men, and then asked to step forward.

As they stepped forward a man's voice came from the darkness at the back of the room, asking, "Are you sure they're the ones who threw the woman off the train?"

They heard the woman, loud and clear. "Yes, I'm positive. But where is the other one? There were three of them."

As Joe and Red were being herded out of the room by two officers, the man from the dark part of the room said, "Don't worry, we'll have him in custody soon enough. We have a description of him from you and the men down at the railroad yard. He won't be hard to find."

"Oh yea, well I hope he gets away!" Joe yelled in the direction of the back of the room.

"Amen to that, brother," Red chimed in.

As they were taken back to their cell, Joe whispered, "As much as I'd like to see him get away, if they catch him, I doubt he'll be able to talk his way out of this one."

Several hours passed before William was brave enough to climb out of the trash container. And by now his clothes stank and were badly stained. Using a great deal of caution, he slowly made his way down the sidewalk, finding it almost barren of people at this time of day, which thrilled him to no end. And the few people he did encounter gave him a wide berth. Several people held their nose as they hurried past him, shaking their heads.

William grinned as his eyes scanned the street and found what he was looking for. A block down the street he saw a large sign that read:

'MISSION OF THE FALLEN ANGELS - FOOD - SHOWERS - BEDS - CLOTHES'

Less than an hour later, William emerged, a new man; showered, clean-shaven and dressed in a three-piece suit that had hardly been worn. He'd also had a meal and was once again feeling good about himself because during his meal he chanced on an idea while overhearing a conversation between some men sitting nearby.

At first, it had been only a glimmer, and then the seed of a plan began to grow in his head until it developed into a full-fledged scheme. It would be risky, but if it worked - oh how sweet it would be.

A block from the police station William hit pay dirt. A bright neon sign read,

BAIL BONDS: OPEN 24 HOURS A DAY

By now it was late, and as he suspected, the office was empty of any personnel - probably in the back, taking a nap. At least that's what he hoped as he eased the door open and quietly let himself in.

Setting on the counter was a sign that read, 'Ring bell for service,' but William had no intention of ringing the small bell sitting next to the sign.

Jared McVay

A wire basket containing bail documents sat conveniently in the middle of the counter. Several of these documents found their way into the inside breast pocket of William's suit coat, along with a fountain pen laying nearby.

With his mission accomplished, he turned and headed for the door, but as his hand touched the doorknob, a voice behind him stopped him dead in his tracks.

"Mister, you just might wind up in jail," the voice said.

William jerked the door open, ready to bolt into the street as the voice continued.

"If you don't let Barney go your bail."

There was a long pause, as William stood there frozen in his tracks. Finally, he turned around and saw a man grinning from ear to ear, walking in his direction with his hand stuck out in greeting and as they shook hands, the man said, "Barney's the name, Bailings the game. What can I do for you, Mister? "

The man was about William's own size and build. His handshake was firm and he held on tightly.

After recuperating from the near coronary, William said, "I was thinking of bailing my brother-in-law out of jail, but I've changed my mind. A few days in the slammer will definitely do him a world of good. Thanks anyway."

The man stuffed a business card into the breast pocket of William's shirt. "If you change your mind, give me a call," he said as he patted William on the shoulder.

William smiled and nodded, indicating he wouldn't forget, as he made his exit. Once he got back out on the sidewalk, it was all he could do to keep from running, and walk causally down the street.

It was too late to put more of his plan into action, and even if he could, he was shaking so badly he was afraid he wouldn't be able to pull it off, so he headed straight back to the mission, where he had reserved a bed.

After a hot shower and a large breakfast, William decided to give his plan another shot. He caught a bus and went downtown to where the big law offices were and walked around until he finally found what he was looking for. He was standing in the lobby of the tallest and most expensive looking building in town, looking at the register. He read the floor number of several attorneys' offices before he selected what he believed to be the most impressive sounding of them all.

On the top floor, William wandered down the expensive hallway with its plush carpet and oil paintings on the walls until he came to a large, mahogany door with gold lettering, announcing, SMYTH, GRIMES AND RUTLEDGE, ATTORNEYS AT LAW.

After taking a deep breath, William opened the door and walked into the waiting room, and to his surprise, the room was already filled with people. It was an expensively decorated room with piped in easy listening music. The receptionist was not at her desk, which suited William's plan just fine.

On a small table under large pictures of the three attorneys, were three stacks of richly embossed business cards. Causally, William sauntered over and studied the three pictures, one of whom he resembled. He reached down and took a few cards from each stack and dropped them into his coat pocket, then turned and walked out the door.

A few blocks from the police station, William ordered a cinnamon roll and a cup of coffee from a tired looking woman with a short, stub of a cigarette hanging from the side of her mouth. The small café was crowded and no one paid him the slightest bit of attention, which suited him just fine.

Nervous tension caused his stomach to growl. The roll and coffee helped a little, but he would rather have had another full breakfast, except he didn't want to waste the time or money.

All the attorney's cards were impressive, but he chose the one he resembled in the picture hanging on the waiting room wall. If no one looked real close, he might be able to pass his or her inspection. He didn't know if anyone he might speak to would know this attorney personally. He hoped not. But it sure didn't hurt anything that the two of them could have passed as brothers, twins almost.

Stopping at the mission once more, William soon found just what he needed for the crowning touch - an impressive walking stick and a homburg dress hat that looked like it had just come from the cleaners. With these new items, he was now ready for action.

Outside the police station, William adjusted the knot of his necktie, then walked inside. At the sergeant's desk, he inquired about the two men who were arrested for throwing a woman off a train, yesterday.

"Yea, we got those two bums back in the tank. Who wants to know?" the square jawed sergeant asked.

William pulled out a stack of business cards and peeled one off and slid it across the sergeant's desk.

"J.P. Rutledge, Attorney at law," William said, hoping the middle aged policeman had never met the man in question.

"I haven't decided yet, whether I will represent them or not. My secretary was a bit vague about it. Would you mind telling me, what are the charges against these men sergeant?"

The sergeant leafed through a stack of papers and whistled.

"Looks like we nabbed ourselves a couple of big timers. Let me see here, John Walker, alias, Johnny Red, is wanted in Texas on charges of rape and murder - and the other guy, Josiah Nathaniel Wilson, is wanted back in New York City for knocking off some big time hoodlum."

William was taking notes on the back of one of the business cards. "Is that it?" he asked as casually as his nerves would let him.

"No, there's more," the sergeant said. "It says here that them two and another dude, who we ain't caught yet, tried ta kill a woman by throwing her off a moving train. Only, she ain't dead; but she is pretty bruised up though, like maybe they roughed her up before they threw her off the train."

"And where is she now? I may want to speak to her," William asked with a very serious attorney look on his face.

The sergeant went through his papers again. "County General, room, one-o-six," he said seriously.

With his pen poised, William asked, "Does she have a name?"

The sergeant looked at William and scratched the back of his neck as the hint of a grin replaced the serious look. "Funny you should ask that. When they asked her, she told the two officers she didn't know her name or anything about herself. And the doctor over there who treats the nut cases said it was possible they hit her in the head while they were beatin' on her, or, she could've hit her head when they threw her off the train. He said that could cause her to lose her memory. Amnesia, he called it."

William looked at the sergeant and smiled. "But I don't suppose that posed any problem for you boys in blue."

The sergeant smiled broadly, "Now that you mention it, with all due modesty, no it wasn't. We have our sources. We checked her prints through the FBI print files and guess what? We found her. One, Jo Ann Fissella, out of Chicago.

William wrote down her name, saying, "Chicago - you don't say. This is getting more interesting by the minute."

Thank you FBI print files, William thought to himself.

The sergeant nodded his head in agreement. "And it gets better. Seems she was mixed up with the mob til she squealed on one of'em. Then she just disappeared. Some district attorney back there wants her pretty bad so she can testify. Said she's his main witness. They're sending a couple of detectives out to escort her back.

"Very interesting," William said. "You've been most helpful, and I want to thank you for your due diligence. Just a couple more questions, if I may. What is the bail set at and who is the presiding judge?"

Once again the sergeant ruffled through his papers. "Let's see, the bail is set at ten thousand dollars, apiece, and the judge is the honorable, W.T. Wilford."

As William turned and headed for the door, he called over his shoulder, "Thank you again, sergeant. You've been most helpful. I'll see to it that your watch commander receives a letter from my office."

The sergeant called back. "Thanks, Mister Rutledge, but I'd stay away from them bums if I was you, they're losers."

William waved his arm as he exited the police station and headed for the café. He had work to do.

It was just after midnight. William was standing across the street from the police station looking over his papers by the light from the streetlamp when he got the break he was looking for. Three paddy wagons loaded with drunks, ladies of the night and a few rowdies, pulled up in front and the officers began unloading them and hustling them into the police station.

William folded the papers and put them in the inside breast pocket of his suit coat and checked his stack of business cards, then settled down to wait.

It was pandemonium from the beginning. The drunks were hard to control and the ladies of the night were resisting by kicking, scratching and biting anyone who came near, while the rowdies began fighting each other.

William waited until they were all inside and then counted to a hundred before he sauntered across the street.

Inside the police station, it was a madhouse as William made his way to the night sergeant's desk.

"I've come for the release of my clients," William said, as he laid the paperwork for their release on the sergeant's desk.

"Who are you?" the sergeant yelled over the noise.

The Legend of Joe, Willy & Red

J.P. Rutledge, their attorney of record," William yelled back.

"You've picked ah hell'va time ta show up," he said, looking at the papers William had placed on his desk.

"I believe you'll find everything is in order. The bail money has been posted and all the paperwork has been recorded and signed by his honor, Judge Wilford."

William was beginning to sweat. He was hoping the sergeant wouldn't scrutinize the signature too closely. The rest he'd done on a typewriter at the library.

Just as the sergeant was reaching for the papers, a fight broke out and two men landed on the sergeant's desk, swinging at each other and cursing a blue streak. Two policemen jumped into the fracas and were trying to break it up. A cup of coffee turned over and dumped into the sergeant's lap and he jumped up, doing a bit of cursing, himself. William saw his opportunity and took it. "Sergeant, please, if you could just release my clients, we'll be happy to get out of your hair."

"Okay, alright already, keep your shirt on, councilor," the sergeant yelled. "Hey, Murray," he called across the room to a man with a large ring of keys. "Release those two bums in seventeen, their mouthpiece is here with bail."

From that point on until they were all out on the street, William felt like everything was moving in slow motion until they were well away from the police station.

In fact, no one spoke a word until they were a block down the street and then Red slapped William on the back and said, "Thank you, friend. Oh man, I thought we were goners for sure. I don't know how you did it! You're a genius! Yes-sir, ah honest ta goodness, genius!"

Joe stopped William and spun him around, taking his hand and shaking it. "What you did was pretty courageous and took some thought and planning, and I thank you. But I think it's like the man back in Colorado said, remember? He called him, Willy the con. So it's no longer, William. From now on you will be known as, Willy, or Willy the con artist."

~ 153 ~

Willy the con, William thought. He liked that. It made him an accepted person.

Both men were surprised to see this side of Joe, especially, Willy, as he was now to be known. And he was glad that it was dark because he was sure he was blushing a dark red, but more than that, he'd finally done something to earn the man's respect.

As they started on down the sidewalk, Red said, "I've got a ton of questions and I ain't sure where ta begin."

"I pretended to be your attorney, forged a judge's name on some papers I stole out of a bail bondsman's office, then gave them to the night sergeant. That's all there was to it," Willy said, a bit modestly.

That was all well and good, but it didn't quite satisfy Red. "Okay, okay, he said, "I can buy that, but how did you know whose name ta forge on those papers?"

"That was easy, I just asked the day sergeant," William said with a wink and a big grin.

Red got a puzzled look on his face. "And just like that, he told you?" Red asked, knowing there was a lot more to the story than Willy boy was telling.

"Well, he did mistake me for an attorney -The honorable barrister, J.P. Rutledge, attorney at law. I happened to pick up a few business cards at an attorney's office I was visiting. I handed the sergeant a card and told him I represented the two of you and he had no reason to doubt me."

Red slapped William on the back again and laughed heartily.

"Where'd you get the new clothes?" Joe asked.

"There's a mission just up the street. I got them there. I also put a little something in the kitty so the man would hold three beds for us. I was sorta hoping we'd need them. In the morning, we can see about getting you some new clothes, too."

"What's wrong with the clothes I've got on?" Joe asked.

The Legend of Joe, Willy & Red

William scratched at his ear and said, meekly, "They won't fit the image we need to make when we rescue Jo Ann, tomorrow."

"Who's Jo Ann," Red asked.

"This is going to take awhile, so maybe we should stop at this little café I know about and grab a bite to eat while I relate all the information I was able to gather while the two of you were lying on your cots, reading books, or magazines or whatever it is they give you to read," Willy said with a big smile.

Jared McVay

Chapter 18

The Great Escape

    Joe slammed his coffee cup down on the table, causing the other customers to momentarily turn their heads in his direction; but a scowl caused them to turn back and mind their own business.
    "No, no, no! This is stupid! Why are we even sittin' here discussin' it? This is the most idiotic thing I've ever heard of! It's hair brained and I want nuthin' ta do with it."
    Joe stopped talking when a very attractive waitress came over and cleaned up the spilled coffee and refilled Joe's cup, then turned and left. Joe watched her enticing walk for a moment, and then indicated his thumb toward Red.
    "Red and me, we just got out of jail, thanks to you and your con man ways. And I ain't speakin' for anybody but myself when I say, I ain't plannin' on goin' back. And, well, I guess that's my final word on the subject."
    William felt tired and worn down. He had talked until his throat was getting sore. There seemed to be nothing else he could do, unless...
    "Okay, Joe, you win," he said with a big sigh.
    Turning to Red, William asked, with a dejected look he'd learned to use, " What about you? Are you turning your back on me, too?"
    Red winced as he picked at his food with his fork.
    "It's not my intent to pressure either one of you into doing anything you don't want to do, but, I want you to know, I'll do this all by myself if I'm forced to," Willy the con man said with a forlorn look in his eyes.
    Red was torn as he stared at his plate. He too reckoned it was ah fools idea, but he couldn't shake the memory of what ole Willy boy had done for him last night and the hair brained scheme he'd used then, too. And it had

worked as smooth as butter on ah hot roll. Plus, he knew William meant what he said about doin' it all by himself. He'd do it just like he did last night.

Red turned his head and asked, "Is she gonna be hangin' around with us again?"

"No, once she's free, she'll go her way and we'll go ours," Willy the con said as he shook his head from side to side and gave a big sigh.

After what seemed an eternity to William, Red finally said, "I guess I'm as crazy as you are. Count me in."

Joe lit a cigarette and blew a long stream of smoke in the direction of a fly that was on the ceiling. When the smoke got near, the fly moved to another spot, away from the smoke. And after a moment, Joe turned to William and asked,

"Why are you doing this? What makes her welfare your responsibility?"

"Well it's clear to me. We owe her that much at the very least. After all it is our fault she got caught."

Both Joe and Red looked at William with raised eyebrows.

"Alright, alright," William said, "It was all my fault. I'm the one who threw her off the train. So sue me for wanting to help. I can't turn my back on her now, any more than I could when you guys were in need of help, yesterday."

Willy the con felt the faintest ray of hope as he watched Joe's face screw itself up into a scowl and blow out a long stream of air as he snubbed out what was left of his cigarette in the ashtray.

"I guess I ain't got the sense god gave a goose. Okay, explain it to me, again."

An hour later, Joe, Willy and Red found themselves walking down the hallway of the County General Hospital, looking for room, one-o-six.

"Are you sure about this?" Red whispered.

"Yes, I'm sure. Trust me and let me do the talking," Willy said with assurance.

Jared McVay

As they turned the corner of the hallway, they saw a young police officer sitting in a chair next to room one-o-six. William walked up and stopped directly in front of him.

The young, police officer looked up from the book he was reading and jumped up. "I'm Lieutenant John Collins, Chicago PD," Willy the con man said with authority.

Nodding his head at Joe and Red, Willy the con, said, "Detectives, Flynn and Marshall. Is this where we pick up a woman named..."

William pulled an official looking paper from his inside jacket pocket, glanced at it, and then put it back in his pocket. "Miss Jo Ann Fissella?"

The young officer turned, and without asking William for identification, or asking to inspect the paperwork, opened the door and led them into the room.

As they entered, Jo Ann bolted upright at the sight of William. "You!" she hissed.

The young police man looked at Jo Ann and asked, "Do you know these men, Miss Fissella?"

There was an awkward silence as they all stared at each other. Both Red and Joe just stood there, not knowing what else to do.

William, who was standing slightly behind the young officer, shook his head no, and formed the word, 'no,' with his lips, hoping she would understand, but before she could respond, the silence was broken by a high pitched scream.

Everyone turned and looked in the direction of the scream and saw an elderly woman sitting in the corner of the room with a knitting basket on her lap. Her mouth was wide open and her eyes were filled with panic.

Both Joe and Red recognized her as the same woman who had identified them from the lineup down at the police station last night.

Willy gave her a look that silenced her, then turned back to face Jo Ann. "Please, just take it easy. We've come to help you get out of here before the real detectives show up and take you back to Chicago."

The Legend of Joe, Willy & Red

"How did you know about that?" she asked with a bewildered look on her face.

"We'll talk about that, later. Right now we need to get you out of this hospital and safely away before anyone else shows up. Where are your clothes?" William asked.

Coming out of his shock, the young police officer reached for his pistol and found his holster was empty.

"You lookin' for this?" Joe asked.

Spinning around, the young officer glared at Joe, who stood too far away to jump at, pointing his own pistol at him.

More than anything, the young man felt embarrassed. He should have checked their credentials and looked at that piece of paper. How was he going to explain this to the captain?

Jo Ann looked at William as she climbed out of the bed and started for the closet.

"You promise not to hurt them?" Jo Ann asked, nodding toward the police officer and the elderly woman.

"I promise." William said with a smile.

"I'm going to hold all of you to that promise," Jo Ann said as she quickly removed her clothes from the closet and headed for the bathroom.

Searching around, William found several rolls of wide surgical tape on the small table next to the bed and handed a roll to Red, who put tape across both, the officer's and the woman's mouths.

William led the woman over to the bed and asked her nicely to lie face down on the bed, crossways, with her arms and legs extending over the sides. Then, he told the officer to lie on his back and scoot under the bed, with his head facing the woman's feet.

William then taped the man's wrists to the woman's ankles and then her wrists to the officer's ankles. When he finished, he stood back and surveyed his work.

Joe and Red stood nearby, smiling, quietly amused by Willy the con's ingenuity.

Jared McVay

Joe looked at Red and said, "He certainly is a source of amazement."

To this, Red nodded an agreement.

Before leaving, Joe wiped his fingerprints off the pistol with a towel and laid it on the bed, saying, "I sure wouldn't want to be in your shoes."

Then, with the same towel, Joe opened the outer door just as Jo Ann came out of the bathroom. They all hurried out of the room and William led them to a rear entrance, and in a few minutes, they were safely away from the hospital, mixing with other people who were walking down the sidewalk.

After a couple of blocks, they entered a park and found a quiet spot and stopped.

Joe took William by the arm and escorted him a few steps away from Jo Ann and Red. He lit a cigarette and said, "Well, you pulled it off just like you said you would."

William shook his head and said, "Not exactly like I said it would. I didn't count on the old woman, or having to tie them up, together. But, I guess it's the end result that counts. I think, somewhere, I remember someone saying something about the best laid plans of mice and men, or something like that."

"Yea, or something like that," Joe said, glancing over his shoulder at Jo Ann.

Before Joe could say anything more, Jo Ann came running up, prattling on and on about how grateful she was for them coming to rescue her and how nice they looked all dressed up in their suits. And yes, she'd regained her memory, and had been terrified she'd have to go back to Chicago where those awful men were. Maybe this time they would kill her. If she never saw Chicago again as long as she lived, it would be too soon for her.

By this time they had walked across the park and came out near a bus station. William told Joe and Red to wait for him up the street. "I want to talk to Jo Ann, alone."

The Legend of Joe, Willy & Red

As Joe and Red walked on down the street, William turned to Jo Ann and said, "This is as far as you go."

"What are you talking about? I'm going with you guys," she said, looking down the street at Joe.

William took her gently by the arm and said, "I'm sorry but it just won't work. I'm sorry, I really am."

"But, why?" she protested, as tears crept into her eyes and she looked again at Joe, who was standing with his back to her.

"I think you know as well as I do," William said with a soft voice.

Jo Ann just stood there, staring at him.

William heard himself saying, "I'd be looking at you and you'd be looking at Joe - and that spells trouble."

William looked down at his feet as he stuck his hands down into the front pockets of his pants. "Those two men over there," he said, nodding toward Joe and Red, "have come to mean a great deal to me; more than even they realize. And I'm not about to lose that friendship, especially because of a woman."

"What do they think?" Jo Ann asked, hopefully.

William sighed and said, "We talked about it at length, and... well, we hope you can understand."

A cloud passed in front of the sun and a sudden gust of wind lifted papers off the street, sending them high into the air.

Jo Ann nodded her head. "I think I do understand. I guess I knew it all along," she said, wiping a tear from her cheek. "But, there is one thing I don't quite understand. Once you got rid of me, why did you risk your necks by coming to rescue me? I mean you could have just kept going."

William blushed and grinned a little boy grin that turned serious. "I figured I owed you that much. After all, I did throw you off the train."

Jo Ann smiled and said, "Yes you did. And that brings up my second question.

Jared McVay

Why did you throw me off the train? I mean, just because I was sitting next to Joe, was no reason to do something like that. You were sleeping. Did you have a wild dream or something; you know, like, a nightmare?"

William straightened up and stared at her. "Let's just say you have a twin sister out there, somewhere. Goodbye and good luck," William said as he reached over and kissed her on the cheek, and with that, he turned and walked away.

There were tears in Jo Ann's eyes as she watched William walk slowly toward his friends. He really must have loved that woman, Jo Ann thought as an idea popped into her head.

"Hey, guys, wait a minute. Don't leave yet, I'll be right back," she called out.

They turned and watched her run into the bus station and in less than a minute, she came running out and down the sidewalk to where they were standing. When she stopped, she handed William a piece of paper.

"If you ever get to San Francisco and need help, go see this man. You can tell him I sent you. He's sort of an uncle, if you know what I mean. He's a good man and he can help you, if anyone can," she said with a big smile.

William looked at the piece of paper, and then said, "Thank you. We just may do that."

There came an awkward moment before Jo Ann went up to each one of them and gave each man a kiss on the cheek. "I'll never forget you guys," she said, and then hurried back toward the bus station.

As they stood watching her go, William had a sudden thought, a panic, actually.

What if she has no money to purchase a bus ticket for where ever it is she wants to go?

He didn't recall anyone asking her if she had funds. For her sake, he hoped she did.

Just before entering the bus station, Jo Ann waved some money in their direction as she mouthed the words, "Thank you, Joe."

"It was the only way I could make sure we got rid of her," Joe said as he turned and headed down the sidewalk at a brisk pace.

William and Red looked at each other and began laughing as they chased after him.

Jared McVay

Chapter 19
The Fight

Black storm clouds filled the sky creating an early dusk. A steady rain fell, making splattering noises as the drops smacked against the surface of the shallow creek next to where the boys had made a meager camp under a bridge, several miles south of Salt Lake City, Utah.

By the light of a small fire, Joe Wilson sat reading a newspaper while Red hunted for what dry wood he could find and William stood a short distance away, alone with his thoughts.

Finally, Joe tossed the newspaper aside with a look on his face that left no doubt that he was upset.

"Well, I hope you're happy," Joe said to William's back. "You've got every lawman from the Atlantic to the Pacific lookin' for us, now - thanks to you and your bright ideas, Mister Willy the con man."

William continued to stare at the rain falling on the small creek, unaffected by Joe and his anger, although it was not lost on him.

Red stopped what he was doing and looked back and forth between William and Joe, wondering if there was going to be trouble. Joe was in a really foul mood, worse than usual.

Joe picked up the newspaper and showed it to William's back. "First, it was theft of legal documents; you know, those bail bond papers you bragged about snatchin'. But that wasn't enough. No, not by a long shot. Next, you lied to the police while posing as an attorney with business cards you stole from a real attorney's office for the purpose of breaking two men out of jail. And still you weren't satisfied, no, no, because you had more tricks in your little bag of deceptions, didn't you? You just had to make the police look even dumber with that little escapade at the hospital."

William didn't look around, even though he was affected by Joe's harsh words.

Joe wasn't the only one who had read the headlines that were spread all over the front page of the newspaper. He'd read them, too, but with a different reaction.

"I guess I could have just let the two of you rot in jail," William said with a bit of contempt in his voice.

"I seriously doubt we would have been in jail if you hadn't thrown that broad off the train!" Joe yelled back.

Something inside William snapped and he whirled around to face Joe, his fists clenched into balls.

"Oh no? Well what about that hoodlum back in New York you murdered in cold blood? Would you like to tell us about that?"

Joe jumped to his feet and stormed in William's direction. "For your information, big mouth, I didn't kill Capaloni, or anybody else, but I just might start with you!"

By this time, Joe was close to William, his anger out of control; so it was without conscious thought when his right fist shot out and caught William on the chin with such force that it lifted William off his feet and dumped him butt first into the shallow creek.

Red dropped the small load of wood he had gathered. Tension between the two of them had been like a rubber band stretched too tight for the past several hours, but this was too much!

Red ran over to Joe and grabbed him by the arm and yelled, "Stop it! Stop it right now! This has gone far enough!"

Joe reacted by pushing Red aside and waded into the creek, reaching for William with his outstretched hands.

William's eyes were wide with fright as he crab walked backwards toward the far shore, kicking his feet and splashing water high into the air.

No matter how infuriated at Joe he might be, he knew he didn't stand a chance in a fight with the big man.

Red definitely had no desires of going toe to toe in a rough and tumble with the big man, either, but he also knew his chances of survival were far better than William's.

Without debating the issue further with himself, Red dove through the air and tackled Joe by the legs, causing Joe to land face down in the water.

When they finally got their footing and were able to stand up, Joe was so mad he was out of control and rushed at Red with his fists swinging like some ole bull gorilla on the rampage.

Taking advantage of Joe's wild rage, Red slipped easily under the wild swing and gave Joe a hard left and a right to his midsection, followed by a right cross that landed squarely on Joe's chin.

The blows staggered Joe and he stepped backward with a surprised look on his face.

Red, not wanting to prolong matters, for reasons concerning his health, grabbed the opportunity and waded back to the shore, waving his arms wildly in the air.

"Now I want this bickering and fighting to stop - right here and now!" he yelled, hoping and praying Joe hadn't followed him out of the water.

Now, all things considered, you'd think that is exactly what Joe would do; but that wasn't what happened - just the opposite. The blow to the chin had brought Joe back to his senses; cooling his rage and making him feel bad about belting William on the chin. After all, William only wanted to help them out of a bad situation and did it the only way he knew how.

Joe had to admit, William had shown brilliance and style the way he thought of the schemes and then pulled them off smooth as any professional ever could have. It was the way the newspaper splashed everything all over the front page that had gotten him all riled up.

Looking over at William, Joe grinned a sheepish grin while raising his hands palm outward and shrugging his shoulders.

It was the closest he would come to getting an actual apology, so William nodded his head in acceptance.

Joe smiled and reached out his hand and helped William to his feet.

Once William was on his feet, Joe leaned in and whispered something in his ear. William grinned and nodded his head in approval as they both tip-toed silently out of the water and as silently as they could, made their way in Red's direction, hoping he would keep his back turned to them until they could accomplish their mission.

Red was standing next to the fire drying himself, but spun around when he heard Joe and William making squishing noises as they came sneaking up from behind.

Red yelled loudly as he was lifted by his armpits and thrown backward into the shallow creek. "Put me down, I'll take on both of you! No, not back in the water!"

Red came up sputtering, ready to take them both on, but when he saw Joe and William standing on the bank, laughing their fool heads off, he had to laugh, too. They were on a friendly basis again, and Red figured that was enough for now.

Later that night, they were able to find an empty boxcar on a freight train headed west.

For a while, they kept watch to make sure no one had seen them get on the train, and when the bull walked across the top, going in the direction of the caboose and didn't check the boxcar, they settled down to get some rest and maybe a little sleep.

Red slumped down on the floor of the boxcar, resting his back against the wall as he looked around to see what Joe and William were doing.

Joe rubbed his jaw and said, "You sure do pack a hard wallop for a short guy."

Red shook his head from side to side. "I'm real sorry about doin' that, Joe. It's just that we've been through so much together and I didn't want ta see you and Willy, here, ah fightin'."

Jared McVay

From deeper in the car, where William lay stretched out, they heard him say, "Amen to that, brother, amen to that!"

Joe grinned as he lit a cigarette and blew the smoke into the sleeve of his jacket.

A few minutes later, Red said in a casual tone, "Ya know, if we ever get into ah town where we ain't in trouble or chased by anybody, I just may settle down and find ah job. Hell, I might even get married."

Joe shook his head as he checked his cigarette pack and found he had only four left. He would have to make them last until they got to the next town, wherever that may be. He put the pack back into his shirt pocket and looked through the open boxcar door at the night sky, wondering what he would do if he got into a town where he didn't have to worry about anything or anybody.

After a few more minutes, Joe looked at the ceiling of the boxcar and said; "I read an article in the newspaper the other day that said there are nearly fifteen million people out of work."

"Yea, I read that too," Red said.

Joe took a long drag off his cigarette before asking, "Knowin' that, how can you sit there and tell us that you're gonna just waltz inta some town where you don't know ah livin' soul, and get ah job, just like that," he said, snapping his fingers.

Red started to respond, but Joe wasn't finished and he raised his hand to stop Red's retort, and then continued with a big smirk on his face.

"Plus, you inform us that some cute little ole bimbo is just sittin' around waitin' for you to show up so she can marry your dumb ass."

Red just shrugged his shoulders and said, "Sure, why not?"

Joe shook his head in bewilderment. "In case you ain't heard, this country is up to its neck with this depression thing. There ain't no jobs! And it's probably more than ah million ta one chance that some cute little gal is sittin' around waitin' for you to show up."

"If it was me, I'd make her a rich girl who wanted to take care of me. That way I wouldn't need to find a job," William added.

To Joe, Red said, "I like to think positive." And to William, he said, "I like the idea of a rich gal, I'll give that some thought."

After a moment, Red continued, "Besides, this new president, Mister Roosevelt, well-sir, he said he's gonna change things around and I believe him. . . I reckon if things turn around, maybe we could start our own business. Between the three of us, why can't we come up with some ideas that could make us rich? What'ya think? You know, like the three musketeers."

From the back of the car they heard William say, "Sure buddy, whatever you say. Maybe if your girlfriend has enough money, maybe we could open a bank."

Joe chuckled and said, "If we do, I vote we make Willy boy the president and Red can be vice president and I'll be in charge of security."

Red shut up and curled up in his blanket and went to sleep.

Chapter 20

The Farmer's Wife

A quarter moon hung low in the western sky as the train came to a stop. William was already up and shaking his friends, awake.

"I think someone's coming," he whispered.

Joe and Red came instantly awake in time to hear the sound of voices mixing with the crunching of rock as whoever it was tromped along beside the train, coming in their direction.

"What's goin' on? And why is the train stoppin' out here in the middle of God only knows where?" a high-pitched male voice asked.

"And you think I would know this, how? If you recall, for the last sixty miles, I was back there in the caboose with you, curled up in my bunk, sleeping like a baby rockin' in a cradle," came a gruff and irritated voice.

Joe, William and Red stared at the half open door of the boxcar, hoping whoever was out there would not notice or come to investigate.

"Maybe one of us should have stayed back there and fixed a pot of coffee," the high-pitched voice said. "I sure could use a cup."

"You're an idiot," the gruff voice said.

The two men walked past the open door of the boxcar without either one noticing it being open and were still trudging along in the direction of the engine, when William sneezed one of those uncontrollable sneezes that happen when you least expect them. His hand flew to his mouth, but he was too late.

"What was that?" the high-pitched voice asked.

"Be quiet," the other voice whispered.

Silence hung in the air like a dense fog; not even the sound of breathing could be heard.

The Legend of Joe, Willy & Red

The two men were about to continue on, when William sneezed, again. This time it was muffled, but not enough.

"Hey, you in there! You in the boxcar, get out here right now!" the gruff voice yelled.

Joe shook his head, wondering why the only luck they seemed to have, was bad, as he moved close to William and whispered, "Okay, since you caused this, you get to be the one who goes out there. Just pretend you're alone, and make sure the door is all the way open. And make sure you stay close to the train, when you get out there. You understand?"

William nodded his head, and then called out, "All right, all right, I'm coming, just hold your water."

William took his time and opened the door all the way, and then turned and stood there peering out into the darkness.

"Why are we stopped here? I don't see a town," William asked as he shielded his eyes with his hand.

"Never you mind about no town. This ain't no passenger train and we ain't porters

you can ask questions or order around, so just haul them chubby jowls outta' that there boxcar, right now!" The gruff voice yelled.

William took his time and sat down on his butt, with his legs dangling out of the boxcar door, then, acting very nervous, which didn't take a lot of doing, scooted out and landed with a grunt.

As he stood up, William immediately stepped close to the boxcar and grabbed a rail, pretending he needed support.

"Now if you gentlemen will just give me a minute, I think..."

That's as far as he got before the two men rushed over and grabbed him roughly by the arms.

The man with the high pitched voice looked at his partner and asked, "You gonna teach him not to ride our train? You gonna do that, Frank?"

Before Frank could answer, a voice coming from the direction of the engine said,

"That you, Frank, Sydney? What's going on?" the engineer asked.

The engineer had just come out of the bushes when he heard the voices back down along the train and came to see what the commotion was all about.

"What are you doin', stoppin' out here in the middle of nowhere, Sam?" Frank called back.

"Too many beans fer dinner; couldn't hold'em any longer. Just barely made it to the bushes as it was," came the engineer's reply. "So, what'a we got? Ah another one trying to hitch a ride to nowhere?"

"Well he won't ride another train after I get through with him," Frank said.

"Yieeeeeee-ahhhh! Yaaaaaaaa, Yaaaaaaaa, yaaaa! Com'on boys! Get'um good! Beat their brains in!"

The high pitched, screaming voices shattered the darkness of the early morning hours like demons from hell as Joe and Red leaped from the open door of the boxcar, their outlines looking like dark shadows against the moon, giving the eerie appearance of giant vultures swooping down to attack their prey.

In less than a heartbeat, Frank and Sydney released William's arms and ran in the direction of the engineer.

"Run! He's got a gang! They mean to kill us!" Sydney screamed as he ran toward the engineer, who didn't need encouragement, and was already twenty feet in front of them and gaining ground.

The train sat there, puffing small clouds of smoke that drifted into the night sky, as its protectors became mere shadows that were finally swallowed up by the darkness.

Grinning, Red and Joe loped off in pursuit of William, who was by now, no more than a shadow, himself; letting no

The Legend of Joe, Willy & Red

grass grow under his feet as he made his way across bare field on the north side of the tracks.

When Joe and Red finally caught up to William, he was huffing and puffing and making more noise than the train setting behind them, waiting for someone to feed it more coal.

Sucking in great quantities of air, William watched his friends run up next to him.

Red patted him on the back and said, "Did you see those guys run off and leave their train? Maybe we should drive into the next town for'em."

"I don't think that would be a very good idea," Joe said.

Between breathes, William said, "They ran off and left the train just sitting there, really? I missed that. I was too busy running the opposite direction."

"If you're rested enough, I think we should get on up to the road. Maybe we can catch a ride if some farmer or salesman comes along. At least we'll be away from those railroad people. I got a feeling they'll be back, with reinforcements."

It seemed to William that they'd been walking for miles, when in reality, it had been only two. Even so, he was worn to a frazzle. His feet hurt and his nose was full of dust - causing him to cough and sneeze. His stomach growled and his teeth chattered from the early morning cold air.

With his short legs and overweight body, which was getting lighter by the minute from lack of nourishment, William decided he definitely was not cut out for this mode of travel.

Shortly, burnt orange threads of light crept their way over the horizon, promising light and warmth. In the glow of the false dawn, they noticed the outline of a farmhouse about a quarter of a mile off the road to their right.

It was one of those big two story affairs, with a barn and some smaller buildings out back. As they watched, someone turned on a light, which made the place a bit more appealing. As another light came on they could see someone moving around.

"Man, am I hungry. When was the last time we ate? What was it, two, three days ago?" William asked, spitting out a brown gob of something as he ran his hand over his growling stomach.

"Yesterday morning," Joe said.

Red thought for a moment, then nodded toward the farmhouse, "Do you reckon that farmer would give us somethin' ta eat if we offered ta do some work?"

"The only way to find out is to ask," William said.

A few minutes later, they found themselves standing at the back door of the farm house, staring at a very sexy looking young woman, dressed only in a sheer nightgown. The light from behind left nothing to the imagination.

Both Joe and William backed up a step, leaving Red standing all alone to do the talking.

Concentrate, concentrate, Red thought to himself as he tried to find his voice, which was for the moment, lost. After a moment, he sucked in some air and said,

"Mornin', mam, sorry ta bother ya so early and all, but we was ah wonderin'. . . " Red stammered as he pointed to Joe and William, "if we could be some help around here in exchange for something ta eat? I'm sure we could be right helpful; you know, clean out the barn, fix some fence - whatever you need done."

She smiled as she ran her hand down across her body. "I'll bet you could be a lot more help than you realize. My husband is always saying he could use more help. He's an older man, you know, and you know older men - well, you know what I mean."

The implications were right there in front of them, loud and clear, and Joe's first impulse was to turn and run as fast as his legs would carry him, far, far away from this piece of trouble. But, instead, he just stood there like his two friends, staring at her with his mouth hanging open.

The Legend of Joe, Willy & Red

Suddenly, a large, meaty hand came out of nowhere, flinging the woman to the side and in her place, stood a very tall, old and ugly man with long white hair and beard.

He was dressed in a pair of faded red long johns and he was bare footed. But it wasn't the man's size or his ugliness that caused Joe, Willy or Red to feel threatened, it was those two giant holes in the end of the double-barreled shotgun he was pointing at them.

"So, you boys are lookin' fer ah little work, are ya?" he asked, as he looked them over from head to foot.

"Yes-sir," Red said, hoping the farmer wasn't really as mean as he looked. "In exchange for somethin' ta eat. We're powerful hungry."

Still pointing the shotgun in their direction, the farmer's eyes became hard and evil looking and they could see him begin to tense up.

"Well you ain't foolin' me none! You jest like all the rest of'em, come ah sniffin' round here, wantin' ta steal me blind and lust after my woman. Well I ain't gonna let it happen, again. Now, you git off'n my land afore I fill yer backsides full of buckshot," he yelled as he pointed the barrels slightly and pulled one of the triggers.

The buzzing of the buckshot passing over their heads was enough to convince them the man had been driven crazy by his sexy, young, wife, and they had no illusions about what he might do if anyone of them even glanced in her direction.

"And don't come back!" they heard him yell as they ran for the road.

They were off the farmer's land and a good piece down the road before William halted and bent over gasping for air. "I don't care, let him shoot me. I can't run another step," he said as his heart hammered like a kettledrum.

"He's not gonna shoot you." Red said, trying to get his wind back. "He's not even chasin' us."

Joe stopped beside them and looked back over his shoulder. In the far distance he could still see the outline of the woman standing on the back porch with her hands on her hips.

"She makes that old man crazy with jealousy the way she runs around practically naked in front of strange men and talkin' the way she does," Joe said, shaking his head.

"Makes you wonder why she married him."

"I'd say, to get the land and whatever money he's got," William said flatly.

"Well she'll have it all before long, the way she's goin'. One way or another that ole man is gonna wind up with a heart attack," Joe said with a grimace.

"But you gotta admit, she sure is somethin' ta look at, with that light shinin' right through that nightgown like that, whoa!" Red said, whistling through his teeth. "What I wouldn't give..."

"Your life, that's what you'd give," William cut in.

As Joe started off down the road, he called over his shoulder, "Com'on, we don't need another broad givin' us trouble."

Chapter 21
Joe and the Restaurant Owner

Heavy thunder rumbled overhead as a warning of the impending storm. Ominous dark clouds overhead were laced with bright streaks of lightning. These warlords of the sky rode in front of the late afternoon sun turning day into night as heavy winds pushed them along.

Joe pointed toward a weather beaten building a couple of hundred yards in front of them. "Looks deserted," he yelled over the sound of the howling wind.

Joe, Willy and Red, ran for the building and as they got close they could see that it was empty and very old. Above the open doorway, hanging from a nail was a lopsided sign. The lettering was faded, but they could still make out what it said.

WINNEMUCCA BLACKSMITH SHOP
HORSES BOARDED

"What'ya think?" Joe asked as the first raindrops began to fall.

"Looks like the place has been out of business for years," Red said as they got close to the open doorway.

"I certainly hope so. I don't relish sleeping with a horse," he said as he peered into the semi-dark interior. It smelled old and musty, like the cellar under his grandparent's house. He didn't like that place, either.

"What's that old saying, any port in a storm? Well there's the storm and here's the port," Joe said as he stepped inside.

Joe and Red kicked around here and there throughout the deserted interior of the barn, just to make sure there were no critters, like rats, or snakes or other creatures that might bite; while William waited patiently close to the door, ready to bolt, should any wild predators be found that wanted to attack him.

Jared McVay

They decided the loft would be the most comfortable since it was well off the floor and full of loose hay, along with being predator free, which they had to convince William of before he would climb the ladder.

Outside, the storm was building with intensity. Large raindrops could be heard, splattering against the roof. A bolt of lightning cracked loudly, causing them to cover their ears as it lit up the interior of the barn momentarily.

Shortly, rainwater could be seen, leaking through the roof in spots where there were rotten shingles. It took a bit of moving around, but finally they found a dry spot and settled in to get some rest until the storm was over.

The storm raged outside as the three men made themselves comfortable in the soft, dry hay - happy to be out of the weather and resting in a place that didn't rattle or bump or wasn't moving and best of all, no one was chasing them.

Red laced his fingers behind his head and sighed as he thought about the young woman with the light shining through her nightgown.

After a few minutes, Red looked at the other two and said, "So far, this here has been quite an adventure. It's been kinda like ridin' some ole mossy bull; lots of ups and downs."

"Riding a bull. That's an interesting way to put it," William said with a big grin.

"And I got ta admit, there was ah couple of times there I wasn't sure whether ta hang on or jump off. But now that it's all behind us, I'll tell ya truthful, it was the most excitin' time of my life. I might even miss it ever once in awhile."

"What makes you think it's all behind us?" Joe asked.

"I don't know," Red said, "Just ah gut feelin,' I guess. I mean, with all the things that have happened to us, what else is there that can go wrong? No-sir, boys, I got ah feelin' things are gonna be ah might dull from now on."

Joe reached under him and pulled out a stickweed that had been poking him in the back, and tossed it aside. "I hope you're right, Texas, I hope you're right."

Red sniffed the air and said, "Ya know, this reminds me of home."

William sniffed the air and said, "Home this is not, but at least it's warm and dry."

He'd no more than gotten the words out of his mouth when the roof gave way and flooded them with rainwater and broken shingles.

"You just had to open your big mouth, didn't you?" Joe yelled as he jumped to his feet.

In fact, all three men jumped up and tried to get away from the huge hole and the water coming through it. The storm had reached almost gale force and whipped the rain far and wide across the hayloft as they scrambled for the ladder with Joe in the lead.

"I guess I spoke too soon," William said as he started down the ladder.

Once they were all on the ground floor of the barn, again, Joe looked at Red and said, "Would you mind telling me again, that part about things bein' dull from now on."

"Yes, I'd like to hear that, too," William said with a twinkle in his eyes.

Red shook his head to get rid of the water in his hair and said, "From now on, I'm keeping my big mouth shut."

They all laughed as they spread out, looking for a dry place to sleep.

The sun was creeping above the horizon, promising a beautiful day when the big white rooster meandered into the barn, searching for some morsel to eat. But when he noticed three men lying here and there, still asleep, some instinct must have kicked in because he reared back, flapped his wings and cut loose with one of his finest crows - high and shrill.

Jared McVay

All three men jumped to their feet, looking around, wild-eyed, as memories of a rooster from their recent past filled their minds.

To everyone's relief, this rooster merely squawked and ran for the door, seeking other people to scare.

Standing there in just their underwear, the incident suddenly became funny and all three of them laughed until their stomachs ached.

William was the first one to stop laughing as he tiptoed over to where his clothes hung draped over the rail of the horse stall where he'd been sleeping. Finding them dry, he began putting them on as he spoke over his shoulder.

"Well, now that we've all had our heart attacks for the day, I would like to suggest we go in search of a place where we can get some much needed nourishment, like real food. As I recall, nothing passed my lips yesterday but dust, and the day before that. . . well, I'm sure you both can remember what meager rations that was."

Both Joe and Red tossed aside the horse blankets they'd found in the tack room last night and began to get dressed.

"Willy, me bucko, ya sure have ah way of getting right to the heart of the matter. Aye, that ya do indeed," Red said in his mock Irish accent as he pulled on his pants.

Not far from the barn, they found a café that was packed with the local residents and went in.

Over a breakfast of eggs, a large slice of ham, fried potatoes, fried bread and several cups of coffee at the town's only eating establishment, they talked about their situation.

"I don't know about you boys but my pocket's getting ah might short on cash, Red confessed.

Both Joe and William nodded their heads to affirm they were in the same fix.

Raising his coffee cup in the direction of the balding, over weight man in a soiled apron coming their way, Red continued, "I was just wonderin', what if we stayed around

The Legend of Joe, Willy & Red

here for awhile; maybe pick up ah little work. I don't like bein' without any walkin' around money jingling in my pockets. What'ya say?"

"Sounds like a good idea to me," William said as the balding, over weight man in the soiled apron walked up and refilled their cups. "This is it," he said. "If you want any more I'm gonna charge ya for it. This ain't no soup kitchen with free handouts."

The sign says, 'Free Refills,' Joe said to the man, taking an instant dislike to him.

"I don't care what the sign says, big mouth, this is my joint and I say, you want more java, you're gonna pay extra for it. You got ah problem with that?" the over weight man said, loud enough for everyone to hear.

Joe felt that, old, familiar tightness building inside his chest as his fists curled into hard knots, under the table.

Seeing the fire grow in Joe's eyes, William sensed his rage was about to explode and knew he needed to do something.

"Excuse me, Sir," William said, drawing the man's attention away from Joe. "It's not our intention to antagonize you. No. You see, it was your excellent coffee. It is the very best we've had in a month of Sundays and, well, I guess we got carried away. We are but three men seeking employment, times being what they are and all. You wouldn't be in need of help, would you?"

The man got a bewildered look on his face and said, "What kind of hogwash talk was that?"

"Who is this overgrown toad, your mouthpiece?" the owner asked as spittle ran down his chin. "I want the three of you outta here, now! Just pay your bill, then don't let the door hit ya in the ass when you leave!"

By now, the man was trembling with rage and his voice had gone up at least four octaves as he held the coffee pot high over his head like a club.

"Easy, Joe, let's just get out of here. Com'on, he ain't worth it," Red said, hoping to calm the fire in Joe's eyes.

Jared McVay

After leaving the restaurant, it took some doing to calm Joe down. He wanted to go back and beat the man into a soggy mass.

Joe smoked the last four cigarettes in his pack, which slowly helped him to calm down. As he finished the last one, he finally promised he wouldn't go back and thrash the man to within an inch of his life.

They stopped at a grocery store and Joe bought a pack of cigarettes and William asked the man if he needed help. The owner shook his head and said, "Sorry."

The rest of the day was spent talking to every storeowner and businessperson in town about the possibility of getting, even menial work.

"Well, we've asked everybody in town for a job," Red said as they walked into the barn.

"And some of them weren't even polite about saying, 'no'," William said.

"That fat slob over at the café was the worst of'em," Joe said. "I still think I should go over there and kick ah mud hole in him and walk it dry."

"You are absolutely correct, my friend. He is the worst of the lot and I've been giving him a lot of thought," William said as he surveyed the interior of the barn.

After a brief description of his plan and a lot of laughter, Red checked the depot and found out that a freight train would be leaving within a few hours, which fit into their plans, perfectly.

Without realizing it, William had become a changed man; had come out of his shell, so to speak. And I suppose some folks might say it wasn't for the best - but on the other hand, Willy the con was just being true to himself.

And of course, there were those who would say that what they were about to do, was not only justified, but inspirational on the part of Willy the Con.

The restaurant was packed with evening diners as William and Red tip-toed up to the back door and crouched down in the shadows to wait, as Joe came strolling down the street with a bulging gunnysack slung over his shoulder.

He marched up the front steps of the restaurant, took a deep breath and entered, causing the bell attached to the front door to jingle.

The smell made Joe's stomach growl, but he was not here to eat.

At the sound of the bell, the restaurant owner headed in that direction to greet his new arrival, but when he saw who it was, he yelled, "What the hell are you doin' back in here? I thought I made myself clear when I told you not ta come back. What's wrong? You don't hear so good, or are you just stupid?"

Joe smiled his widest smile. "Oh yea, absolutely, you made yourself real clear this mornin'. And no, I ain't stupid. At least I don't think so. But whether I'm stupid or not ain't the reason I'm here. The reason I'm here is because I got ah delivery for ya."

"I don't recall ordering nuthin', especially somethin' you might be deliverin'," the owner said, eyeing the bag suspiciously. "What ya got in the bag, boy?"

Joe walked directly into the dining room and lowered the bag to the floor.

By now all the patrons had stopped eating and sat, staring in his direction.

"I'm right glad you asked," Joe said, speaking loud enough for everyone to hear.

"What's in that sack? Well-sir, I'll tell ya. It's the essence of your soul. At least that's how the man that sent me here, described it."

"Are you crazy?" the restaurant owner yelled. "I don't even know what the hell you're talkin' about! Now, for the last time, get out of my restaurant and stay out! And take your sack with ya!"

Shaking his head, Joe said with a very serious tone, "Oh, no-sir, I can't do that. I promised ta share it with all these nice folks, and you wouldn't want me ta go back on my word, would ya?"

By now, the owner was full of rage and lunged at Joe with his hands balled into fists, yelling at the top of his lungs, "I've had all I'm gonna take from you!"

Joe grabbed the gunnysack and slipped easily under the owners' wild swing.

As the owner tried to turn, Joe stuck his foot out, causing the owner to do a belly flop onto the nearest table, breaking the table in half and scattering plates, silverware, cups, glasses and food all over the floor.

As the patrons sat in stunned shock, Joe opened the top of the gunnysack, then grabbed it by the bottom and lifted it over his head and began swinging it around and around as he ran through the restaurant.

Women screamed and men cursed as dry horse manure sailed through the air, landing in their food, on their heads and on their laps. One piece even landed in a glass of water a woman was holding. She screamed and threw it all over her husband.

Bedlam broke out as people trampled over one another, trying to escape being hit by the flying horse manure. Two women fainted while another climbed under a table to hide, only to find her husband already there.

The restaurant owner got to his feet and chased after Joe like an enraged bull, screaming obscenities while slipping and sliding in the muck.

"You won't get away from me! And when I get my hands on you, you're ah dead man!" he yelled.

All the yelling and screaming, mixed with dishes breaking in the dining room, sent the kitchen help scurrying into the dining room to find out what was happening.

And while everyone was occupied in the dining room, William and Red sneaked into the kitchen and began loading several sacks with anything that looked good to eat. Red couldn't contain his curiosity and before they left, took a sneak peek into the dining room, then turned and followed

The Legend of Joe, Willy & Red

William out the back door and down the alley, barely able to contain his laughter.

What he saw was total chaos and destruction. There were broken tables and chairs, food and drinks mixed with horse manure, covering not only the floor, but the people too. Joe was ducking and dodging people, while the owner was shoving them out of the way, trying to get to Joe. It was like something out of one of those Laurel and Hardy movies. It was even more outrageous than the episode with the rooster and the farmer.

Through the plate glass window, Joe saw William and Red running off into the darkness, which was his signal to make an exit.

Joe turned back just in time to see the owner make a frantic lunge for him. Joe sidestepped and watched as the owner crashed headfirst into a table that had been tipped onto its' side. The owner climbed to his feet, momentarily dazed and Joe seized the opportunity, and shoved the gunnysack down over the owner's head and spun him around several times.

The man staggered about crazily, bumping into things before crashing through the plate glass window, falling face down on the sidewalk. Joe followed him through the broken window and kneeled down to make sure the man wasn't seriously hurt. It wasn't their intention for the man to be injured, just humiliated. And that is what they'd done. The man didn't have a scratch on him.

Relieved, Joe sprinted off into the darkness in the same direction he'd seen Red and William go, as the rest of the people fled the restaurant, running in all directions.

Not one person challenged Joe or stopped to see if the restaurant owner was in any danger. Even the kitchen help deserted the now destroyed dining room, which said a lot about how the people of the town felt about the man.

A few minutes later the freight train was heading west with Joe, Willy and Red, tucked safely in one of the empty boxcars, laughing and joking at the fruits of their labor.

"You should have seen his face when I started slingin' that horse manure all over the restaurant. It landed on their food, in their hair. It was a riot! "

Joe could hardly tell about it without erupting with uncontrollable laughter and his eyes watering so hard he could hardly see.

William and Red laughed right along with him as they stuffed themselves with the food they'd stolen from the kitchen.

"I couldn't help myself," Red said with a mouth full of food. "I sneaked over and watched some of it from the kitchen door. It was hysterical!"

William became serious. "He wasn't hurt, was he? I mean it wasn't our intent to do him any physical harm."

"Not ah scratch," Joe replied as he raised the roast beef sandwich to his mouth.

The sandwich flew through the air as Joe, Willy and Red tumbled end over end as the train came to an unceremonious stop; cars ramming into the one in front of it, steel grinding against steel, sparks flying and a tremendous amount of noise.

After slamming into the end wall of the boxcar, Red bounded to his feet and ran to the door, which was now, standing wide open.

"Holy beejesus! We gotta get off this train, muy pronto!" Red hissed as he turned around and saw Joe and William, just climbing to their feet.

"What's wrong?" Joe asked as he headed for the door.

"What's wrong? I'll tell ya what's wrong. Wyatt Earp and all his deputies are out there!" Red said, running to the open door on the opposite side of the boxcar.

William looked at Joe and asked, "What's he talking about?"

Joe took a quick peek around the edge of the door, then pulled back inside. "The Sheriff, the restaurant owner and at least half the town is out there, with guns and clubs and none of'em look like a welcoming committee. That... is what he's talking about."

"Com'on, this side is clear," Red said in a loud whisper.

Joe, Willy and Red scrambled out of the boxcar, running hard for a nearby stand of trees.

Once they were inside the tree line, they stopped momentarily to see if they were being pursued.

They saw men running along side the train, checking each car, but the small field they'd just crossed, was clear.

"We need to put a lot of distance between them and us, in a big hurry. It won't take'em long to put two and two, together."

Even as they turned and followed Joe at a dogtrot, one of the men from the train turned and looked toward the trees.

The boys continued to travel through the night. Joe was relentless in pushing for them to stay away from roads of any kind and allowed very few breaks; only when they saw the lights of the posse close by would he have them stop and hunker down until the men had passed on. And each time, Joe led them away from the lights, but somehow kept them moving, west.

As the sun climbed into the eastern sky, Joe, Willy and Red raised themselves out of the ditch where they'd slept for a short period. They stretched and tried to get the kinks out of their necks, backs, knees and anywhere else that ached.

It had been a hard night of traveling, mostly across open fields and through any wooded area that might keep them out of sight. Lucky for them it had been one of those cloudy, moonless nights and they had made good progress.

During the early morning hours, not long before daybreak, Joe found a stand of weeds in a gully not far from the highway and they were able to get some much-needed rest. But now the sun was up and it was time to move on.

Jared McVay

Chapter 22
Capaloni's Real Killer

"No more of your schemes!" Joe said bitterly. "I don't know why I let you sucker me into going along with your hair brained ideas. One of these days they're gonna land us in jail, or maybe worse, get us killed. I've been coned for the last time; do you hear me? The last time."

William nodded his head as he shuffled down the long, narrow strip of highway that seemed to have no end. And even though he felt dead on his feet, in need of a bath and hungry enough to eat almost anything that was put in front of him - a strange, new feeling also engulfed him; a kind of fulfilled excitement.

The three of them had walked along in silence for the past twenty minutes when William broke the silence.

"I guess I've lived what you might call, a sheltered life, always doing what other people expected of me. First it was my parents, then the teachers, my wife, my boss and finally society. I was never an adventurer. Oh, I had dreams, but never followed up on any of them. Mister dull, that was me. So, at this time, please let me apologize for bringing danger into your lives. I've never meant to get anyone hurt. My intentions were always for what I believed to be good." When no one said anything, he continued.

"Again, I'm sorry, but for me, this has been the most exciting time I've ever had or probably will have, and I can't thank you enough for allowing me to share it with you."

"Don't mention it," Red said, slapping William on the back. "Like somebody once said, 'you only go around once,' and believe me, after all this, I ain't sure I want ta try ah second go round. And trust me, knowin' you ain't been dull."

Joe just shrugged his shoulders and didn't say anything, because if the truth be known, he was enjoying the company of these two guys. Red was congenial and what

The Legend of Joe, Willy & Red

could you say about William, or Willy the con man, except he seemed to be releasing a whole new personality that had been hidden so deep that Willy himself didn't suspect he had it. And the end result had been a wild and memorable ride.

Joe's thoughts were interrupted by the sound of a high-powered engine coming in their direction, and when he turned around, a large black sedan topped the small rise just behind them and for a moment, went airborne before landing hard on the road, and before they could jump into the ditch to get out of its way, the car roared past them.

Taillights came on and smoke came off the tires as the car skidded to a halt, then began to back up.

A young man stuck his head out of the passenger's window and yelled, "Hey, you boys want a lift?"

As the sedan skidded to a stop next to them, Joe, William and Red stared at the two young men in the big, black car. Puffs of blue smoke exited the tailpipe and drifted off into the sky as the two boys stared back.

"I don't think they're part of the posse," William whispered.

"Me either," Red agreed. "They seem ta be havin' too much fun."

"Well, What'ya say? You ridin' with us or not? We're in a bit of a hurry," the young man on the passenger side of the car said.

The need to put a greater distance between themselves and that angry mob of men, who just might still be searching for them, was more than enough reason to accept the offer of a ride.

But. . . as they climbed into the back seat of the big car, Joe eyed the two young men with a speculative eye and got a nagging feeling in his gut. Something wasn't right, but it wasn't anything he could pin down, exactly. It was more like those ocean riptides you can't see, but even so, you know the danger is there.

Jared McVay

The inside of the car reeked of alcohol, but that wasn't it. Maybe it had something to do with their age and appearance. The filthy clothes they were wearing just didn't go with an automobile like this. Plus, those I've just done something bad grins they had on their faces, made Joe wearisome.

The idea that the car might be stolen hit him all of a sudden, but before he had a chance to say or do anything, the driver stomped down on the accelerator, slamming them back onto the seat as the tires squealed and the car sped off down the highway, the odometer quickly climbing to sixty miles an hour.

The car finally leveled out at eighty miles an hour and Joe, Willy and Red looked at each other with here we go again looks on their faces.

After taking a long pull from a bottle of whiskey, the driver handed the bottle back toward the back seat and said, "My name is Bob and that ugly brute sittin' next ta me is called, Tom. You boys want ah drink ta help us celebrate our new found fortune?"

"What new found fortune would that be?" William asked, cautiously.

"We just robbed ah bank and stole the mayor's car," Tom said through stained yellow teeth, as he took the bottle from Bob and chugged a goodly portion of the clear liquid called white lightning.

When Tom finished, he handed the bottle back to Bob and then gave out with a long belch, banging his chest with his fist, after which he turned to face the back seat.

"Here, have some," he said, tossing a wad of bills into their laps. "We got plenty."

Joe groaned, William sucked in a huge gulp of air and Red scooped up the cash and stuffed it into his pocket.

"Yea, the sheriff and all the men in that little ole Podunk town back there are out lookin' for some ole boy who raised hell in their restaurant last night; really tore it apart," Bob said, taking another swig of moonshine.

The Legend of Joe, Willy & Red

"So, we decided, since nobody was around ta stop us, we'd rob the bank and steal the mayor's car. What ah hoot."

"And we figure they'll blame it on that dude that tore up the restaurant. Now, ain't that ah kick?" Tom added.

Under his breath, Red whispered, "What do we do, now?"

Joe squeezed his arm and said, quietly, "Just stay calm."

Once again, William's mouth functioned before his brain did. "Well now, isn't that a coincidence - and ironic, too."

"Coincidence? Ironic? What'er you talkin' about, mister?" Tom asked, looking over at Bob, who just shrugged his shoulders, indicating that he didn't understand what William was talking about, either.

Tom turned back and looked at William. "You wanna explain what ya mean?"

"I just find it funny, that's all." William said. "Here you are, driving down the road with a notorious man in your car and don't even know it," William said, smiling broadly.

Bob and Tom looked at each other, again, confused. Suffice to say, there were no geniuses in either family and even at the best of times, information was slow to reach the understanding portion of their brains. Add a goodly amount of rotgut and they were practically brain dead.

After a moment, William decided they needed a smidgen more clarification and said, "Do you remember the man you were just talking about - the one who tore up the restaurant - the one the sheriff and everyone is looking for?"

Both Tom and Bob shook their heads, yes.

"Well right here he sits," William said, pointing at Joe. "And can you imagine what will happen to anyone who is with him if they catch up to us?"

This time the information went from their ears to their brain, setting a new record as the car burned half the rubber off the tires sliding to a stop, and before they could turn around twice, Joe, Red and Willy were once again standing along the side of the road, laughing as the big sedan sped down the highway.

The car was nothing more than a dark spot against the western horizon when they heard the wail of sirens.

The boys barely had time to dive into the tall weeds standing in the ditch at the side of the road when two police cars came screaming down the highway and as they roared past, they could see both cars were loaded with men armed to the teeth.

Red fingered the wad of bills in his pocket and said, "Like I said, hangin' round with you ain't been dull, Willy boy. No-sir, not dull at all."

As the police cars disappeared down the highway, William gave a big sigh. "That was close."

Joe shook his head in agreement, "Too close. We need to find a way to put some distance between this part of the country and us, quick. As soon as they catch up to that pair of morons in the mayor's car, they'll squeal like a couple of stuck hogs and then the sheriff and his goons will come backtracking."

Red snorted and swept his arm around at the wide-open countryside. "And just where do you think we can run to? There's nothin' but wide-open country out there and I don't see any freight trains within runnin' distance. So, unless we can sprout wings and fly away, I reckon that leaves us between ah rock and ah hard spot."

William stood up and began dusting off his clothes, running his fingers through his hair, and in general, making himself presentable. "Red, I agree with you completely, but consider this. They haven't had time to set up any roadblocks and I don't think they will be looking for paying customers on public conveyances, do you?"

Joe and Red looked at William like he'd lost his mind.

"Red, how much money do we have?" William asked.

"Two hundred and forty one dollars. Why"

The Legend of Joe, Willy & Red

"Because, fellow travelers, here comes our way out of this part of the country," William said, pointing back down the highway at the Greyhound bus moving in their direction.

Joe turned and saw what William was talking about. Grinning, he stepped onto the highway and began waving his arms to flag down the bus.

The bus pulled to a stop next to them and opened the door with a, whoosh.

After following Joe and William up the steps of the bus, Red inquired of the driver what the final destination would be and when the driver told him, Red smiled and purchased three tickets.

As the bus continued on down the highway, Red meandered toward the back to give Joe and William the good news.

"Well?" William said. "Where are we headed?"

"San Francisco. Is that far enough?" Red asked as he flopped down on the rear bench seat.

"If we actually get there," Joe said, pointing toward the front windshield and the scene just beyond.

As the bus passed by, the boys turned and looked out the rear window of the bus and what they saw made their stomachs turn.

The big, black sedan was in the ditch, turned over on its side, covered from the front to the rear with bullet holes. While next to the road laid the bloody, bullet ridden bodies of the two young men who had given them a ride, and also, without realizing it, the money to hopefully get them out of harm's way.

Shaken by what they'd seen, all three men sat back in their seats and listened to the other passengers as they discussed the gory sight they'd witnessed.

After a couple of minutes, Joe said, "That could have been us back there, but we got lucky, again. But I'm tellin' ya, if we don't change our ways, one of these days we're gonna get into somethin' that no amount of luck can get us out of. I didn't come all the way from New York to wind up in jail or dead. I came out here to hide from lunatics and crazy policemen and that's just what I mean to do. "

Joe turned in his seat and looked directly at William. "Let me tell you something right now, Mister William Conrad Bains, or Willy the con man, or whoever you wind up calling yourself, if you want to continue pullin' these shenanigans, so be it, but I don't want any part of it. In fact, I'm thinkin' San Francisco would be a good place to get rid of the two of you. You been taggin' along on my shirttail long enough."

"Getting into that car wasn't anything I had anything to do with. They just came by on their own. And you have to admit I did get them to stop so we could get out."

"That's ah fact. He sure did that," Red said. "You might say he saved our butts, again."

"Yea, yea," Joe said as he leaned his head back against the seat and closed his eyes. That had been the longest speech he could remember making in a long time and he hadn't meant to throw in that last part, it had just come out. The real truth as he saw it, was his friendship with these guys was getting out of hand and he knew what could happen when you let people get too close. He'd been there, done that. And had vowed never to let it happen again.

Yea, he thought to himself, it would be better to end it in San Francisco before he got himself deeper involved. But even as these thoughts roamed around in his head, he knew it would be tough because he'd already gotten himself in too deep. He'd let these guys become his friends and he wasn't sure what to think about that.

Red spoke just above a whisper. "I reckon I can speak for Willy when I say we don't want to split up. We think we make ah pretty good team."

William nodded his head as he stared at his shoes. "We've never done anything really and truly bad. We've just looked after each other.

"Yea, I know," Joe said, feeling uncomfortable. "But there's times when you don't have to do anything at all.

The Legend of Joe, Willy & Red

Sometimes all you have to do is be at the wrong place at the wrong time and bingo, you're in more trouble than you can handle. And it doesn't matter that you didn't do anything wrong."

"Ain't that the truth," Red said, thinking of his own situation?

"Anyway, I don't want to talk about it right now. I'm gonna take a nap," Joe said, and with that, he settled back against the seat and closed his eyes before they had a chance to protest.

Joe was more tired than he'd let on. Staying awake all night last night, plus the excitement of today had taken a lot out of him and he allowed his weariness to pull him down into a darkness where he hadn't expected to go, but couldn't help himself.

It was a place where dreams are not dreams, but reliving the past in such vivid clarity that you believe you're actually there, seeing things that happened as though they were happening for the very first time.

The pool hall was crowded and he stood with his back against the wall, smoking a cigarette, waiting his turn. Joe was an excellent pool player and he liked to pick up extra money when he needed some fast cash. The pool halls down along the docks were full of young men who were eager to challenge him, but these guys today were like shootin' ducks in a barrel.

After seeing some of them take their turns, he refused to let them throw their money away, at least to him, and told them to come back in a couple of years when they'd learned to shoot better.

Joe was about to put his cigarette in the butt can when the room got very quiet.

Joe turned his head and saw Tony Capaloni and two of his henchmen marching through the silent crowd of men. Tony walked straight up to him and stopped about a foot in front of him and gave him an evil grin as he sucked on a toothpick.

Jared McVay

Joe blew a puff of smoke in Tony's face and waited for his reaction. Tony's thugs started forward, but Tony held up his hand, ignoring the insult.

"Well, well, well, if it ain't Mister Hotshot himself, Joe Wilson. Fancy runnin' inta youse. Mister Scaballini said, should I happen ta run inta ya, I should maybe collect the money you owe him."

Joe shoved away from the wall and stood nose to nose with Tony and said, "I'll pay Mister Scaballini, personally, not through some two bit punk like you."

Joe turned and walked over to the pool table, bent down and took his shot.

Tony smiled, liking the way events were going. If things worked out like he hoped they would, he would break all of Joe's fingers and maybe even cut a couple of them off so that Joe Wilson would not be able to hold a pool cue again. Next he would put on his new brass knuckles and beat Joe's face until it was nothing but a scared up bloody pulp.

And the best part was, the dude would still owe the money at twice the interest rate.

When Joe finished his shot and stood up, Tony approached him, saying, "Mister Scaballini says you owe him ah chunk of bread - ah grand. That means ah thousand bucks in case I gotta spell it out for ya. And Mister Scaballini, he don't like wise guys dat don't pay up what they owe. Mister Scaballini says ta me, he says, Tony, you see that Joe Wilson guy, you collect my money. So, here I am. You got ah thousand bucks on ya?"

Tony winked at his two henchmen, already knowing the answer.

"What thousand bucks? I only borrowed ah lousy hundred, and that was only two weeks ago," Joe said, looking Tony straight in the eyes.

Tony raised the palm of his hands upward and shrugged his shoulders. "Hey, I don't deal in finance. I'm in charge of collections and Mister Scaballini, he said I should

~ 196 ~

The Legend of Joe, Willy & Red

collect the money or I should break both your legs and throw youse in the East River... Me, I like the second choice best."

Tony knew Joe didn't owe a thousand dollars, but he always liked to add a little something extra for himself. His goons and lady friends didn't come cheap, and besides, as long as Mister Scaballini got his, what was the big deal?

Joe took his time, knowing every eye in the place was watching to see what he was going to do. As he thought about the situation and what to do about it, he dropped what was left of his cigarette onto the floor and crushed it out with the toe of his shoe.

He knew Tony was not going to let this thing go. Tony was like a vampire lusting for blood. And it was his blood Tony wanted to see, but Joe wasn't ready to just hand it over, not just yet.

He wasn't afraid of Tony, even though Tony's reputation for brutality was known throughout the city. It was his henchmen that gave him superiority. If it was one on one, Joe figured he had the upper hand. But right now, it didn't look like one on one was an option, not with those two goons bein' so eager to prove to Tony they were worth every penny he was paying them. And the chance of getting help from any of the men who were standing around watching was slim to none. They were all afraid of Tony and his goons. But most of all, they were afraid of the mob because even if they somehow got rid of Tony, the mob would just replace him with someone just as mean.

Out of the corner of his eye, Joe saw Tony slipping a pair of brass knuckles over the fingers of his right hand. Whatever he was going to do, he needed to do it now.

Joe turned his head toward the front door and called out, "Sergeant O'Banion!"

Along with Tony and his too hoods, every man in the room jerked their heads around to look at the front door. And as they did, Joe swung the heavy end of his pool stick down across the head of the hood nearest to him, then gave the second hood a right cross. Both men dropped to the floor. Tony saw what had happened and swung his fist at Joe's head. Joe easily slipped beneath Tony's brass knuckled roundhouse punch and drove his own fist into Tony's soft gut, which doubled him over. Tony went to the floor with an astonished look on his face.

By the time Tony was able to get to his feet and stagger after him, Joe was out the back door and running hard down the alley.

Reaching the street, Joe zigzagged between the cars coming and going up and down the busy street, amid tires screeching, honking horns, loud yells and the shaking of fists, then vanished among the throng of people walking up and down the sidewalk on the far side of the street.

Half a block later, Joe turned into another alley and began running, again.

What Joe hadn't seen or anticipated was the man who had quietly slipped out the front door of the pool hall just prior to Joe yelling out Sergeant O'Banion's name, then hurrying as fast as his crippled legs would carry him, down to the entryway of the alley, hoping he'd guessed correctly. He didn't have to wait long for his prayer to be answered and he smiled when he heard Joe's footfalls coming down the alley. Now he hoped his timing would be good. Everything depended on it.

He turned his face away as Joe ran from the alley and made his way across the street. And as soon as the man heard the second set of footsteps pounding down the alleyway, he pulled a switchblade knife from his pocket, hit the button that released the blade, and waited, knowing this would probably be his only chance for revenge. It was now or never.

Tony never saw the knife coming. There was only a sharp pain in his gut, then a second pain as the knife was twisted and drawn upward toward his heart.

As the knife was yanked free, Tony's life had already ebbed from his body as he toppled over onto his back, his

The Legend of Joe, Willy & Red

cold, dead eyes staring blankly at the fiery orb shining brightly in the sky.

By the time more footsteps came down the alleyway, the man was already gone, limping down the sidewalk to where an empty cab sat next to the curb, waiting for him. The knife had been tucked safely back into his pocket and not a living soul had seen a thing.

As the cab pulled away from the curb and became just another automobile on the busy street, the men from the pool hall ran up and stopped at the sight of Tony Capaloni staring at the blazing sun. It took a moment for them to fathom what had happened and what they were seeing.

One of the hoods turned to the crowd of men and said, "Joe Wilson is gonna pay for this, big time."

In the meantime, unaware of Tony's demise, Joe was wondering where he might hide out for a few days until things calmed down a bit. He couldn't go to his apartment, which would be one of the first places they'd look.

Joe rented a sleazy hotel room in a dumpy hotel down on the lower East Side of the city, a place where Tony and his hoods rarely ever came. He bought Italian from a small café next to the hotel and took his supper back to his room with him.

After a restless night on a lumpy mattress and jumping to his feet to peer out the window every time he heard a siren, early morning found Joe sitting in a back booth of the hotel dining room, which was almost as run down as the hotel.

His breakfast of greasy eggs and over cooked bacon, along with burnt toast was hardly touched and his coffee just sat there getting cold.

Now that he thought about it, what he'd done yesterday had been stupid. Oh yea, he'd made Tony and his two goons look bad, but the only thing he'd accomplished was to put the mark of Cain on himself. Which meant in

Jared McVay

layman's terms, he was a dead man, and all because he was so damn hardheaded, or stupid, or maybe both.

Tony Capaloni had been publicly humiliated and he would not be satisfied until Joe Wilson had been made an example of. After being made to suffer publicly for a long time, he would then be beaten to a bloody pulp and thrown in the East River to rot along with the others whose bones resided there as a monument to Tony's anger.

Joe looked up to order fresh coffee and saw a small black man standing in the entryway, staring in his direction. Joe waved the man over. The man grinned and then headed in Joe's direction, showing a noticeable limp.

Joe knew the small black man with a limp and felt no fear of him squealing to the mob about seeing him. He was one of the few survivors of Tony's beatings. Tony, in his benevolent way had allowed the man to live - in pain and a cripple for life to show to the others what might be.

After shaking hands, the small black man said, "Been lookin' fer ya all night. You got troubles, Joe, real troubles. You seen the mornin' paper, yet?"

When Joe shook his head, no, the man slid into the booth opposite of Joe and slid a newspaper across the table in front of Joe.

Joe stared at the headlines in shocked confusion, trying to comprehend what he was reading, but the only thing that was clear was that Tony Capaloni was dead and he, Joe Wilson, was the fall guy.

"Well, I don't feel sorry that he's dead. He was no good and he deserved what he got, but I didn't do it," Joe said, looking directly into the black man's eyes. "I almost wish I had."

The black man sat there silently as the waitress came up and poured fresh coffee for the both of them.

After the waitress had gone, Joe looked across the booth and thought the man looked a bit uncomfortable.

"If I didn't know that in my heart, I wouldn't be here now," the black man said, unable to look Joe in the eyes.

The Legend of Joe, Willy & Red

"You and me and ah whole lot of folks is glad he's gone and rottin' in hell. Look what he done ta me. I'll never walk straight again and he sure nuff made sure I won't never have no chil'ren of my own. They's been ah many ah time I wished I could stick ah knife in'em and watch him die."

As Joe sat there and listened to the man talking, he felt there was something in the man's eyes and voice that was trying to tell him something that wasn't being said outright, but finally sluffed it off as an old hatred. He knew about old hatreds and how they could influence your thoughts and words.

"You got both the police and the mob lookin' fer ya, boy. You got any idea what you gonna do?" Joe heard the man say.

"I guess the best thing to do would be to get outta town for a while," Joe said with a grin.

The small black man grinned back at Joe and said, "I was kinda hopin' you would say that. I'd like ta help ya if'n ya'll let me."

Once again Joe got that strange feeling, but this time chalked it up to something akin to friendship, even though he knew they were not much more than acquaintances.

"You come with me, Joe," the man was saying. "You jest stay ah layin' down in the back seat of my cab and I'll haul ya down ta the train yard where you can mayhap catch ah fast freight train headed west, or someplace."

Joe could see sweat popping out on the man's forehead and he seemed anxious all of a sudden.

Actually the idea sounded good to Joe. He didn't have anything at his apartment that he would miss and the landlord wouldn't have any trouble renting his place to one of the guys down at the dock. He knew of at least three who would move in tomorrow. Plus, yesterday had been payday, so he wasn't leaving any money behind.

"That's real decent of you," he heard himself say. "I don't know how to thank you except to give you some cash for the ride."

Jared McVay

"Don't want yer money. You jest git outta town thout gettin caught, that'll sure be thanks enough for me," the man said as he slid out of the booth and laid a wad of bills on the table. "Breakfast is on me."

The black man hurried toward the front door, pulling his car keys out as he went.

As Joe climbed into the back seat of the cab, he felt that nervousness come over him, again. There was something he was missing, but what was it?

As the cab pulled out into traffic, Joe closed his eyes for some much needed rest, and hadn't gone far when a voice called to him from far, far away.

"Joe, Joe, wake up. Com'on, sleepyhead, wake up," Red's voice was saying.

Joe stirred and opened his eyes, unsure of where he was. "Where am I?" he said to no one in particular. Where was the black man? And why was he on a bus and not a freight train?

The smiling face of William appeared before him and said, "San Francisco, we're in San Francisco."

Like a flood, it all came back to him. He'd been dreaming and now it made sense! The small black man with the limp, the same man who had helped him escape, the man who had a reason to kill Tony, it was him! He'd stabbed Tony! And with Joe Wilson out of the way, he'd be in the clear and no one would even consider him.

And if Joe Wilson ran away, that would make him look guilty, so the obvious thing to do would be to help make Joe Wilson disappear.

At first it made him angry, but looking at it from the black man's point of view, he might have done the same thing.

Joe chuckled, thinking it was strange how things worked out, sometimes.

Chapter 23

Welcome To San Francisco

After all the trials and tribulations Joe, Willy and Red had been through a person would think they would be ecstatic about finally reaching San Francisco and the west coast virtually unscathed. And they were, too, but it was that first sight of the famous city by the bay that made San Francisco somewhat foreboding.

Fog drifted aimlessly down the streets, leaving a cold, wet blanket on everything it touched, creating a dismal picture; at least in this part of the city.

Trash lay in heaps along the curbs and loose trash was scattered here and there on the sidewalk. Hidden inside cardboard boxes or anything else that might keep them out of the cold and wetness of the nightly fog, were gaunt, hollow eyed men who spent each day walking the streets, searching for non-existent work.

From time to time there would be jobs on the docks, or in the warehouses, but they rarely lasted more than one day. And the number of men who applied for the jobs far out numbered the jobs available. And for the most part it was the guys who got there first, who got the few jobs available. Sometimes, if a foreman saw somebody he knew and liked, the man might get preference over the others, but those times were few and far between.

Nationwide, the depression hit the big cities the hardest.

"Reminds me of home," Joe said with a sigh. "New York City has been just like this ever since the depression hit. I'd guess all the big cities probably turned out to be pretty much the same."

"I sure am glad I didn't live in no big city. Maybe Dallas or Houston is like this, I don't know," Red said, shaking his head. "But it wasn't like this out where I was from. We were ah small farm and ranch community and most everybody had ah garden and plenty ta eat. Oh sure, we read about the depression and the bad times and all, and we had ah few inconveniences, but nuthin' like this."

William saw the way things were going and decided to change the subject. "It's too bad we weren't able to save any of that food from that restaurant. I'm starving."

"Ain't you always," Joe said with a grin.

"I sure could use some vittles, too. My belly button feels like it's rubbin' against my backbone," Red said, laughing.

A few blocks down the street they found a small diner with only two early morning customers and as they entered, a very pretty, young waitress with a big smile and even bigger breasts, greeted them. She showed them to a booth and then bent over so low that Joe got an eye full of cleavage while she took their orders. And as she sash-shayed off to get their food, the view from the rear was just as nice as it was from the front, and that was saying a lot.

"Mister Wilson, I do believe you have an admirer," William said with a grin.

"She can admire me any time she wants to," Red said with a big smile.

"You're both crazy," Joe said. "She just wants us to spend money and that's how she keeps men comin' back. It's strictly business."

"Well I reckon she don't care much one way or the other whether me or William comes back or not," Red said, indicating William and himself. "Cause we sure didn't get ah gander at them big boobs like you did."

"You're full of it," Joe said as he sipped his coffee, enjoying the warmth he felt all the way down into the pit of his stomach, not wanting to admit she just may have been flirting with him, and he sure wasn't going to admit it to Red or William.

During breakfast Red's prediction came true as the waitress openly flirted with Joe several times - and even

The Legend of Joe, Willy & Red

went so far as telling him what time she would be getting off work and suggesting he drop by about then.

Normally, Joe would have been very receptive to a woman as pretty as she was and being right up front about her intentions, but not this morning. Not with William and Red sitting across from him, winking and grinning like a couple of idiots. They made him feel uncomfortable with the whole situation for some reason.

When the waitress had cleared all the dishes and they sat drinking their coffee, Joe lit a cigarette from the fresh pack the waitress had brought him and then asked,

"So, what do we do now? Are you two ready ta quit hangin' onto my shirttail now that we've reached the big city? That was something we'd talked about as I recall."

Joe wasn't quite sure why he'd said that. Maybe it was out of habit or because he secretly wanted to see the waitress.

The simple truth of the matter was, he was getting used to their company and it wasn't all bad - and that made him nervous. He'd never had feelings like this before. Was he getting soft, or what, he wondered? Joe shook his head to clear his thoughts. He didn't let people get under his skin. That rule couldn't be broken, or could it?

William was the first one to speak, "I think we should take our time and not make any rash decisions right now. After all, we just got here. Maybe we should take the day to relax; give ourselves time to think. We have what you might call, found money. . . so we're not destitute. We can give ourselves some time to look the city over. We just may want to change our minds and go someplace else. We can decide tomorrow, or possibly the next day. Why rush things?"

At the mention of splitting up, William had almost panicked. William had come to think of them like those classical heroes in the book, 'The Three Musketeers,' one for all and all for one. And he wasn't going to let that change - not if he could help it.

"I ain't for splittin' up, either," Red said, noticing the panic in William's eyes. He'd kinda gotten used to hangin' around with these two. They'd become the closest thing to family he could remember in a long, long time.

Joe turned his head in the direction of the waitress and blew out a long stream of smoke. She smiled broadly and gave him another come-hither look that made his blood begin to boil. It had been a long dry spell and right in front of him was a beautiful, very tempting sacrificial lamb waiting to bring him much needed relief.

"So, what'a ya think? We gonna stick together for ah while longer?" Joe heard Red say.

After taking another drag on his cigarette, Joe looked at the two men who were waiting for him to say something.

William was stirring his coffee, making noises as the spoon bounced off the edge of the cup. And Red was just sitting there, staring at him.

The waitress put a nickel in the jute box and played, 'Everything I have is yours.'

So, it was settled then, Joe thought to himself. At least for the time being they would continue to hang around together, with only a couple of slight changes that were already forming in his mind.

He took a drink of coffee and realized that for the first time in his life, he had two real friends; men he could trust and depend on.

He was on unfamiliar ground here and still not sure how to deal with it, but there was one thing he was sure of; he wasn't ready to tell them how he felt; that would be exposing too much of himself.

"Okay," Joe said, "It appears you two chicks aren't ready to leave the nest, yet. So be it - at least for a day or two. Now, just how un-destitute are we?"

Red thought for a minute and then said, "Let's see, we had two hundred forty-one dollars when we got on the bus. The tickets cost four dollars apiece. . ."

"Twelve dollars," William said.

The Legend of Joe, Willy & Red

"Right," Red said as he picked up the meal check. "A pack of butts, ten cents, three breakfasts at forty cents apiece, add ah twenty cent tip because of the view and that comes to..."

"One dollar and fifty cents," William stated.

Red looked at William out of the corner of his eye and then went on. "Right again. Now we add twelve bucks and a buck fifty; that comes to..."

"Thirteen fifty."

"Would you like ta do this?" Red asked.

"No, no, no, you're doing just fine," William said, smiling. "I'll just sit here and sip on my coffee."

Red nodded and pulled the fat wad of bills out of his jeans pocket and began to unfold and count the money. "That leaves us with Ahhh; let's see..."

"Two hundred and twenty-seven dollars and fifty cents - which comes to, seventy five dollars and eighty three cents apiece," William said, with the assurance of a man who knew exactly what he was saying.

Both Joe and Red stared hard at William.

"What? I used to work in a bank. I'm good with figures," William said holding up both hands, palms out.

"Then you should be doing this," Red said with a grin as he shoved the money in front of William. "I never had my very own personal banker before."

Joe found it interesting that William automatically accepted his roll of banker and smiled at the good-natured ribbing from Red.

After holding out enough to pay the waitress, who gave Joe a look and received a hidden wink, William gave each man his share.

They left the restaurant and found the fog had disappeared, leaving a bright blue sky with soft puffs of white clouds drifting lazily overhead.

The walk down to the bay - to a place called, Fisherman's Wharf, was made in silence because there were too many sights to be seen. In the daylight, the city looked

Jared McVay

somewhat different - like the depression hadn't beaten the city down or crippled it as much as it had other big cities.

On this bright morning, San Francisco looked like a city that wouldn't totally give up on itself. Even though work was scarce, many stores still opened their door and sold their goods at discounted prices.

Standing at the edge of the bay, Alcatraz Island loomed dark and mysterious a short distance away.

"That place is ah Federal Prison, now. Used ta be ah military prison, but ah while back, the government decided it would be the ideal place ta keep the hard cases. They say it's impossible ta escape from The Rock as it's called," Red said as a matter of fact.

"Let's hope we never have to test that theory," William said, poking Red in the ribs with his elbow.

Joe, Willy and Red stood, enthralled as they watched several sailboats gliding along with the wind, seemingly without a care in the world, tacking back and forth, first this way and then that away, heading for an unknown destination, or no destination at all.

Coming in from the Pacific ocean, a beautiful ketch, maybe sixty feet from her bow to her stern, with two tall masts pointing at the sky, entered the bay, her three sails full and billowing as she skimmed through the water with grace and poise.

Joe, Willy and Red stood watching the large sailboat as it came toward them, mesmerized by her beauty and the majesty in which she carried herself, as though she stood head and shoulders above the other sailboats.

Joe finally broke their trance. "Now that's the way to live and travel, boys. If a man had a boat like that he could go anywhere - see the whole world!" Joe said with wanderlust in his eyes.

Red nodded in agreement. "There sure ain't nuthin' like that down where I come from, except in picture books. Never thought I'd ever see one this close. Course I never thought I'd ever be in San Francisco, either."

The Legend of Joe, Willy & Red

"Nor in Minneapolis," William said. "She most certainly is a thing of beauty."

They watched as the ketch passed a large freighter anchored in the middle of the bay, waiting to unload her cargo. Down to a man of them, the crew of the freighter stood on deck, waving at the people on the ketch, who waved back.

The crew watched until the beautiful ketch sailed beyond the huge freighter, then tacked and veered off to the north.

"Probably headed for Sausalito," Joe said. "I hear tell some rich folks live over there and you sure need a couple of bucks in your pocket to own a boat like that."

A loud noise interrupted their thoughts and they turned and looked to see where it was coming from and saw a group of men working on a piece of land that jutted out from the shore near the entrance to the bay.

"Looks like there might be some work ta be had down there," Red said, pointing toward the worksite.

"Not unless you're a specialist at bridge building," William interjected.

"They're building a bridge? To where?" Red asked in an astonished tone.

"To that piece of land over there," William said, pointing across the bay.

"You gotta be kiddin' me." Red said, staring across the bay. "That's gotta be over ah mile. Ain't no way they can build ah bridge that long."

"You're right about the first part." William said. "When they get finished, it will be the longest suspension bridge in the world; six thousand, four hundred and fifty feet from end to end."

"Hooooeeee, that's incredible! How do you know all this stuff, you livin' way back there in Minnesota?"

"It was in the newspapers all over the country, some time back," Joe said. "They think it's a pretty big deal, I guess. It was designed by a man by the name of. . . Joseph B.

Strauss. The New York Times said the center section will be connected to a very tall structure on either end and will be four thousand, two hundred feet long and ninety feet wide. The road, or driving surface will be a mere height of two hundred and twenty feet above the water and the bridge should be capable of withstanding one hundred mile an hour winds."

Both men were impressed by Joe's knowledge of current events and the grins on their faces showed it.

"That's impressive," William said, offering him a salute.

For the first time, Joe let his hair down, a little, by bowing with a wide swoop of his arm.

As they headed back in the direction of the city, Joe felt a kinship that he'd never experienced before, and it felt good.

"So, what's next?" Red asked as they walked along.

"I'm gonna get a hotel room where I can get myself cleaned up, have the bellhop get me a bottle of booze, and then I am going to pick up this gorgeous woman I know of and take her up to my room where we will attempt to relieve all this pent up tension that you guys caused," Joe said, grinning broadly.

"That sounds like ah fine idea to me. Think I might try ta find me a good lookin' woman ta help relieve all my tension, too, which of course was caused by ole Willy boy, here. And speakin' of Willy boy, what are you gonna do, mister banker man, now that you're footloose and fancy free?"

Assuming an air of sophistication and speaking with his best banker-like voice, William said, "Yes, I too will seek accommodations, but as for those vices of women and liquor, I believe I will pass. A good meal, a long soak in a tub of hot, steaming water and a good night's sleep will do me just fine. Thereby saving myself a large expense."

"Sometimes I just don't know how ta figure you Mister Banker man," Red said . . .

"But as they say, 'to each his own.'"

A few blocks from the bay they found a somewhat, middle of the road hotel - not expensive and not run down.

"How about this one?" William asked, after checking out the lobby and declaring it better than the last three he'd looked at.

"Fine," Joe said. "As long as they have clean rooms, a private bath and a firm bed, that's good enough for me."

The skinny little man with a pencil thin moustache and slicked down hair standing behind the front desk assured them the hotel was clean, the beds were as good as any hotel in town and that all their needs would be promptly taken care of.

"The rooms are a dollar a night, paid in advance. You will find clean towels in the bathrooms, changed daily, as are the sheets, and should you need anything else, ring me day or night. Any and all special services are also paid in advance. Please enjoy your stay at the Savoy."

Counting out seven one-dollar bills, William said, "My good man, I believe I shall rent by the week."

The greedy little clerk scooped up the money before William could change his mind and slid a room key across the counter with the speed of a striking snake.

Joe and Red followed suit, and shortly, each man was in his very own room, after promising to meet at the diner around eight, for breakfast.

Well, as you can imagine, that old expression, 'to each his own,' held true on this particular night. Except for Red, the other two, each in the privacy of his room, fulfilled his pleasures in his own way.

Joe, of course, had a grand tay-ta-tay with the pretty and buxom young waitress from the diner, who turned out to be quite talented in the art of lovemaking, leaving very little time for drinking or anything else for that matter - such as talking or sleeping.

But on this night, Joe didn't care because she made him feel younger than he had in a long, long time. And that was good enough for him.

Red, on the other hand, had a much different night than he had planned. He had eaten too little and drank too much prior to the arrival of the pretty little blonde the hotel clerk sent to him.

Red wasn't much of a drinker to begin with and the bottle of John Barley Corn the desk clerk had given him earlier, produced a kick similar to that of a Missouri Mule. Pour that stuff into an almost empty stomach and the combination was practically lethal. Poor ole Red didn't stand a chance. He was done for before the party even got started.

When the pretty little blonde arrived, she sized up the situation and quickly got him undressed and into bed, then slipped out of her own clothes. But she was already to late. By the time she climbed in next to him, Red was snoring loudly and that told her all she needed to know. She'd seen this before.

So, while the Texan tried to raise the roof with his snoring, the pretty young lady decided not to let the entire night be a waste and got her cosmetic case out of her bag.

While the Texan lay dead to the world, the young lady sat on the edge of the bed and painted, first, her long fingernails and then her tiny toenails, bright red, not wanting the night to be a total waste. Besides, she had already been paid.

She would have gone home, but she'd seen clients who woke up after awhile and if she wasn't there, the hotel manager would be angry and possibly stop using her. No, it would be better if she waited, jobs were not easy to come by.

Just down the hall, Mister William Conrad Bains, banker and all around con man sat in a tub of steaming hot water with bubbles covering the surface, as classical music played on the radio in his adjoining room.

The Legend of Joe, Willy & Red

William leaned back and puffed on a fat cigar while he sipped champagne from the crystal glass he shared with the beautiful young Chinese woman whose long, jet-black hair hung nearly to her waist, covering her naked breasts.

Kneeling next to the tub, she hummed to the music as she gently and soothingly massaged his body with a large sponge. Shortly, when he was fully aroused, she smiled and said, "I think it is time I joined you," as she stood up and stretched, allowing William to fill his eyes with her beauty.

William could not believe how fortune had smiled on him as he watched her ease into the tub and slowly straddle him, just as the sound of the Blue Danube Waltz filled the air. It didn't get any better than this, he thought to himself. Yes, life could have its beautiful moments after all.

At this particular moment in time, Brenda, the woman who had betrayed him and left him grief stricken, was no longer a part of his conscious mind. He was lost in the dark eyes, long black hair and olive skin of this gorgeous, tender loving oriental girl.

For William, this was his way of letting go of his marriage and the hurt and pain Brenda had caused him. It was his way of saying goodbye and allowing what she had done to him to become a forgotten moment of unhappiness.

Even though he didn't have a piece of paper that said divorced, he was finally a free man and his new life was just beginning.

William took a long puff of his cigar, blew out the smoke and took another sip of his champagne as he settled back in the tub to enjoy life and what it had to offer.

Chapter 24

Breakfast At The Diner

A few minutes before eight o'clock the following morning, William was sitting in a booth at the diner, enjoying a leisurely breakfast, and feeling like he'd been given a new lease on life. He was full of more vim, vigor and vitality than he'd felt in quite some time.

His appetite was never better and his taste buds were at their peak as he savored the rich taste of orange marmalade mixed with the sweet flavor of butter on his toast. Next came the zesty, country fried ham, combined with a large bite of eggs, which made the ensemble complete. He chewed his breakfast slowly before washing it down with hot, black coffee, whose aroma filled his nostrils. He was a happy man.

Red entered the diner holding his head with both hands. When he slid, gingerly into the booth, across from William, the waitress came bouncing over to take his order. Like William, she seemed to be on top of the world. Red groaned at the sound of her footsteps.

"What's your pleasure, honey, " she said with a bright smile as she poured coffee into a cup and set it in front of him.

"You don't half'ta yell," Red whispered. "Just bring me ah whole pot of coffee and make it black and strong. And please, do it quietly."

The waitress gave Red a knowing wink and a nod that said she understood what he was suffering before returning to her space behind the counter and busied herself at something, while humming a happy tune.

Red sat with his elbows propped on the counter, holding the sides of his head as he massaged his temples with his fingers. "Oh man. . . I'd have ta get better ta die," he hissed.

After a couple of moments, Red gripped the mug of coffee with trembling hands and lifted the steaming brew to his lips, taking only a small sip.

The loud blaring of a car horn tore through the diner, causing Red to shutter and set the coffee mug down hard, spilling some of it.

William wanted to do something for his friend, but there was nothing he could do, except feel sympathy. Red was suffering from an old fashioned, king-sized hangover; it was as simple as that.

Basically it leaned toward the side of irony that two men could indulge in similar types of recreational activity and have the results turn out to be totally and completely different.

Here he was, a man who the previous evening had indulged in alcohol libation and the wonderful, rapturous joys of a beautiful young woman and wound up feeling so full of life he could hardly stand it, while his good friend was sitting directly across from him looking like something the cat had dragged in.

For a fleeting moment, William recalled a similar feeling of nearly unbearable pain ripping through his head the morning he'd awakened and found himself inside a moving boxcar and the rattling of the train nearly driving him crazy. There had been no strong, black coffee or food to help his tortured stomach. His only recourse had been to hang his head out of the open doorway and empty his stomach of the terrible rotgut that had gotten him into this situation to begin with.

"You really should try to eat something," William pleaded, softly. " Honestly, it will make you feel better. Honest Injun."

Red's bloodshot eyes moved up and stared directly at William. "Please, do me ah favor and don't mention food, or even talk. Just let me die in peace, okay?"

Jared McVay

About then, the waitress walked up and set a tall glass of brownish-red liquid on the table in front of Red. It resembled thick, rusty water with frothy foam on top.

"A little something special I make," she said. "I call it 'the hangover breakfast,' I promise it will make that nasty ole headache go bye, bye."

Red turned his head and looked up at the waitress with the intention of saying something vile to her for interrupting his grieving, painful last moments here on earth. But when he saw the soft, tender, caring look on her face, the words hung in his throat unsaid. Finding himself unable to resist the pleading in her eyes, he picked up the glass and raised it to his lips.

"Go ahead, drink it all down at once and you'll see. In a few minutes you'll begin to feel better, I promise, Girl Scouts honor," she said holding up her hand.

Red held the glass close to his mouth for a moment, then took the plunge and downed the thick, spicy tasting liquid in one tip of the glass and almost immediately, felt a reaction as the concoction lined the walls of his stomach and dulled the throbbing in his head.

"See, that wasn't so bad, now was it?" she asked, smiling at him.

"It's okay, I guess," Red said offhandedly, not wanting to give in too easily to her charm. "What's in this stuff? You need to get a patent."

She smiled again and said, "It's an old recipe that's been in our family for eons of time. All the men in my family were robust drinkers. Actually it's pretty simple to make. You start off with a glass of tomato juice, a few shakes of salt and pepper, a healthy dab of hot sauce, three crushed up aspirin and last, two raw eggs. Then, all you do is stir it all together real good and drink it down, and walla, it does the trick."

Red clamped his hand over his mouth, slid out of the booth and hotfooted it in the direction of the men's room at a fast trot.

The Legend of Joe, Willy & Red

Joe entered the diner just as Red went sailing past with his hand covering his mouth, trying desperately not to throw up on the floor.

Joe was still grinning as he slapped the waitress on the fanny and slid past her and took the spot Red had just vacated. "Mornin' Sugar," he said to the waitress.

Very waitress like, she said, "May I take your order, sir."

"You sure can," he said, smiling up at her. "Bring me a big slice of ham, and eggs over easy, fried potatoes, biscuits and gravy, light toast and black coffee. And be quick about it, wench!"

"You certainly are chipper this morning. You must have had quite some time last night to have such an appetite this morning. Did you get any sleep at all?" she asked in a mischievous tone.

Joe took his time and lit a cigarette, blowing smoke in the direction of the suction fan on the ceiling, as she poured coffee into an empty mug and pushed it in front of him, then gave a grinning William, a refill and a wink.

"I had an incredible night and sleep had nothin' to do with it," Joe said. "How bout you? You look pretty chipper yourself."

Once again that mischievous twinkle gleamed brightly in her eyes as she tilted her head slightly and stared at the ceiling, contemplating her answer. Finally she looked back at Joe and said, "I guess you could say my evening was somewhat enjoyable."

Joe's smiled disappeared. This was not the answer he was expecting to hear and it stunned him, momentarily.

William sat quietly watching - amused as she played Joe like you would a fish on a hook, and him taking the bait, hook, line and sinker.

She placed a hand on her hip and said, "I had a first date with this guy I recently met and, well, you know how first dates can be. I don't date often because they usually turn bad. You know, a girl gets her hopes up - looking for

~ 217 ~

prince charming and all that. Then I wind up getting disappointed. It's such a hassle. I guess if I had to rate this guy I went out with last night on a scale of one to ten, oh, I don't know, maybe I'd have to give him an eleven."

With that said, she whirled and headed for the kitchen. "I'll get your breakfast now, sire," she called out over her shoulder, swinging her hips back and forth for Joe's benefit.

"Well, I'll be dammed," Joe, said, realizing she'd been toying with him and he'd fallen for it like a schoolboy.

"Quite the young lady, isn't she?" William said, observing the way Joe watched her as she sashayed toward the kitchen.

"Yea, there's more to her than meets the eye," Joe said. "She's got brains, too."

She must be quite the young lady, indeed, William thought. In one night she had single handily turned this hardnosed warhorse of a man into a frolicking young colt. . . How very interesting.

Muttering to himself, William said, "I wonder if they realize the power they have."

"Booze and broads," Joe said. "If the good lord made anything better, he kept it for himself."

"What did you say?" William asked, coming out of his own thoughts.

"I said, booze and broads. If the good lord made anything better, he kept it all to himself." Joe repeated, grinning broadly.

"May I assume the young lady was to your liking?"

William felt the question was not necessary, but thought he'd ask it anyway. Joe was in too good a mood to waste the moment.

"To my liking? I've never met anyone like her. She's exquisite!" Joe said as she walked up and set his breakfast on the table in front of him.

The Legend of Joe, Willy & Red

William almost laughed out loud when Joe's face turned a bright pink once he realized she'd heard what he said.

Without a word, she leaned forward and gave Joe an ample view as she placed the silverware next to his plate, never hinting she'd heard a word he'd said.

But what she did next surprised both of them as she reached over and kissed Joe on the forehead, then turned on her heels and walked away, speaking to no one in general.

"If a person likes to dance, there's a swell band playing at the Starlight Ballroom tonight."

Joe sat there in stunned silence, wondering what was going on. His world as he knew it had been turned upside down, again.

"Okay, I think I get the picture," William said, chuckling to himself as Joe tried to recover from his embarrassment.

Joe picked up his knife and fork and attacked his breakfast wanting very much to change the subject. Between bites he looked at William and asked, "What about you? Did you get that long soak in the tub and a good night's sleep you were talking about?"

William closed his eyes as he remembered the beautiful, young oriental woman.

"Let me just say that my time in the tub was the most satisfying I can remember in my entire life, and when sleep finally came, it was a glorious, peaceful rapture."

Joe stopped a mouthful of food halfway to his mouth. With a bewildered look on his face he was about to ask what all that mumbo-jumbo meant. A yes or a no would have been good enough. But before he could say anything, Red returned and sat down, gingerly, next to William.

Joe smiled and pointed a large piece of ham that was stuck on the end of his fork in Red's direction. "This is great. You should try some," he said, waving it back and forth under Red's nose.

Jared McVay

Red took one look at the chunk of ham with yellow egg yolk dripping from it and bolted for the men's room, again.

"Oh, you've got a mean streak in you, don't you," William said as he watched Red running across the diner. "Where's your compassion for your fellow man? Don't you feel sorry for him?"

It seemed like everyone in the diner felt sorry for Red, but Joe.

Unmoved, Joe continued eating his breakfast. After a minute he looked up and said, "The sooner he gets that rot gut out of his system and some solid food in his belly, the faster he'll get back on his feet and be his old self again and we can get on with the things that need getting done. I hope he doesn't do this often, because I can't and won't tolerate a drunk."

William saw the hardness return to Joe's eyes and a chill ran down his spine. If that turned out to be the case, he had no illusions that Joe would call it quits flat out with no room for argument. Joe would tell Red in no uncertain terms how he felt and leave and that would be that, this time.

Actually, he didn't like being around drunks either, and he hoped and prayed this wasn't a side of Red they'd never seen before.

William tried to remember and as he reflected back, there had been times when Red could have gotten a bottle of alcohol if he'd needed it, but he hadn't and William hoped that said something in Red's favor.

Nor, could he remember Red ever showing any symptoms of a man in need - like having the shakes, or talking about finding a place to get a drink.

William's nerves began to simmer down a little as these thoughts ran through his mind. His worries about Red being a drunk and them breaking up slowly began to fade. It had been a toot and that was all; a celebration that had gotten out of hand, that was it.

The Legend of Joe, Willy & Red

He felt even better when he saw Red come out of the men's room and go over to where the waitress was standing and ask her for another one of her concoctions and when she brought it to him, he turned it up and downed it and then smiled and patted his stomach as he sat the glass back on the counter.

This time it stayed down and he came back and slid into the booth saying, "Sorry about that, guys. I'm not much of ah drinker and I reckon I got carried away some last night, you know the excitement and all. But I can and will promise both of you that it will be a long, long time before it ever happens again because I can't even remember if I got lucky or not."

William noticed relief wash over Joe's face as they all had a good laugh, with Red holding his head for the effort.

The waitress sat a bowl of steaming oatmeal, some dry toast and a tall glass of milk in front of Red.

"Poor baby, do me a favor and eat this and I promise it will make you feel better, and in no time at all, you'll be all well again."

There was a tenderness in her voice, like a mother speaking to her child as Red lifted a spoonful of oatmeal to his mouth, blew on it, then took his first bite.

She stroked the top of his head softly and said, "That's a good boy. While you eat your breakfast, I'll get you some coffee."

Before she left, she gave Joe one of those smiles that would melt an iceberg and said, "Give him about a half an hour and he'll be okay."

Joe smiled at her and winked. "Thank you Miss Florence Nightingale, there are no doubts whatsoever that under your care, the patient will recover fully and stand on his own two feet again."

At first she pouted, thinking he was making fun of her, until she saw the twinkle in his eyes. Her curtsy was that of a fair maiden, with a finger under her chin.

Jared McVay

"Thank you, kind sir," she said before turning and heading for the coffee pot.

This girl is quick on her feet, William thought as he watched her walk away. She could give as good as she got. She just might be what Joe needed in his life and by the look in his eyes, he just might be thinking along the same lines.

Once they'd finished eating and Red had downed several mugs of coffee, it was Joe who suggested they look the city over and see what it had to offer.

They paid their bills, with Red leaving a large tip before he and William walked outside and stood waiting as Joe lingered, speaking to the waitress.

As Joe walked out and joined his friends, the waitress watched the smooth way he walked and felt warmth begin to grow inside her. He'd asked her to go dancing this evening and she'd said, yes. There was something about this man that was different... She hadn't known many men, but none of them had made her feel the way he did.

Suddenly, she began to tremble. A feeling came over her as though something terrible was about to happen to Joe. She started for the door to warn him, but stopped short. What could she actually tell him? She wasn't a fortuneteller who could predict the future and she hadn't actually had any visions of what the disaster might be. He would think she had gone off the deep end, and she wouldn't blame him.

The truth was, she wasn't even sure what she'd felt really had anything to do with Joe. And as they disappeared down the street, the feeling went away as she greeted a man and a woman who entered the diner.

But it wasn't over. Several times during the day the feeling had returned and it was always at a time when she least expected it. There were no pictures in her mind, no premonitions - just that uncontrollable trembling and a feeling of disaster. And the scary thing was, she never had any warning.

All of a sudden her hands and body would begin to shake violently, like when she was pouring coffee for one of the customers and her hand had jerked suddenly, spilling coffee all over the counter and the customer, too.

She had apologized and the man had said there was no problem and thanked her when she told him there would be no charge. But when it happened two more times, she became almost frantic with worry.

Two hours before her shift was over, she called the woman who was to relieve her and asked her to come in early.

By now she had convinced herself that she was coming down with something, but by the time she got back to her apartment she was feeling her old self again and the trembling had disappeared completely. She took a long soak in a steaming tub of hot water anyway, along with a glass of wine and two aspirin. She was going dancing this evening with a great guy and no little cold or whatever it was, was going to keep her from it.

Jared McVay

Chapter 25

The Address

"Well, gentlemen, and I use the term advisedly, it's time to begin our new lives," William said as they walked down the sidewalk.

The first thing they did after leaving the diner was to stop at a used clothing store a few blocks down the street. And within a short time, they each found presentable suits and shoes, along with shirts, socks, and clean underwear.

Dressed in their newly acquired clothes, all three stepped out of the store feeling good about themselves. The sky was blue, a warm, yellow sun was shining brightly and William was full of optimism.

They had reached their destination, San Francisco, California, the city that butted up against the Pacific Ocean and at this very moment all was right with the world. Willy felt like they could finally put their troubles behind them because something inside him told him good fortune was headed their way.

But three hours later, Willy's hopes and dreams began to diminish. Even though the depression had not devastated San Francisco as hard as it had many other cities, it still felt the effects all the way down to the edge of the water. And what few people who were still able to keep their doors open, barely made enough profit to pay the bills.

It staggered the mind to see the long lines of gaunt eyed men standing in line to get into the soup kitchens for possibly their only meal of the day, or sleeping along the sidewalks and in the alleyways.

NOT HIRING and NO WORK signs were posted everywhere. On one block alone they counted five, OUT OF BUSINESS signs.

William had not been prepared for this. He wondered if Minneapolis had been like this. Most of his time had been

The Legend of Joe, Willy & Red

spent at the bank and he hadn't really ventured out into the city much. Brenda did the shopping and he'd been left to his music and books.

By late afternoon, the three men found themselves at a small beanery café near a group of warehouses close to the bay, where a sign in the window boasted the owner specialized in navy beans and the best veal sandwiches on the west coast.

As they walked in, they noticed the place was packed with men from the docks and warehouses. There were two men waiting in front of them and William asked one of them what was so special about the sandwiches.

The man was a little taller than William, but built pretty much from the same mold except this man had a hard stubble of beard and calloused hands. And when he spoke, his voice sounded like it was coming from the bottom of a barrel.

"If you've never eaten here before, you're in for a treat. Been eatin' here for the past three years. For fifteen cents you get a large bowl of navy beans, oyster crackers, hot peppers, a cup of coffee and a specially breaded veal sandwich about five inches thick, with a large dollop of his secret recipe chili on top, all between two thick slices of his homemade bread. It's a meal you'll remember for a long time."

"I think we should give it a try," William said to Joe and Red.

They had to admit, it was worth the wait, but once they were outside again, and had to face the dreariness of the city and remembering the stories the men in the café had told them about how bad things were, their conversation was sparse.

They were approximately three blocks from the café before William finally broke the silence. "After what we've seen today, I would suggest we reconsider our options...

San Francisco is obviously not what we expected it to be. I think we should conserve what cash we have until we

Jared McVay

decide what we're going to do. Finding work is not going to be easy if we stay here. Maybe we should give some thought to going somewhere else, like, Los Angeles or up north to Portland or even Seattle. . ." He let the sentence trail off as he waited for some kind of a reaction.

Red scratched his nose and said, "In all fairness, we've only been here one day and I ain't sure that's long enough ta make an honest opinion. Besides our rooms are paid in full for six more days. But if we do decide ta leave, I suggest we try ah smaller town. Maybe ah farm community. As I recall, we didn't have these kinds of problems back home."

Joe exhaled a long stream of smoke. "I go along with Red. I think we should give this place a fair chance, then if it doesn't pan out. . ."

He didn't want to leave San Francisco quite yet, not until he figured out how he felt about the young woman at the diner and how she felt about him. He liked the new feelings he was having and wasn't anxious to just walk away from them. Besides, Red and William wouldn't leave until he did, he was sure of that.

Once again they fell into a silence that allowed each man his own thoughts, each one trying to think of what was best for all of them.

There was something jumping around in Red's head, but he couldn't pin it down.

It was something he needed to remember; a nagging feeling like it might be important, but for the life of him, he couldn't think of what it might be. Maybe if he just let it go, then it would come to him, he thought, and just like that it was gone.

As they turned the corner Red looked up and stared at the large billboard on top of one of the buildings. And like a flash of lightning, it came to him. The girl in the picture on the billboard reminded him of that gal on the train, Jo Ann.

"Hey, I just thought of something. What about that guy Jo Ann told us about, you know, the one she said was her uncle or somethin'? She said he'd give us some help if we needed it and I think now would be about as good ah time as any. What'ya think?"

"William slapped himself on the forehead and said, "Of course. Why didn't I think of that?"

Joe put his arm around William's shoulder and said, "It doesn't matter which one of us remembered, just as long as one of us did. Now, where's the address. It was on a small piece of paper that you stuck in your pocket."

William searched his pockets, turning them wrong side out, but there was nothing that resembled a name and address.

"It must be back at the hotel," William said, weakly. "Yes I must have left it in my room."

William searched his room from top to bottom, every nook and cranny where the information might be, but came up empty each time. Finally, he slumped onto the bed with his head in his hands and said, "It's no use. . . It's not here. . . I've lost it."

Joe was pacing back and forth, slamming his fist into the palm of his hand.

"Think, man! What was the guy's name? His address? Anything that can give us a lead," Joe said as he stopped his pacing and looked down at William.

When William just sat there, Joe looked up at Red and said, "You talk to him. Tell him to think!"

Red laid his hand on William's shoulder and said in a gentle tone, "Calm down good buddy. Just try to relax and think back to the last time you saw the piece of paper and what you did with it. Go clear back to when she gave it to you, if you have to."

After a moment William raised his head and said, "It seems to me that I put it in the front pocket of my pants. . . Yes, I'm sure that's what I did with it."

"Which you left at the used clothing store this morning!" Red shouted in triumph, smiling at Joe like an attorney who had just solved the big case and won the jury at the same time.

The doorway to William's room got crowded when all three men tried to exit at the same time. But it was Joe who was in the lead as they ran down the stairs, through the lobby and out onto the sidewalk where he turned and ran for the clothing store. Red wasn't far behind, while William came huffing and puffing twenty steps to the rear.

Their heated energy was quickly deflated like air rushing out of a big balloon with a hole in it. Their hearts sank as they read the red and white sign on the front door that read, 'CLOSED'. It was like a barrier between them and their destiny.

"Damn the luck," Joe said as he glared at the sign.

"I reckon we'll just have ta come back in the mornin'," Red said as he pointed at a star just winking its way into the night. "Besides, it's way too late ta see the man today. I reckon he's already gone home."

Having to wait until morning seemed to be a major let down, but the truth was, there was nothing else they could do - short of breaking into the place, and they weren't about to do that.

The only thing they could do was to hope and pray that William's old pants would still be there, with the piece of paper still folded safely in the front pocket.

Back at the hotel, William purchased a newspaper for a nickel and Red bought a dime novel - a western.

"I've read a lot of these dime novels about the old west, but this is a new one. It might take my mind off things," Red said as they headed up the stairs.

"I guess I'll spend the evening looking the paper over from front to back," William declared as they neared his room. "Especially the help wanted section, if there is a help wanted section in this rag. And if they do, since we have a wide range of skills between us, maybe one of us will get lucky."

The Legend of Joe, Willy & Red

Joe patted William on the shoulder, "You do that, Willy boy. You do just that," he said as he walked to his door and slid the key into the lock. "I'll be seein' you boys in the morning. Get plenty of rest and ah good night's sleep. I want you gentlemen sharp when we go see that Sugar Daddy of Miss Jo Ann Fissella - especially you, Mister Willy the con man."

As Red entered his room, he called over his shoulder, "Right. And the same to you, too, big guy."

William's attitude was a bit more subdued as Joe's words wondered around in his head. "Sugar Daddy?" he mumbled to himself. "I thought she'd told them he was her uncle?"

Then he remembered what else she'd said after calling him, her uncle. She had added, 'if you know what I mean.' Only now did it come to him what she'd meant and it made him feel stupid.

And so, the night passed quietly with William and his young oriental girl enjoying dinner and listening to classical music.

Red was found in the company of the cute little blonde with red fingernails, who turned out to be a really nice gal who was originally from Texas.

Joe went dancing with his waitress and afterward, sat up until the wee hours, just talking.

Morning found Joe, William and Red pacing the sidewalk back and forth in front of the used clothing store, waiting for the man to come and open up.

When he finally arrived, the man was beside himself as he watched them tear the place apart looking for William's pants. He tried in vane to protest, but his words fell on deaf ears.

It was William who finally called out, "Here they are! They were right where I left them."

Joe and Red ran over to him as William pulled a small piece of paper out of the right front pocket and held it high over his head. "Here it is! Here it is! I found it! It was still

Jared McVay

there!" he shouted like a man who'd just won the Kentucky Derby.

"Well open it up and make sure it's what we're lookin' for," Joe said, bringing a halt to William's dancing.

It only took a moment before William screamed, "Yes!" and they headed for the front door.

The owner wiped his forehead with a rag and patted his chest. "Well, I'm certainly glad you finally found what you were looking for. Otherwise my store would have been demolished for sure," he said indignantly, as he rushed around picking up clothes that had been thrown on the floor.

Joe, William and Red stopped and looked around at the mess they'd made of the man's store. It did indeed look like a tornado had come charging through the place.

Joe collected a dollar apiece from Red and William and then walked over to the storeowner and handed him the three one-dollar bills.

"We're real sorry about this," Joe said, waving his arms around. "It's just that . . . that piece of paper was kinda important to us. It has the name and address of someone we need to find. But I guess we sort of got carried away. I hope this will help make up for the trouble we've caused you."

The storeowner smiled as he took the money and stuffed it deep into his pocket. This was as much as he'd hoped to make today. Looking at Joe, he said, "Sure, sure, you got money, you can search every pocket in the whole store."

After a quick breakfast at the diner and then a fast stop at their hotel rooms to make themselves presentable - William's idea - they got directions from the hotel clerk and then headed out to see the man Jo Ann Fissella called, her uncle - if you know what I mean.

The building turned out to be a three-story brick warehouse that overlooked the docks and the bay. A large sign on the front of the building said,

ABRAM SHIPPING AND WAREHOUSING COMPANY
HARRY ABRAM, PROP.

"Well boys, it looks like we've found dear old uncle Harry. Now, lets go see if he remembers his dear, sweet little ole niece," Red said as he opened the front door.

After climbing three flights of stairs, they found the door to his office. All three of them took a deep breath before entering.

The office was clean and had nice furniture, which surprised them; being in the location it was.

Sitting at a desk on the far side of the room was an elderly woman, maybe sixty years old and dressed very much like the spinster she was. She looked in their direction when they entered, took their measure, frowned and then resumed working at whatever it was she was doing before they entered.

As they neared her desk, William spoke up, "Excuse me, please. We're here to see Mister Harry Abram."

Without looking up, she asked, "Do you have an appointment?"

"Well.... no... not exactly... you see... we're here,"

"Mister Abram doesn't see anyone without an appointment. And if you're from the unions you're wasting your time. He does not grant appointments to any of your kind," she said, raising her head and boring a hole through them with a look of contempt. Her eyes were as cold and hard as a glacier.

It became instantly apparent that this woman was not only his secretary, but also his defense line for anyone she determined to be unworthy of his time. She made it very clear there would be no conference with Harry Abram without going through her, first.

Red nudged William in the back, trying to encourage him to say something that would allow them to walk through the door, marked, 'PRIVATE.'

Jared McVay

William took a step closer, clearly intimidated by this woman, cleared his throat and said, "Well. . . you see. . . we, ah. . . met his niece, and. . . well. . ."

The secretary raised her head once more, her eyes releasing all the rage and anger she could muster, making all three men feel as though they were facing, Attila the Hun.

Standing up to her full height of five feet, two inches, she said, "I don't care who you met, or who you say you know. I don't even care if you say you're related to him. If you don't have an appointment, you cannot see Mister Abram. Do I make myself clear? And I hope you won't make me repeat myself. Now, will you please leave! Or do you prefer I call the police? It makes no difference to me. So, which will it be?"

Joe placed his hand on William's shoulder, drawing him back two steps, then stepped up to her desk and said as politely as he could so she wouldn't see the rage he was feeling.

"No, ma'am, there's no call to bring in the police. We'll leave quietly. But just for the record, we're not with any union and we're not salesmen, nor are we looking for a handout. . . Just wanted you to know that. Sorry to have taken up your valuable time."

By the time Joe had finished having his say, Miss Iceberg of 1933, had already dismissed them and was back at her paperwork.

As they reached the door and were about to leave, there was a commotion and the door marked, 'PRIVATE', swung open as a burly man in his sixties came escorting another man, none too easy like, out through the door.

The man being thrown out looked scared and gave no resistance. The heavyset man they assumed to be, Harry Abram, shoved the man toward the front door and said,

"You come around here again and I swear I will break every bone in your body, and I'll take pleasure in doing it! Now get out and don't come back!" he screamed as the man ran past them and out the door.

The Legend of Joe, Willy & Red

He was about to turn back toward his office when he noticed Joe, William and Red standing there. "What the hell do you want?" he yelled.

William took a half a step forward and said, "Jo Ann requested we stop by and talk with you."

Harry glared at them and said, "I don't know anybody named, Jo Ann. Now get outta here!"

With that, Harry Abram spun on his heel and headed for his office.

"The man is apparently in a foul mood for some reason and just possibly we have chosen an inopportune time to come calling," William whispered to Joe and Red. "I think we should leave and possibly come back tomorrow."

"Tomorrow? I don't care if I never see him or that old, bony necked secretary of his again as long as I live," Joe said in a voice, loud and clear.

Harry Abram had just placed his hand on the doorknob to his office and heard Joe's speech. He held the doorknob in his hand for a moment and then spun around and walked toward them.

Joe balled his hands into fists and stepped forward two steps in front of William and Red. This whole situation had grated on his nerves and put him in the mood for a fight. Mister Harry Abram would find out Joe Wilson could not be tossed out as easily as that other dude. Before he went, he would put a big hurt on Mister Harry Abram that he wouldn't soon forget and he'd enjoy doin' it, too.

Harry Abram was half way across the office floor, with a curious look on his face when he said, "Gentlemen, please, wait just a minute." When he got close, he said, "Jo Ann, who?"

William stepped up next to Joe and spoke as quietly as he could, even though he knew the secretary was eavesdropping as she pretended to work at her desk and would not miss a word.

"Jo Ann Fissella, from Chicago. She asked us to look you up when we got to San Francisco. That's why we're here. At her request, you see."

Harry Abram's whole attitude changed immediately. His eyes began to twinkle as a broad grin spread across his face. He opened his arms wide like he was welcoming a long lost friend.

"So, you know my favorite niece?" he said - now looking like a big kid, grinning from ear to ear at Christmas time.

"Yes-sir, we sorta met her on a train, you might say," Red said, encouraged by the man's change of attitude.

Both William and Joe gave Red a look that told him to be careful what he said, as Harry herded them toward his office.

"Why didn't you say so in the first place? Come into my office, gentlemen. We have much to talk about."

The stiff-necked secretary eyed them coldly as they walked into Harry Abram's office.

Joe gave her a big grin as they passed her desk. The pencil she was holding in her fingers broke in two with a loud snap, which pleased Joe to no end.

Chapter 26
The Proposition

Harry Abram's office was larger than the reception area. The furniture was done in good taste. More than likely a decorator had been hired to do both rooms.

Floor to ceiling bookshelves filled one wall and several file cabinets stood against another. Harry's desk was a huge, wooden affair that was polished to a bright sheen of mahogany color and sat with it's back to a line of four windows that overlooked the bay.

The desk was covered with papers and manifests and other things. Harry's chair was large and smelled of polished leather. In front of the desk sat two overstuffed chairs that also smelled of polished leather.

On the far side of the room, there was an oval table with six chairs that fit in with the décor. To this table and chairs, Harry directed his guests.

"Sit down, sit down, please. Relax. Make yourselves comfortable... Can I get you something to drink?" he said as he walked across to a bar in the corner of the room, which was hidden by louvered doors, giving the impression that it was a closet.

"I know it's a bit early in the day, but how about a beer? Its very good beer, even if I do say so, myself. I make it from an old German recipe that has been in my family for several generations."

Even though it was still morning, a good, cold bottle of homemade German beer sounded good to Joe - except sitting around drinking beer wasn't why they were here.

Joe watched Harry take four bottles of beer out of the refrigerator behind the bar and then head back to the table. When he arrived, Joe decided to come right to it.

"I'm not one for beatin' around the bush, Mister Abram. The reason we're here is to see you about getting some work. Jo Ann told us you might need some good hands, which we are, and well, that's why we're here. So if you don't want to waste your good homemade beer on us, we'll understand."

Harry smiled that broad, boyish like grin he had and set a bottle of cold beer on the table in front of each man, then took a chair himself.

"We'll talk about that later," he said with a twinkle in his eyes. "First, I want you to tell me all about Jo Ann. Is she alright? I heard she had some trouble back in Chicago, and then just up and disappeared."

Leaving his beer untouched, William cleared his throat and said, "Yes, there was a bit of trouble back in Chicago. But when we last saw her in Salt Lake City, she was just fine."

During the time William was talking to Harry, a smile crossed Joe's face and his eyes began to glow, as a new side of him was about to make itself known. The ornery side of Joe's personality was about to show itself.

After taking a long pull on his beer, Joe said, "Actually, Mister Abram, Willy boy here is being way too modest. You see, when we first met, 'your niece,' she had been hurt real bad."

Joe took another sip of his cold beer to let the information sink in, then continued.

"As we found out later, some guys back in Chicago had beaten her up pretty bad and tossed her into an empty freight car headed west. And, well. . . to make a long story short, ole Willy here, well. . . he made sure Jo Ann got medical attention."

Harry Abram was by now sitting ramrod straight in his chair and acting nervous.

"Medical attention? I thought you said she was fine," he said, looking at William.

"What hospital is she in?" he said, slamming the open bottle of beer down on the table causing it to foam over and spill onto the table.

The Legend of Joe, Willy & Red

With William beginning to sweat, Red decided to join in on the fun. "Now you just relax, Mister Abram," Red said in that good ole boy way he had. "She is fine as frog hair and goin' strong. And she's not in the hospital anymore. When ole Willy boy here, found out she was okay, bein' the kind of fella he is, he made all the arrangements ta get her released. Shortly after that is when she told us to look you up if we got out this way."

Harry Abram came around the table and grabbed William by the hand and began pumping it up and down profusely, while patting him on the back with his other hand.

William glared at his two friends for putting him in a predicament; hoping Mister Abram wouldn't notice his heart pounding like a jackhammer.

"Makes me proud to shake the hand of a man like you. Jo Ann is a mighty fine young lady. It's good to know there's still men around like you who care; not enough would have."

Harry turned and walked over to his desk and picked up his pen. "The very least I can do is reimburse you for your expenses. How much was her hospital bill?" he asked, opening his checkbook.

Joe and Red turned and looked at William to see what he would do.

William stared down at his lap while his mind raced at the speed of light, trying to think of something. After a moment, he said, "Thank you, sir, but, the truth is, I never actually spent any out of pocket money to get her released from the hospital."

Harry sat down in the chair behind his desk and asked, "What are you saying, young man?"

"You see. . . as it turned out, there were some unsavory characters hanging out around the nurses station, asking questions about her and if she could travel; you know, things like that."

~ 237 ~

"And you thought they might be the same ones who had caused her harm, back in Chicago?" Harry asked, with real concern in his eyes.

"Possibly," William said as sincerely as he could. "Or friends of theirs. Either way, I, we," William said, pointing at Joe and Red," felt it wouldn't be in Jo Ann's best interest if they got their hands on her, and neither did she. So, we sort of sneaked her out the back way."

Joe and Red were struggling to keep a straight face and not burst out laughing as they sat there and watched Willy the con work his verbal magic.

"Gentlemen," Harry said, "I'm impressed. That took bravery and cunning. They were at the very least, men who worked for the mob. I knew she was about to testify against one of them in court. They have people everywhere. And I'm sure every hospital in the country was being watched. It just may be that you saved her life, and for that I will be eternally grateful."

Joe, William and Red looked at each other, wondering what the term, eternally and grateful actually meant to Harry Abram.

Harry stood up and leaned his fists on the top of the desk. "As you have correctly suspected, Jo Ann and I aren't really blood kin. But she is very special to me - and I do mean very special."

There being no need to speak, Joe, William and Red sat in their chairs, sipped their beer and waited for Harry to continue.

Harry stared at the ceiling for a moment, then slumped into his chair. "Salt Lake City, huh. Did she say where she was going from there? Did she mention coming to San Francisco?" he asked, hopefully.

William was in his stride now and looked Harry straight in the eyes as he spoke.

"We did ask her if she wanted to come along, urged her as I recall, but she said to tell you that she would see you

The Legend of Joe, Willy & Red

soon. I believe she was going to see a relative, to rest up and let her bruises heal. It had been quite an ordeal for her."

William took a short pause and took a sip of his beer. He was beginning to enjoy this. "At any rate, she gave us your name and address and said to come and see you if we decided to look for work, here. Mister Abram, we're not looking for a handout, and we're not looking for sympathy - or even a reward. We're just three men who have been caught up in the system and are looking for honest work. Jo Ann believed that you could possibly be of some help."

When William finished speaking, he looked directly at Harry Abram, and knew he had reached something in the man. He could see it in his eyes. He had accomplished exactly what he set out to do - get the man on their side. He was in their debt and honor bound.

"And she was right, too!" Harry shouted.

Joe, William and Red, all gave a silent, sigh.

Joe shook his head, thinking, 'Willy the con had come through, again. The man was good when the chips were down'. Had he been in Harry Abram's shoes he would have bought the story, himself.

While on the other hand, Red was quietly congratulating himself on his good luck to have fallen in with these two guys. He could have gotten tangled up with a couple of nobody's and still be stuck in ah hobo camp out there somewhere, or maybe back down in Texas, waitin' ta stretch a rope. He'd had an adventure that he would be able to tell his kids and grandkids about, someday, if he ever had any.

Harry reached across his desk to the cedar-lined box where he kept his cigars. He was always at his best when he was puffing on a good Cuban cigar. It was an old habit that allowed him to think before making any rash decisions and he needed that moment right now.

The truth was, Harry Abram had been expecting them. He knew they would be coming to see him sooner or later. Jo Ann had called him and told him the whole story a couple of days ago. So, when they showed up today, he decided to make a game of it - give them some rope to see if they hung themselves. But in the end, they hadn't.

Oh yea, their version was somewhat different from Jo Ann's version. But even so, it wasn't so far a field as to be unbelievable. And it was definitely understandable why they had left out certain details - like that William guy throwing her off the train, which at first had made him mad. But when Jo Ann explained it to him, he was able to let his anger go and forgive him. Especially when she asked him not to be mad at them - she wasn't. And in the end, he knew he'd do whatever she asked him to do.

At any rate, they had helped her get away from the Chicago police and possibly the mob as well. Those men coming from Chicago may or may not have actually been from the police department, and if they were, it was more than likely they were on the mob's payroll. And if they had gotten their hands on her, Jo Ann would probably be at the bottom of some river by now.

Harry didn't think these three men really knew the danger they faced when they sneaked Jo Ann out of the hospital. But that was in the past. They had all gotten away without anyone getting hurt and because of that he was truly grateful, which meant he would overlook any slight deviations from the truth, which he also found interesting.

After lighting his cigar, Harry leaned back in his overstuffed desk chair, letting an idea take shape in his mind. And after a couple of moments, Harry sat upright.

"What can you boys do? I mean, what kind of work did you do before you came to San Francisco? I assume you did have jobs?"

"I'm very good with figures. I worked in a bank for the past nine years," William said, proudly.

"I'm ah fair ta medlin' mechanic. I know both gasoline and diesel engines and the electrical workin's of cars and trucks," Red said with a big grin.

The Legend of Joe, Willy & Red

Looking at Joe, Harry asked, "How about you, big guy. You look like a man who can handle men. Ever done anything like that?"

"Some," Joe said nonchalantly. "I worked on the docks for several years, cargo handling mostly - roustabout at first, then crane operator. Did some foreman work for a few years, mostly big freighters."

Mister Harry Abrams stared at the three men, taking their measure.

Joe decided that a little information wouldn't hurt, as long as the man didn't get too nosy about what docks or what city; not that his work history was bad because it wasn't. In fact the big bosses had always liked him and the way he handled both men and equipment. It was that bum murder rap he wasn't keen for Harry Abram to find out about.

Fortunately for Joe, Harry Abrams had other things on his mind. Plus, he had already pretty much made up his mind about these three men. He just needed a little more information.

As of late, there were things that were worrying him to distraction. He took a puff from his cigar and slowly blew the smoke into the room.

"Are any of you boys part of the union, or union organizing?" Harry asked, staring intently in their direction, cigar smoke circling his head in a cloud of blue that drifted slowly toward the ceiling.

When all three men shook their heads, 'no,' Harry continued. "That man you saw me throw out of here a few minutes ago was a no good union organizer! He is the scum of the earth!"

Harry's voice was beginning to rise and his face was getting red, along with his blood pressure going sky high.

"I pay good wages and I take care of the people who work for me, on or off the job, and I don't need some dumb ass union man coming in here and telling me how to run my business!"

By now, Harry was wound up tighter than one of those rubber bands you use on one of those little airplanes.

"They'll ruin a man's business and I won't have it. I've talked to all the men who work for me and they're satisfied with the way things are." he said. "But I can't always be around when they show up. I need somebody on my team that I can trust," Harry said with conviction.

When none of them said anything, Harry propped both his elbows on his desk and leaned his chin into the palms of his hands and studied each man with meticulous care.

His efforts were rewarded by one of the things he regarded highly in a man. To a man, they looked right back at him with no signs of fear. Not one of them squirmed in his chair or shifted to avert his look. No-sir, they stared right back at him, and that was what made up his mind for him.

"You boys wouldn't mind going abroad for awhile, would you? Get out and see the world for, say, six months or so?" Harry asked with mischief in his eyes.

Joe was the one to speak. And then it was brief and to the point. "Are you making an offer of some kind?"

"Gentlemen, I'll not beat around the bush," Harry said as he sat back and relit his cigar. "As I said earlier, I need people on my team; people who will be loyal to me and the people who work for me - people I can trust to be my eyes and ears against those union organizers."

With nothing more than eye contact, Joe, William and Red all silently agreed that this was not what they were looking for. And with Joe leading the way, all three of them stood up and headed for the door.

Harry Abram took a long puff on his cigar before he spoke.

"Gentlemen, please. Just hear me out. I didn't mean to give the impression that I was looking for snitches. Far from it," he said in a sincere tone.

They all stopped and turned. But instead of going back to their chairs, they stood looking at him, waiting for

The Legend of Joe, Willy & Red

an explanation. If they didn't like what they heard, they would be out the door and gone.

Harry laid his cigar in the big ashtray on his desk, and then stood up, meeting their stares. He pulled a handkerchief from his hip pocket, blew his nose and returned the handkerchief to his back pocket before he started walking in their direction, giving himself a moment before confronting these three, stone-faced men.

They were strong men who couldn't be treated as common day laborers. And he needed them more than they needed him.

He wasn't smiling now. He was serious as a heartbeat. He needed to be straight forward, with no fancy words or empty promises.

Stopping directly in front of them he said, "Please, hear me out. When I'm done, if you still want to leave, I won't try to stop you," he said as he indicated for them to sit in the chairs once more.

When they were seated, Harry folded his arms across his chest and said, "I have a ship leaving tomorrow for the orient. And without any doubt, there will be several union organizers on board, disguised in several areas of the work force. They will not only disrupt my crew, but will do anything and everything they can to see that the cargo is trashed as well. It will be their jobs to see that my company either goes union or goes bankrupt. I don't say the unions aren't needed in some places - they are. But not in mine because I look after my people like they're family."

Harry walked over to his desk and took a sip from his bottle of beer, then went on with his presentation. "I know all of the regular members of my crews. They're good men. The union organizers are slipped in when we need extra help and I do not want to lose my men or the company because of a few bad apples in the barrel, who can spoil the whole barrel."

Harry took another sip from his bottle of beer and a puff from his cigar. "Not only do I pay higher than normal

~ 243 ~

Jared McVay

wages, but I also give bonuses at the end of every trip. It's my way of saying thank you for a job well done; plus, it makes for a smooth running ship and that means a lot in my business."

After a brief pause, Harry shook his head and said, "I know every man who works for me by name, as well as their families - you can ask any of them. Good wages and working conditions, along with sharing the profits is what makes Abram's shipping what it is - a happy family."

"Then why don't you get one of them to do the squealin' for you?" Joe asked.

Harry looked directly at Joe. "I'm not looking for squealers, as you so aptly put it. I'm looking for men to work directly with the captain, whom I trust explicitly. And I don't expect these men to just run crying to the captain, either. I want them to keep their ears and eyes open - to find out what their plan is and then, and only then, with the captain, plan a strategy to stifle their attempts, without the crew having anything to do with it if they don't have to. In other words, I don't want the crew in harm's way or connected so they or their families can be harmed, then or later."

Harry took another puff from his cigar before saying, "You will be working with the captain exclusively. Even the crew won't know who you really are."

"Let me get this straight, Mister Abram," William said. "You want us, the three of us, to sabotage the saboteurs. Like undercover agents, or something. Except we work for you. Is that about the jest of it?"

Harry thought for no more than a second, and then, grinning broadly, said, "I do believe you've hit the nail squarely on the head. And it is my firm belief that the three of you could do very well in this line of work, yes, very well indeed. And the pay would be handsome, plus allowing the three of you to, let's say, disappear for a while."

At that moment, the realization of his meaning, slammed into their brains like a giant steel ball slamming into the side of a brick building. Of course! Jo Ann had called

The Legend of Joe, Willy & Red

him and told him all about what had happened. He'd known about Jo Ann all along, but let them play their hands out to see where they would go with it. This had all been a big test and they had apparently passed. Life sure had some mind-boggling twists of fate.

"May we discuss this privately?" William asked.

"Sure, sure. Take your time. Have another bottle of beer. I'll be in the other room.

Just open the door when you're finished," Harry said as he made his way out.

The boys discussed the fact that Harry had known about them all along and said nothing. At first, they were puzzled as to why, but Joe explained it to their satisfaction. He said Harry was sizing them up - seeing if they were just hustlers or regular guys prior to making a decision whether to offer them jobs, or not. They must have passed the test or Harry never would have mentioned the jobs. He went on to say that it was his belief that Harry had been won over when William told him they weren't looking for rewards, just a job. And Joe also believed that Harry needed someone or some ones who had the chutzpa to carry off his plan.

After a little more discussion, they decided to take Harry up on his offer. Not only would the job get them out of the country for awhile and let things cool down a bit, but they would have three squares a day, a place to live, money in their pockets and a new adventure to look forward to.

Plus, none of them had ever been to the orient. Red and William had never even been out of the United States - although Red did mention something about a weekend in a Mexican border town, but that really didn't count. The orient, a land filled with many mysteries and. . . And just where in the orient were they going? As far as any of them could remember, he hadn't said, exactly. That was a question they would have to ask.

"Well I for one ain't worried. My gut feelin' is, he's a good man and he'll take real good care of us. And I'm not worried about those union guys, either. They can't be any

~ 245 ~

Jared McVay

worse than some of the creeps we've dealt with - like those railroad bulls. I'll bet we can handle ourselves real good," Red said. "Why, I'll tell ya for ah fact, with Willy here doin' the talkin' and me and Joe..."

Joe clamped his hand over Red's mouth, while William guided him to a chair, where they sat him down before Red could get himself more worked up than he already was.

"We get your meaning. Now just calm down a mite, okay?" Joe said.

Red nodded his head and Joe took his hand away from Red's mouth as William walked over and opened the door and motioned for Harry to come back in.

Harry was delighted at their decision and had his secretary call the captain of the ship and request that he come over immediately. He also told her to order lunch - to be brought in from the Chinese restaurant just down the street.

While they waited on lunch and the captain, Harry told them they would be going to New Zealand, Australia and Hawaii and then back home.

When William asked about the orient, Harry told him that was just to throw them off the track in case things didn't work out.

Harry went on to explain their pay plan. Each of them would receive two hundred dollars a month, cash, along with a bonus of one thousand dollars apiece if they brought the mission to a successful ending.

They would not, for obvious reasons, be on the regular payroll, or even crew list, except for ports of entry. Harry also asked them to think up phony names to go by just in case things didn't go as planned, that way the union people would be hard pressed to track them down.

He didn't like to talk about that side of it, but in all reality, these things need to be discussed and planned for. It was also his hope that, somehow, the saboteurs might be accidentally left on shore in Australia - with no identification papers, of course. Harry also hoped that paperwork of how the union was planning to take over all the shipping trade might somehow be found on one or both of the abandoned men. He said he would leave that to them and the captain's discretion.

When the captain arrived, Joe, William and Red, each scrutinized him carefully from the moment he entered the room.

Like Harry Abram, the captain was a large man of the same age and demeanor. But one thing Joe noticed in particular, were the captain's hands. He had big ham like hands with scars on his knuckles. For Joe, that meant the man had sand, and that was important if they were going to work together.

For William it was the captain's voice and he listened carefully. The man's voice had a nice resonance to it, which William believed to be a baritone. And when the man spoke, his voice had that certain quality to it that said, authority, yet friendly. He took an instant liking to the captain and the man.

Last but not least, Red liked, not only the way the man shook hands, but that something in his eyes that said he could be trusted. The handshake, his father had told him, was where it all started when you were sizing up another man, and the captain's handshake had been firm, but not crushing, even though the man's hands were large enough to do so.

Next came the eyes. He'd read somewhere that the eyes were the mirrors of the soul and to Red's satisfaction, that theory had proven true many times.

Maybe fifteen minutes after the captain's arrival, the young man from the Chinese restaurant arrived with enough food to feed an army. After paying the bill and giving the young man a nice tip for being so speedy, he told his secretary to fix herself a plate, and should anyone want to see him, to tell them he was not available until tomorrow.

She gave Joe, William and Red an icy look and then nodded to Harry.

After fixing her plate, she walked primly out of the room. They would not be interrupted.

Chapter 27
The Shortcut

Standing near the edge of the bay, its waters lapping the shore not far from their feet, Joe, William and Red looked around to make sure no one could see or hear them. When it was apparent they were alone, they cut loose with whoops and yells as they danced around like wild men, while overhead a dozen sea gulls cawed at these crazy humans who were disturbing their normal activity.

It seemed that good fortune had smiled on them at last. They had the world by the tail and they had no intentions of letting go.

Red did a war dance as he chanted, "Thank you Jo Ann. Thank you Harry Abram and your wonderful shipping company. And thank you Willy for throwing Jo Ann off the train in the first place!"

After shaking hands with Harry Abram to seal the bargain, Harry had given them a hundred dollars apiece - a sign on bonus, he'd called it. "Just a little something to see you through to your first payday."

Harry Abram was happy to share his wealth, especially if he could see a return, and the scheme they had devised should allow his shipping to continue operating like a well-oiled machine and showing a substantial profit.

He was also instrumental in selecting their new names. Since there were three of them, Harry thought it would be a kick to coin the old phrase, Tom, Dick and Harry. So, William would be called, Tom Snow, in reference to the snow each winter in Minnesota. Joe was dubbed, Dick York, because he was from New York, and Red got the name, Harry Longhorn in honor of the famous cattle from Texas.

They laughed at their new names as they ate lunch and discussed Harry's plan, which left an area for them and the captain to improvise should they need to.

Jared McVay

After lunch, with the plan agreed on, the captain took them aboard the freighter and gave them a tour from the tower to the engine room and all the freight areas; along with introducing them to various members of the crew that they came in contact with.

Joe, in particular, noticed how cheerful the crew seemed to be and the familiarity with which they spoke to the captain, which was different than the crews he'd met and known in the east. Plus, the ship was cleaner than the ones back east. Everywhere he looked, the ship was freshly painted and in tip-top condition and the crew was dressed better than the ones he'd seen on any other ship.

For the first time, Joe was finally beginning to believe what Harry Abram had said about treating his people well. If this was the way it was going to be, working for Harry was going to be the best job he'd ever had. Yes, he could find a home here.

The captain took them to the dining room, where they had coffee and discussed what each man's job would be and where they could store their personal gear and what the sleeping arrangements would be. Both Joe and Red would eat and sleep with the crew, while William, as bookkeeper, would have accommodations to himself - a small stateroom where they could meet and talk in privacy.

The captain preferred they meet in William's stateroom rather than his quarters because it would be less suspicious that way. Also, William was to eat with the officers so he could keep an ear and eye open in that area - even though the captain assured him that that was one area where infiltration was safe from union organizers. Even so they would take no chances that one of his officers had been compromised.

Joe, or Dick, as he was now called, would be one of the men in charge of cargo, which allowed him free access above and below decks in the cargo areas.

The Legend of Joe, Willy & Red

Red, or Harry, as a mechanical and electrical technician, slash, inspector would be free to roam the entire ship, making friends and listening to the gossip.

William, or Tom, was the only one who was somewhat confined, but not entirely. Even though his job as bookkeeper kept him stuck to a desk most of the time, as the owner's pincher of pennies, he was free to poke around anywhere he pleased. With a handful of manifests, he could be found checking new pieces of equipment, purchased items, like food or medicines. Bookkeepers had full run of the ship and an open ear.

They all agreed it was an ideal arrangement and for some reason never brought up the fact that this game they were playing, could turn out to be dangerous.

They would find out who the union men were and what they planned to do; and then make sure it didn't happen. It was as simple as that.

Tom, or William was already devising a scheme to leave the union men ashore in Australia, without passports, nearly broke and their plans for wrecking the shipping industry hidden on each man's body.

The captain said he could hardly wait to see what kind of scheme William came up with.

Given the opportunity to move aboard immediately, they told the captain they would bring their things aboard within the next couple of hours, but in all likelihood be spending their last night ashore, to take care of some unfinished business.

Knowingly, the captain smiled and bid them an enjoyable evening.

Now, ten minutes after leaving the ship, they stood near the edge of the bay - laughing and hollering like men who'd lost their minds, causing the sea gulls to squawk and fly around in circles wondering what these fool creatures were up to.

Had anyone seen them, they would have believed the depression had finally gotten to them and the only thing left was to have the men in white coats come and pick them up with their nets and straightjackets - then haul them away to the funny farm.

But, fortunately, there was no one around to see them or call for the men in the white coats, and when the laughter calmed down, William waved his arms and said,

"Gentlemen, gentlemen, enough. I believe we have matters to attend to and I suggest we get them taken care of. Tomorrow we begin a new adventure; one that may prove to be the best of our lives, but tonight." William let the sentence trail off, knowing each man had his own plans, which he hoped would include spending his time with the beautiful oriental woman, May Wong, who was quickly becoming someone he could talk and share common interests with.

"The captain said the ship weighs anchor at ten o'clock tomorrow mornin'," Red stated. "I reckon that means that's when the ship leaves, right?"

"That is precisely what it means, landlubber," Joe said with a grin. "So exactly what is your point?"

Red squinted his eyes and looked toward the sky.

"Well. . . I was just thinkin', since none of us have much ta take with us, we could wait until tomorrow mornin' and take it with us then."

"A splendid idea," William chimed in. "We could meet at the diner at, say, around eight o'clock tomorrow morning, have breakfast, and still get to the ship with plenty of time to spare."

"Well then, I guess it's settled," Joe said, grinning, his mind already thinking of the extra time he'd be able to spend with Patricia King, the gorgeous waitress from the diner and how he was going to explain to her why he would be leaving so soon.

Leaving her would be his only regret. There was nothing or no one else to hold him here. He had no family. In fact he'd never heard a word about his parents since the day they deserted him. And because he'd always been a loner,

The Legend of Joe, Willy & Red

he'd never let anyone get inside the invisible shell that protected him by keeping them at arms length. But now it all came pounding down on him like a heavy weight on his shoulders.

Suddenly, it seemed to Joe that his entire life had been based on leaving, only this time it felt different, somehow more painful. Leaving Patricia seemed akin to cutting out a part of him and leaving it behind, and not sure it would be here when he returned. And not sure what he would do if it wasn't. It wasn't like they were engaged or anything. You let somebody inside your shell and right away there's complications.

Absorbed with his thoughts, Joe had unconsciously dropped a few steps behind Red and William.

Neither of them seemed to have a care in the world. They were deeply engaged in conversation about what living on board a large ship would be like and what it would be like to have hot showers, three meals a day and a decent place to sleep every night.

Red wondered if they would get sea sick, and what they would do when they reached New Zealand, Australia and Hawaii. There would be so many places to see.

It was like Red and William were just beginning to live. From here on they would be living in a world filled with hopes, dreams and fantasies. They would be like gypsies.

For Joe, it was totally different. It was like he was beginning to see the world for the first time, and it all looked and felt different. Had the change started when he first met William? He wasn't sure, but he thought that might have been when it was.

Joe wasn't sure he believed in the super natural powers that be and all that crap, but his life and the way he looked and felt about things sure had changed a lot since he hooked up with William and Red. He shook himself out of his reverie. This was all too much to think about right now. He needed to clear his mind.

Jared McVay

Propped against a building was a lean jawed man with several days' growth of beard on his face, playing a lively tune on an old concertina. His clothes were clean but patched in several places. Next to the man stood a pair of crutches.

Joe looked down and noticed the man's foot and part of his leg was missing and on the sidewalk in front of him was an old cigar box with thirty cents in it.

Joe dropped a five-dollar bill into the box and continued on.

"Thank you, friend," the man called to him. "My wife and I can eat for a week on that," he said as he began playing with wild abandon.

Joe waved his hand in the air as he hurried on down the sidewalk. He'd given money to people on the street before, but it had never felt like this. This time he felt like he was actually helping someone. The money would be used to buy food for the man and his wife, not back alley rotgut.

Joe decided that later he would take some time and give these new feelings a whole lot more thought, but right now he had a pretty little gal to see who had eyes so deep blue they could swallow you up like sinking into a shimmering pool and kisses that could melt an iceberg,

And on the other side of the coin, she was smart, and easy to talk to. She could talk intelligently on almost any subject you wanted to talk about and hold her own in a debate as well.

For the past two years she'd been taking a business course three nights a week at the university. She was saving her money and when this depression finally came to an end, she planned to open a chain of stores that catered exclusively to women. Her professor was helping her put the plan on paper.

Joe looked up and noticed that farther down the sidewalk, William and Red were escorting two men into a diner. He hurried up and watched through the front window as his friends paid for two meals with all the trimmings;

The Legend of Joe, Willy & Red

even desert. The two men couldn't seem to thank William and Red enough.

Joe noticed that one of them had no teeth, but planned on tackling a big, juicy steak anyway. Joe smiled as the picture ran through his mind.

Back on the sidewalk, William said, "Makes a man feel good to be able to share his good fortune."

Joe nodded as he thought of the man with no foot and only part of his leg.

Two blocks down the street, Red stopped next to the entryway to an alleyway and called out to Joe and William, "Hey guys, I think if we cut down this alley it will put us on the same street as the hotel. Make ah nice shortcut. What'ya think?"

Joe shrugged his shoulders and entered the alley along with Red. But as William started to follow, a cold feeling of danger swept over him like an ill wind blowing in from the sea.

William stopped and looked around, searching for the danger he felt - but could see nothing that would cause him to feel this way. Still, as he started into the alley, he broke out in a sweat that he couldn't explain.

He raised his hand and started to call out to his friends, but what could he tell them? That he was afraid of an empty alley. Except for a car parked at the far end of the alley with a man sitting behind the steering wheel, smoking a cigarette, the alley was empty.

"Com'on, Pokey," Red called over his shoulder.

William wiped sweat from his forehead onto the sleeve of his jacket, hesitating as Joe and Red walked deeper into the alley. William watched, but nothing happened.

Then he remembered; as a young boy, he'd been chased down an alley by a big, mean dog. As he recalled, he'd been around ten at the time. That was it! It was just a memory from his past. It was as simple as that.

William took another look around and saw no mean dog ready to attack him as he hurried to catch up with his friends.

Had William had the wisdom of a fortuneteller, he would not have entered the alley, nor would he have allowed his friends to enter it, either. He would have found some way to persuade them to go the long way around.

But he did not have such wisdom, only a gut feeling - and that he misread.

Chapter 28

The Man In The Car

The man who was sitting in the car smoking a cigarette saw the three men as they came toward him and hoped they would hurry on by and not get curious about what he was doing sitting in a car with the motor running. He didn't want complications.

But the fickle finger of fate must have been having a field day full of mischief, for Red could not have picked a worse time to enter this particular alley and the danger it held at this moment in time.

To the left of the far entrance to the alley was a bank, and at that very moment, was being held up at gunpoint by three men; men who very much resembled, Joe, Red and William.

Except for the president, the tellers and an elderly guard, the bank was empty as the three men came charging in just as the elderly guard was about to lock the door.

The curtains had already been drawn, so no one from outside could see what was happening.

The job had been well thought out and planned down to the last detail. The whole job should take no more than five minutes. The bank president had assured them this would be a sweet deal that would make them all rich.

The guard was knocked down and disarmed by the first man through the door. The second man came charging in with a shotgun and stuck the end of the barrel in the president's face as he winked at him.

"You got two choices, mister bank president. Give us your money or get your head blown off."

"Don't argue with them. Just give them the money and we'll be all right," the bank president said to his tellers as he stared down the business end of the shotgun.

Jared McVay

The third man, the short, fat one was already passing out bags to the tellers who immediately began filling them, while the first man who'd come through the door; the one who had disarmed the guard, leaped over the counter with a large bag and entered the open vault and began stuffing money into his bag.

At the same time, Joe, William and Red were walking past the big sedan where the man was sitting. As they walked past, Joe threw his arms over William and Red's shoulders.

"Ya know life sure is funny. Yesterday we were on the run, didn't know where our next meal was coming from and now here we are with good paying jobs that allows us to take a ship ride across the big pond to erotic places like New Zealand, Australia and Hawaii. How's that for ironic?"

"Yea, life sure is crazy, ain't it? Ya never know from one minute to the next what's gonna happen," Red said.

William forced a smile along with his two friends, but there was no real joy in it because the feeling of danger was still with him. Just because there wasn't a mean dog snapping at his heels, didn't mean he wasn't there.

William took a deep breath, trying to steady his nerves. The end of the alley and freedom was just ahead.

Glancing over his shoulder, William suddenly felt a shiver run down his spine as he noticed that smoke was coming out of the tailpipe of the car. Why would someone be sitting in an alley with the engine running, he wondered?

Suddenly, he wanted to run, get out of this alley as fast as he could and take Joe and Red with him. His heart began to pound and his breathing became labored, but he couldn't run. In fact his legs didn't want to move at all. It was like his feet were glued to the alley. He felt like he was hyperventilating and he couldn't speak.

The man in the car tossed what was left of his cigarette out of the window and glanced in the side view mirror.

The Legend of Joe, Willy & Red

The three men had stopped and the fat one was staring in his direction. After a moment, the man gave a sigh of relief as the other two men, forced the fat man into moving again, in the direction of the end of the alley.

The fat man balked at first, but finally gave in and continued on down the alley with his two friends.

Chapter 29

Mistaken Identity

The first glitch in this well thought out plan where nothing can go wrong when robbing a bank, was believing that they had all of the angles covered. Their second mistake was that no one checked the guard for a gun other than the one he had in his holster.

So, as the three bank robbers backed toward the door with their sacks of money, they never suspected having any trouble.

Why the old guard reached beneath his jacket and pulled out a thirty-two-caliber hide out gun from his shoulder holster instead of just lying there until they were gone is still a mystery.

Maybe it can be attributed to the fact that he was first, last and always an officer of the law and had been his entire adult life. He'd taken this job two years prior, when he retired from the police department after forty years of faithful service.

Between his bad eyesight and awkward position face down on the floor, it made it difficult for him to roll over quickly and take aim. And in his haste, he pulled the trigger of his gun six times as fast as he could, shooting in their general direction.

His first bullet hit one of the bank robbers in the thigh, while the other bullets, missed their targets by inches and killed the wall and a door.

More from nervous reaction than anything else, the robber carrying the shotgun swung the barrel in the guard's direction and pulled the trigger.

A loud boom reverberated off the walls of the bank, rattled the windows, and in less than the blink of an eye, the guard's face disappeared as the pellets ripped into his brain.

The Legend of Joe, Willy & Red

The guard's retirement was now permanent and there was no more resistance as the robbers exited the bank.

The boys were nearing the end of the alley when they heard the loud blast of the shotgun. William jumped like he'd been snake-bit, his heart racing a hundred miles an hour and his eyes wide with fright as he searched for the demons he was sure would be attacking them.

"What was that?" he screamed, looking back down the alley.

"It was just ah truck backfirin'," Red said, staring at him.

"Why are you so jumpy all of a sudden?" Joe asked.

Still wild eyed, William tried to calm his frazzled nerves. He was just being overly sensitive again, he told himself as he turned away, too embarrassed to let his friends see him this way.

Joe looked at Red, who just shrugged his shoulders, as both of them wondered what had come over William so suddenly. They'd never seen him this nervous.

"So, do you want to tell us what's wrong?" Joe asked. "You've been jumpy ever since we started down this alley."

"It's nothing, just an old fear of alleys. Com'on let's get out of here," William said.

The man in the car had also heard the shot and knew it had not been a truck backfiring. For some reason, Harold had fired his shotgun. Something must have gone wrong. He slapped the steering wheel with the palm of his hand. From the beginning he had had the feeling that the plan wouldn't work but his need for money far outweighed his fear of going to jail. So here he was sitting in a getaway car, waiting for his friends to come running down the alley. He'd wait another minute, but no longer. If they weren't here by then, they wouldn't be coming.

A nervous twitch began at the corner of his left eye that he couldn't control and his hands began to shake.

He shoved down on the clutch with his left foot as he shifted the gearshift into first gear. His right foot hovered nervously over the accelerator, ready for a quick get away. It took all his efforts to just sit there. The palms of his hands began to sweat.

Within seconds, the three bank robbers came charging into the alley, colliding with Joe, William and Red, who were by now, very close to the end of the alley.

The man with the leg wound ran into William and lost his balance, dropping the bag of money and his pistol when his knee struck the alleyway.

Struggling to stand up, he was at the same time, looking around for the bag of money and his pistol, but Red had already scooped them up and stepped away.

Hearing the getaway driver yell, "Com'on, com'on, forget it! We gotta get outta here!" he headed for the car that was already beginning to move slowly down the alley.

"I'm comin', don't leave me!" he yelled. "I've been shot!"

One of the robbers jumped out and helped him to the car and shoved him inside and then jumped in himself, as the big sedan began to pick up speed.

Joe, William and Red watched as the big sedan sped down the alley with its tires screaming and black exhaust smoke filling the air.

Looking down at the bag and the pistol he still held tightly in his hand, Red said, "What the hell was that all about?"

Joe looked toward the street, and then said, "I think we just witnessed part of a holdup of some kind."

"You don't think there's money in this bag, do ya?" Red said, looking down at the bag.

During this same time, one of the tellers by the name of Harvey Rosenthal, had pushed the alarm button and called the police, who informed them a squad car was less than a block away and would be there in just a few moments.

Harvey ran outside just as a black and white pulled up next to the curb with two young officers inside. Harvey

The Legend of Joe, Willy & Red

leaned into the passenger's side window and told them what had happened, in detail.

It was about then that things started going crazy, because when the young police officers heard that a retired policeman had been shot and killed in the line of duty, it was like waving a red flag in front of a bull.

The driver pulled the squad car forward slowly to look down the alley and the two young policemen saw three men standing in the alley. One of them had a large bag in one hand and a pistol in the other.

"It's them!" the driver yelled as he slammed on the brakes.

Both police officers scrambled out the driver's side of the police car, grabbing for their weapons.

The fact that they were both rookies, nervous, fresh out of the academy and this being not just a bank robbery, but a shooting as well, procedure vanished from their minds.

The second officer crawled across the seat on his belly and began shooting out through the passenger side window, while the other officer moved to the left front of the squad car and began shooting down the alley at the three men and the big sedan that was heading for the other end.

The second officer scooted back inside and grabbed the microphone. "This is squad car three-one-six, engaged in gun battle with three of the suspects. Black, Buick sedan proceeding down the alley at high speed toward Front Street. Considered to be armed and dangerous. Bank guard dead from shotgun blast; send all the backup you can spare."

The radio barked back at him, "Two-twelve turning onto Front Street as we speak."

"One-eleven, on the scene from other end of block in twenty seconds."

The radio barked again. "This is Sergeant Mills. Do not take chances; these men are bank robbers and killers. Use whatever means it takes to bring them down!"

Jared McVay

Joe, William and Red, heard the voices coming through the speaker of the squad car and realized the men they'd bumped into were the ones who had robbed a bank and killed the security guard.

Their first intention was to give the money back to the people at the bank or let the police return it, but when bullets began whizzing past them and ricocheting off the brick walls of the buildings on each side of the alley, they panicked.

Joe led the way as they raced for the far end of the alley with Red close behind, still carrying the pistol in his hand, but not returning fire. He was weaving one way, then another, trying to escape the barrage of lead coming their way.

Why he didn't just drop the pistol and the bag of money and surrender will never be known, because just close to half way down the alley, Red took a bullet in the back that made it's way to his heart. The impact drove him face down onto the alleyway and he was dead before he landed.

William, who was only a few steps behind Red, saw him go down and stopped and looked down at the small hole in the back of Red's jacket. Blood was beginning to ooze from the place where the bullet had entered.

Without thinking about it, William reached down and picked up the bag of money and the pistol and began chasing after Joe, hoping to give the money and the pistol to someone and explain their innocence, his fear overpowering his common sense.

When the shooting first started, Joe raised his hands in an attempt to surrender and stop this craziness before someone got hurt.

"Wait a minute! We surrender! I can explain. We're not with them!" he'd yelled.

But the two young officers were so keyed up they paid no attention and in all likelihood, hadn't even heard what Joe was yelling. As far as they were concerned, they

The Legend of Joe, Willy & Red

had the men who had robbed the bank and killed the security guard right in front of them and they were going to bring them down!

This was a time for action, not talking. By tomorrow they would be heroes! Their pictures would be in all the papers and they might even get a medal! Hell, the mayor himself might pin their medals on them.

When Joe felt the searing pain of a bullet striking his left side and heard the whiz from another bullet that nicked his ear, he realized any attempt to surrender or explain what had happened would more than likely mean his death, so he turned and began to run.

"Let's get outta here before those lunatics kill somebody," Joe yelled at William and Red who were already doing just that.

As he passed them, he yelled again, "Let's go! Let's go!" trying to urge them to run faster as bullets continued to bounce off the walls on both sides of them.

Further down the alley Joe turned to see where they were and saw Red go down and he felt anger begin to rise within him. He also saw William scoop up the pistol and the bag of money and continue running toward him.

Why had he done that, Joe wondered? But as another bullet whizzed past close enough to hear, he decided the answer to that would have to wait until later, if there was to be a later. Right now he needed two things. First and foremost, they needed to get out of this alley and second, he needed to find a doctor. Raw pain was shooting through his left side and his shirt and hand were soaked with blood. Joe pressed harder on the wound, trying to stop his life from flowing out of him.

Somehow, both Joe and William made it to the end of the alley and turned left around the corner of the building, away from bullets bouncing all around them. As they stopped for a moment to catch their breath, Joe peeked around the edge of the building and saw the two young policemen running hard in their direction. One of them fired

Jared McVay

and a piece of brick chipped the brick wall near his head and he jerked his head back.

"Head for Mister Abram's office, maybe he can help us if anybody can."

William touched Joe on the arm and said, "I'm not sure that will be possible."

"What do you mean?" Joe said as he turned to look at William who was staring at the street and pointing.

In the middle of the street sat the black sedan, riddled with bullet holes and four dead men inside. Further down the block each way, the street was blocked with black and white police cars with armed policemen standing behind them.

Twenty guns were pointed at them, waiting to see what was going to happen. Each policeman's finger was poised and ready to fire if they made the slightest wrong move.

William looked at Joe with tears in his eyes. "They killed Red because of this lousy bag of money. They murdered our friend," William said in a subdued tone of voice as he tried to understand it all and his hands began to tremble. He was so mixed up and distraught by this time that he'd lost all reason. He didn't care that a bank guard had been killed, or that the two policemen who had been shooting at them were rookies. All he knew was that his feeling of danger was showing it's ugly face.

Thoughts and pictures raced through his mind - being accused of embezzlement, his wife making love to another man, watching Jo Ann flying through the air when he'd thrown her from the train, that crazy farmer who'd shot at them because he was jealous of his young wife, the farmer and his dog and that mean rooster, along with Red lying face down in the alley, blood seeping from the hole in his back, along with many other things that came to him as he stood there, wondering why his world had been turned upside-down again. He felt like he was slowly losing his mind.

The Legend of Joe, Willy & Red

"Have to stay out of the alley," he muttered to himself.

About then, William noticed Joe's bloody hand and in his delirium said, "Did they have to kill you, too. Why did they do that? We didn't do anything."

Joe could see by the look in William's eyes that he was no longer the easy going, glib tongued Willy the con man who could talk his way out of most any situation. He had let his mind had take him to a place where reason no longer meant anything.

Joe wanted to say something, to tell William that things would be okay. But he knew he couldn't say that because in his heart he knew it wouldn't be true. Things could never be the same again. Red had been shot down - killed for no reason he could think of. And he'd been shot, too. And maybe he was also dying. Nothing made any sense.

What he did know was that just when everything they'd wanted was within their grasp, somehow the world had been turned upside down and they were on the bottom, hanging on by their fingertips. And for the first time in his life, he didn't have a clue as to what to do to make things right again.

His tongue felt dry and he could feel himself getting weaker as his blood seeped through his fingers and dripped onto the street, making a small puddle next to his shoe.

For some reason William had taken several steps into the street - and when the two young policemen came running out of the alley, William turned and looked at the men who'd shot his friend, oblivious of the strong wind that was coming down the street from the ocean, tossing dirt and paper into the air and whisking it away.

William could feel it biting his face and messing up his hair, but it meant nothing because the two men who'd murdered his friends were pointing their guns at him.

"Is this what you want?" William shouted, raising the bag of money high over his head. "Is this why you murdered my friends? Because of a lousy bag of money?"

Suddenly, William turned the bag upside down, shaking it. The loose bills came tumbling out and before they could hit the street, the wind grabbed them and lifted them into the air, swirling them around and around, filling the sky with paper money.

The sky was filled with five, ten, twenty and even hundred dollar bills that were flitting here and there like a flock of birds swarming overhead.

By now, people hearing the gunfire had come running to see what the shooting was about and had formed in groups on both sides of the street, watching in awe as the money floated on the wind. Many of them had their hands up in the air, just in case any of it drifted their way - but it didn't. It just kept swirling around and around, just above Joe and William's head.

"There! You can have it back! We weren't the ones who stole it in the first place, but you didn't take the time to ask, did you? No. You just pulled your guns and started shooting," William shouted as be began walking toward the two young policemen, the pistol still in his hand.

Chapter 30

The Last Hoorah

    Having heard the police sirens, Harry Abram went down to the street to see what all the commotion was about and pushed his way to the front of the crowd just in time to see William dumping a bag of money into the air. William was saying something, but between the people next to him talking to each other and the noise of the wind he could only catch a word or two, but it was enough to understand that they had nothing to do with whatever was going on.

    Next, Harry saw Joe standing on the sidewalk with his left hand holding his side as blood oozed between his fingers. He also saw the sedan filled with bullet holes and the dead men inside. Turning his head back and forth he counted ten police cars and twenty police officers with guns pointed at Joe and William. What the hell was going on, he wondered as he looked around for Red, but the little Texan was nowhere to be seen on the sidewalk or the street.

    About then, William began walking toward two young policemen standing in the entryway to the alley. Harry noticed that William had a pistol in his hand. He couldn't believe what he was seeing. William seemed to be walking in a daze.

    Joe called out to him in a weak voice, "No, Willy, don't."

    "William, no! Come back here!" Harry also shouted.

    But William didn't seem to hear either of them, or he was too far-gone to care.

    William hadn't taken more than three steps when one of the young policemen yelled, "He's got a gun!'

    At this point, Harry Abram wasn't sure who commenced firing first, the young officers or the group of policemen behind the cars. Not that it made any difference because the end result was the same.

Jared McVay

When the sound of gunfire ceased and the smoke cleared, Mister William Conrad Bains staggered once, twisted and stretched his arm out in Joe's direction and then fell over, his bullet riddled body landing face up in the street, his dead eyes staring blankly at the swirling cloud of money above him.

Suddenly, there was total silence. No guns were being fired and the gusting wind stopped as quickly as it had come. It became as quiet as a church on Monday morning. Then, like gentle flakes of snow, the money descended from the sky, covering the bullet riddled body of Mister William Conrad Bains.

Like petrified trees, the people stood on the sidewalk - in shock over what they'd just witnessed. They could only stare at the dead man lying in the street, covered with money, while only a few feet away, the other man stood leaning against the building and stared at his dead friend.

Tears flowed freely from Joe's eyes like small streams, while blood dripped from the hand that was pressed to his side. He looked around at the policemen pointing guns at him and grinned. Joe knew he wasn't far from drawing his last breath and he could deal with that, as long as he could hold on long enough to do one more thing.

Everyone seemed to be holding his or her breath. Even the police stood silently behind their squad cars, watching and waiting to see what would happen next as though no one wanted to be the first one to break the silence.

Harry Abram stood there, dumbfounded. He wanted to go to Joe, but his feet seemed to be stuck to the street, his mind still trying to figure out how this could have happened in such a short time since leaving the ship. The captain had called him and congratulated him on his choice of men within minutes after they'd left.

Joe felt his heart breaking as tears continued to spill down his cheeks. His friend would never know if the plan to oust the unions would work or not. There would be no more

The Legend of Joe, Willy & Red

sheepish grins over concocting some wild scheme to rescue him and Red from the trouble they'd gotten into. There would be no more outlandish stories told with such fever that people had no choice but to believe them.

From this day forward, Willy the con man would cease to exist and there would never again be a little fat man tagging along on his shirttail, badgering him into going along with one of his wild schemes, like slinging dried horse manure throughout the interior of a restaurant full of people trying to eat, or rescuing a damsel in distress.

Joe staggered into the street next to where William lay and let his tear filled eyes look down the alleyway to where the body of the once happy go lucky, red haired Texan lay - shot in the back by some over zealous officer of the law.

Joe felt his throat choke up as he recalled memories of the man who had tracked him through the forest, sneaked into that farmer's house and, borrowed, as he called it, food, blankets and other stuff. Joe also remembered the Texan's infectious laughter and the burden he carried. Well that lynch mob would never get their hands on him now.

Staring once again at the body of his friend, William, Joe recalled the narrow escapes they'd had together and telling them that one of these days they just might get into something they couldn't get out of. Well, today that prediction had come true. But this time it had nothing to do with any wild scheme. They were just in the wrong place at the wrong time.

Joe looked around, wondering how long he'd been standing there? When in real time it had only been a few minutes since they had exited the alley and all of the dying had taken place, and only moments since he'd staggered up to stand next to William.

All of a sudden his sadness turned to anger. He was mad through and through. His anger ran all the way down into the marrow of his bones. Never before had he ever felt this much rage.

Jared McVay

Not even the thundering force of ten thousand buffalo racing across the prairie, shaking the earth for miles in all directions, nor the worst hurricane known to man could compare to the rage that was consuming Joe at this very moment. A mixture of hurt and anger and sorrow and a whole bunch of other feelings he couldn't distinguish were tearing at his insides.

The world began to spin as the pain in his side increased and it was getting hard to breathe. He knew his time was getting short and it was too late for anyone to help him. He'd lost too much blood. He would be joining his friends soon. He regretted not being able to tell Patricia goodbye and he hoped she'd understand.

Joe felt his legs move, but had no control over them, or his actions thereafter as he knelt next to William and placed his hand over William's eyes and closed them as the blood continued to ebb from William's body and mixed with the tears from Joe's eyes.

"I love you, my friend," Joe whispered and without conscious thought took the pistol from William's hand and with horrendous pain, stood up and fired two quick shots at the two young policemen who'd killed his only real friends; men who had become like brothers to him.

It didn't matter which one had actually killed them, they were both guilty as far as he was concerned.

The shots had come fast, before any of the policemen could react. The first shot caught the officer on the left just above his right eyebrow and tore a gaping hole through his brain. The second shot slammed against the other officer's chest and burst his heart.

And before the two young policemen hit the ground, Joe whirled and faced the stunned police officers behind the squad cars, his pistol spouting flame, shattering the windows of the police cars.

No more policemen were killed in the bloody shootout, but Joe was slammed backward as twenty or more chunks of lead punctured his chest - his body landing next to

The Legend of Joe, Willy & Red

William, their arms touching, as though they were taking the trip to the next world, together.

The first person to reach the bodies was Harry Abram and as he looked down at the two men, Joe's eyes opened.

A gasp emitted throughout the crowd of people who had followed Harry. Harry knelt down and whispered to Joe, "Hang on. There's an ambulance on the way."

Blood was seeping from the corners of Joe's mouth and it was difficult for him to speak above a whisper. Joe coughed up a mouthful of blood that ran down over his chin and Harry had to lean close to hear what Joe had to say.

"We didn't steal the money. . . three other guys. . . police just started shootin', never gave us. . . "

Joe gave one last sigh and then joined his new found brothers.

As Harry stared at William and Joe, he very quietly muttered to himself, "If you're a benevolent God, please let these three men in. They're good men who just became victims of this crazy depression."

With that Harry stood up and felt his jaws tightening and the muscles in his back go ridged as the crowd of people began grabbing money off William's body.

Harry pushed his way through the crowd as the police took charge and ordered the crowd to back away from the bodies and the money. In the far distance the sound of ambulances could be heard as their sirens filled the air.

Jared McVay

Epilogue

Harry Abrams went back to his office and called his cousin, the chief of police, who pulled some strings, which allowed Harry to take custody of the bodies.

The following morning, as planned, the captain guided the ship into the open waters of the Pacific Ocean and set a course for New Zealand. In the cooler below, were the bodies of Josiah Nathaniel Wilson, William Conrad Bains and Johnny 'Red' Walker.

Two weeks later - the bodies of Tom Snow, Dick York and Harry Longhorn were buried at sea somewhere in the Pacific Ocean as full crew members, with every man aboard standing at attention.

As sad as their untimely deaths had been, Joe finally found in William and Red, a bond of friendship far greater than any he had ever dreamed about - plus - a promising bonus - Joe's feelings about a pretty waitress named Patricia King and their possibilities of having a future together.

For William, the inner courage and strength that he'd always dreamed about for so many years had finally shown itself, but surprisingly not for himself, but in coming to the aid of other people - his two new friends and a woman who reminded him so much of his wife.

As for Red, well, he had always longed for excitement and a grand adventure, which, during his time spent with the tough guy, Joe Wilson and the little fat guy, Willy the con man, he had been party to more excitement and wild adventures then he had ever hoped for. They had been the type that people write stories about. And he had been a part of it all and had laughed longer and louder and had been happier than he could ever remember.

The next day when the newspaper hit the streets with their pictures all over the front page, the little blonde haired woman thought it was such a shame. She and Red were just beginning to hit it off. He was such a nice guy.

While the oriental woman went to her place of worship and lit candles for all of them, but especially for William, whom she had come to have deep feelings for.

When Patricia King, the pretty waitress at the diner read the news, she fainted right there in the diner and went home for three days to mourn the man she had fallen in love with, never realizing she would have something to remember him by.

Six weeks later, Jo Ann Fissella arrived at the office of Harry Abrams and three days later, disappeared, and then reappeared in the name of, Mrs. Carol Abrams.

It took twenty-seven years before the wild antics of Joe, William and Red became legendary - when a young journalist wrote his first book, entitled - 'The Man Who Rode The 106.' The young author's name was, J. N. Wilson II.

As it turned out, his mother, Patricia King, the pretty waitress from the diner, had named her son after his father, Josiah Nathaniel Wilson.

~~~~~~~~~~~~~~~~~~~~~~~~

Jared McVay

Made in the USA
Charleston, SC
23 August 2011